SHY

John Inman

Dreamspinner Press

Published by
Dreamspinner Press
5032 Capital Circle SW
Ste 2, PMB# 279
Tallahassee, FL 32305-7886
USA
http://www.dreamspinnerpress.com/

Shy

Cover Art by Paul Richmond
http://www.paulrichmondstudio.com

ISBN: 978-1-62380-148-9

Printed in the United States of America
First Edition
November 2012

eBook edition available
eBook ISBN: 978-1-62380-149-6

For John B., as always.

Chapter One

IT BEGAN innocently enough.

A simple invitation to my ex's birthday celebration. Just a few people. Nothing to get antsy about. I had purchased a new shirt that looked pretty good on me. My hair had been cut just the week before, so it wasn't poking up like blowfish spines, as it tended to do when too long. I had a nice bottle of Chianti tied with a cute bow and a funny card to go along with it. Jerry would like that. It might even make Stanley, his current lover, jealous. That would be nice. Checking the mirror, I could see no zits on the rise, thank God. Dermatologically speaking, things were copacetic.

But then, out of nowhere, came a tingle of warning. Just a glimmer of trepidation at first, like a warning shot fired across the bow, followed by a distant spark of harsh light, growing brighter by the second. Then there it was, that old familiar lightning bolt. It smashed into my gut and quickly turned all those rosy hopes of having a good time at Jerry's little get-together into a twisted pile of rubble smoldering at my feet. Mental thunder rumbled in the back of my head like an F5 tornado gathering on the horizon. A sudden fluttering in my upper colon made me blink. A sheen of perspiration gathered at my hairline. One right after the other, all the usual symptomatic suspects converged on me *en masse*. Nausea. Tingling fingertips. Cold toes. Knocking knees. Thumping heart.

Aw geez, I thought. Here we go again. And the party was still two days away!

Like a trumpeting elephant stomping through the apartment, tossing furniture and smashing everything in its path, the fear was impossible to ignore. In a matter of five seconds, I went from vague unease to sheer, unmitigated terror.

I couldn't go to this party. I couldn't. But how the hell was I going to get out of it? Jerry would be hurt. And even worse than that, his lover would be ecstatic. Of course, he would be even more ecstatic if I actually showed up, had a panic attack, went into convulsions in front of everybody, then threw up on the cat. God, I hate people. Well, no I don't. I hate me. No, that's not right either.

I just hate me and people thrown together. Yeah, that's it.

That's it *exactly.*

And Stanley. I really hate Stanley.

I WAS first diagnosed with social anxiety disorder a year and a half ago. Imagine how surprised I was to learn that the extreme shyness from which I had suffered my whole life wasn't really shyness at all, but something with an actual name. And an embarrassing name at that. SAD.

Sad is right. Why did they have to make it sound so gothic? Why couldn't they call it something frivolous and lightly charming, like party pooper paranoia. "I have PPP," I'd tell people. Doesn't sound too bad. Sounds kind of perky. I can't tell them I have SAD. It's just too pathetic. I'm not a sad person. I'm a happy person.

As long as I never have to interact with anybody in any sort of social situation.

Like Jerry's goddamn birthday party!

I squinted into the foggy bathroom mirror, and my eyeballs were bulging out of the front of my head like ping-pong balls. The body looked good though, I reflected, trying to take my mind off the panic. I stood there fresh out of the shower, dripping on the rug, gazing into the mirror with my buggy-assed eyes. I was nicely tanned from hours on the beach, my brown hair tipped platinum from sun and sea water. A little trail of fuzz wended a path down my flat stomach to a very attractive package, if I say so myself, uncut, nestling in a velvety pillow of light brown pubic hair. A smattering of soft hair was splashed across my chest, my nipples erect. (The bathroom was cold.) One of my ears was twitching. That was new.

I watched in the mirror as my fingers gently circled my penis and slid my foreskin back. I considered taking Tom Junior out for a little spin just to take my mind off the upcoming birthday party, but no sooner had I thought that than my telephone rang. With a twinge of regret, I stopped ogling myself and, still dripping in more ways than one, dragged my naked ass into the living room to pick it up.

"You're panicking, aren't you, Tom?" It was Jerry. "The party is two days away and you're already going into meltdown mode."

I wiped the sweat off my upper lip. My hands were shaking. I wasn't sure if it was a residual symptom from my social anxiety attack, or guilt at having been caught with my pecker in my hand. "Why would I be panicking?"

Jerry and I were both twenty-seven years old. We had been lovers for five years. We broke up more than a year ago but still remained friends. I wanted him back. He didn't want me. He knew me inside out. Literally. And I could close my eyes and recall the taste of every one of his bodily secretions. Sometimes, just to torture myself, I did exactly that.

(I know what you must be thinking. *Tom and Jerry?* These two were a couple and their names were *Tom and Jerry?* Well, we did hear a lot about that, as you can imagine. Later in the relationship, however, we weren't a cartoon cat and mouse anymore. We were cartoon magpies. Heckle and Jeckle. According to Jerry, I was Heckle, the more annoying of the two. My opinion differed.)

"Well?" Jerry asked again. "Are you panicked or not?"

I knew he would hear a tremor in my voice if I said anything, so I opted for silence. Dead silence. What a coward I am.

"Listen, Tom," Jerry crooned. "Stanley says not to worry. He'll make it as comfortable for you as possible."

Right. Stanley. My old lover's new squeeze. A gorgeous package of manhood enclosing a soul with all the warmth and compassion of a frozen bag of chicken legs. He'll probably drag me up to the front of the room for charades the minute I walk in the door, then stand in the kitchen and giggle as I swallow my tongue and have a stroke while everyone is staring at me. He knows I hate charades. Stanley's such a dick.

"Yes," I said. "I'm sure he's terribly concerned. Kiss him for me, won't you? Then kick him in the nuts."

Jerry laughed. "I wish you two would get along."

"Keep wishing."

"Have you taken your meds?"

"What, I don't have enough problems with the shyness, but I have to be impotent too? Those pills put my dick to sleep. They put everything to sleep. I was a zombie. Well, no, zombies are interesting. They actually make movies about zombies."

"You're interesting."

"Oh shut up."

"And when your dick does wake up, it's a wonder to behold. The term 'sleeping giant' comes to mind. I remember it fondly, your dick."

"Thanks," I said. "What do you want?"

"Just checking on you."

"Bullshit."

"Okay. I need a favor."

"Stanley require a kidney?" A heart, more like it. Or maybe he needs a dick, since Jerry was remembering mine so fondly. I smiled at that thought. Stanley, dickless. I could die a happy man if I thought those two words were somehow permanently connected.

"No, dearest. We need someone to squire his brother around. Show him the town. He's in the process of moving here from Indiana. For some reason he doesn't get along with Stanley."

"Hmm," I said. "Now there's a shocker. Is he gay?"

"As the flowers that bloom in the spring, tra la."

I guess I thought about it a little longer than Jerry was willing to wait.

"He's cu-u-ute," Jerry cooed, waving the two words in front of my face like a farmer dangling a carrot in front of a recalcitrant jackass. As if I could really be bribed so easily.

"*How* cute?" I asked. Okay, maybe I could. And before that thought could travel from the back of my brain to the front then dribble out my mouth, the old demon rose up and stopped me cold. Butterflies. Tingles. Annoying flashes of light. Shit.

"I'm sorry, Jerry. I'm not up to it. Right now it's all I can do to come to grips with your birthday party. Besides, if he's anything like Stanley I'd probably hate his guts right off the bat. You do know I hate Stanley, don't you?"

I could hear fingernails tapping a tabletop through the receiver. I thought I could also hear eyeballs rolling around inside a human head like two marbles in a plastic bucket, but that might have been my imagination. "I've suspected it all along," he droned, sarcastic as hell. "Look, Tom, the reason we're asking you is because the two of you have something in common."

"We both hate your lover?"

"No, jerkwad. He's shy. According to Stanley, his brother is really, really shy."

"How shy?"

"He's had some therapy for social anxiety."

"So he's nuts."

"Yeah, Tom, he's nuts. Just like you. So you oughta get along. How about it?"

"And you say he's cute?"

"For Christ's sake, yes! He's cute!"

"How old is he?"

"Twenty-four."

"What's his name?"

"Frank."

I nibbled a fingernail for about thirty seconds, gazed out the window, dusted a piece of lint off the phone table, and bent down to pet my Chihuahua, Pedro, who was peeing on my foot. I'd have to take another shower.

"Okay, I'll do it."

"Great." He sounded relieved, probably afraid he'd have to squire the guy around himself. I guess after five years with me he'd had enough of social anxiety disorder to last a lifetime. Jerry has never been shy in his life. Most sluts aren't. Not that he's a slut. Well, yes he is. He cheated on me with Stanley. That's pretty slutty.

"But only once," I firmly stated. "I'll show the poor guy around town, maybe take him out to eat, show him where the bars are, the insane asylums, then I'm outta there. Deal?"

"Deal."

I slammed down the phone, scooped Pedro off the floor, and plopped him down in the kitchen sink before he pooped on my foot as well. I could tell he was considering it by the sneaky look in his eyes, and I'd rather scrub the sink than the floor. Less bending.

Chihuahuas. You gotta love 'em. Exes not so much.

IF MY life were a soap opera, then my typical workday would simply be one more boring scene stuck in the middle of a long string of dull-as-hell episodes, with every script just as poorly written as the one before it. And every day would be an experiment in terror. Every single one. No fun, no lover, no excitement. Scared to speak to anyone. Scared to get close. Scared to be myself. I knew there was a different me lurking beneath the surface, a better me, a *fun* me. But tapping into that other me was *far* beyond my capabilities. Shit, it was all I could do to *pretend* to be normal. *Actual* normality was *far* beyond my grasp.

Nothing maudlin about me, huh?

I was fine, sitting at my desk in the First National Bank behind the little laminated sign that read THOMAS MORGAN, SENIOR RELATIONSHIP BANKER, signing up new accounts, handling questions from depositors, dealing with nervous mortgagees or anxious senior citizens, and sometimes covering for a teller or two when break time rolled around.

However, interacting with my fellow employees on a *social* level, such as fending off their invitations to the Starbucks around the corner for a quick latte and a midmorning side of gossip, was another story altogether. Customers I could deal with. No problem. But put me on any sort of social playing field with my comrades in arms, and the old demons began swooping in. As a matter of fact, the invitations to share a latte or lunch had become increasingly rare of late. You can only say no to people so many times before they stop asking altogether. Of course, my self-imposed isolation only served to make me more paranoid than I already was. SAD sucks. It really does.

And to make matters worse, even I was smart enough to know the problem was worsening. I was pondering this disturbing state of affairs and surreptitiously picking my nose (not really mining for gold, more of a gentle reconnaissance) when the phone light for line one blinked on. An outside call. I jauntily scooped it up, seeing as my boss, Mr. Moonhouse, was eyeing me from just inside the vault where he was probably beating off on the thousand dollar bills. It was a slow day. If I wasn't so damned shy, and he wasn't so damned ugly, I'd join him.

"First National Bank. Tom Morgan speaking. How may I help you?"

I could hear the sound of breathing on the line but that was it. I cleared my throat and tried again. "First National Bank. Tom Mor—"

"Sorry, wrong number," a male voice said and the caller softly hung up.

Two seconds later, I forgot the phone call. And two seconds after *that* the phone rang again.

"First National Bank. Tom Mor—"

"I'm sorry," the same male voice said. "Are you busy?"

Moony was still watching so I put a businesslike smile in my voice and tried to look interested.

"No, sir. How can I help you?"

Silence lasted so long that I was beginning to think my caller had hung up again. Finally, he said, "I'm Frank. Frank Wells. Stanley's brother."

I blinked. "Oh. Well… hi." One lone butterfly flapped his wings somewhere in the vicinity of my spleen. He was probably a scout. No doubt six million other butterflies were hot on his heels, if butterflies even *have* heels.

Since I couldn't think of another thing to say, I just sat there like a moron with the phone stuck to my ear, waiting.

Apparently Stanley's brother didn't know what to say either. The silence stretched out so long I was beginning to wonder if maybe I was starting to need another haircut.

God, I thought. *We're two peas in a pod.* A trickle of sweat skated down my ribcage as the silence went on and on. I heard the big regulator clock ticking on the wall behind the teller cages. Tick. Tick. Tick. What next? A cricket?

"So—" I began.

"I'm sorry—" he sputtered at the same time.

Taking the bull by the horns, I made my move. Fueled by jangled nerves, my voice boomed out slightly below a roar, making the tellers jump thirty feet away. "Going to Jerry's party?" I blared.

Mr. Moonhouse frowned, someone giggled in the counting room, and I waited for my heart to explode and end my misery.

To my amazement, Frank let out a nervous chuckle. "Jerry *said* we'd get along."

"Yes," I said. "We're doing swimmingly."

From the corner of my eye, I caught the glint of Mr. Moonhouse's horn-rimmed glasses headed my way. I assumed an officious tone. "So if you just come on in, sir, we'll have the forms for you to fill out and everything will be set."

Frank said, "Uh—"

And I hung up. Poor guy. Probably set his therapy back six months.

Moony walked on by, the phone remained silent, and the day kept grinding along. After a lifetime or two, five o'clock rolled around and I stumbled out the bank door like a convict set free after thirty years in Chino State Pen. Gulping in the un-air-conditioned air like a fish, only fish don't sigh, at least I don't think they do, I headed for my car and the Brass Rail.

I needed a drink.

And while I was *needing* that drink, I found myself wondering just how cute Frank Wells really was.

IT WAS happy hour at the Brass Rail, and judging by the number of cars parked around the bar, and the number of guys milling around the front door, and the happy chatter of male voices drifting out into the street from the patio out back, I knew the place was packed. It took me all of five seconds to decide to skip the mayhem and toddle on home. I told myself it was because I just didn't feel like fighting my way through the crowd, and once inside, pushing my way through the mob of warm bodies to belly up to the bar just for the privilege of ordering what would probably turn out to be a watered-down drink. But deep inside I knew the truth: I was too shy to run the gauntlet of all those gay guys lurking on the sidewalk outside. Lacking anything better to do, they would be checking me out from head to toe to basket to ass as I slunk through the front door, trying to enter unnoticed. They wouldn't be checking me out because I'm all that cute, you understand, but because that's what gay guys *always* do when they congregate in a group. They swarm. Like sharks. And God help the poor seal pup that gets in the middle of them. Sweat broke out in my armpits just thinking about it.

So rather than elegantly sipping my way through a six-dollar Effin and tonic and acting nonchalant while a horde of beautiful men lusted after me, or so I imagined, I was reduced to slinking home, slipping on a pair of rubber gloves, and slurping a Miller Lite from a can while I scrubbed Chihuahua caca off my best chair. Pedro seemed to be as proud as punch about the mess he had made, dancing around the room like he had just won a Tony Award for Best Original Poop.

Two beers later, the chair was clean and Pedro had worn himself out, thank God. So while he was sleeping the sleep of the unjust on his little doggie bed in front of the TV and snoring like a lumberjack, I changed the ribbon on Jerry's bottle of Chianti. I changed it three times, using a different color ribbon each time, finally deciding I didn't like any of them. Disgusted, I decanted the wine and drank every last drop while watching the news. After the news, I walked down to the market. (After two beers and a bottle of wine I thought it prudent not to drive.) Once there, I bought a nice box of chocolates for Jerry to replace the wine. Halfway home, I cracked open the box, ate six pieces, did an about-face, and returned to the store to purchase the exact same bottle of Chianti I had tossed down earlier.

Then I bought a different card.

Back home, I rewrapped the new bottle of Chianti, tossed the old birthday card, addressed the new one, polished off the chocolates, and stumbled into bed with Pedro snuggling up next to me around eleven o'clock. As I lay there thinking about Frank and once again wondering if he was as cute as Jerry said he was, I also mulled over the possibility that I may have just manifested the first concrete symptoms of OCD. Well, good. I hated being a one-trick pony. Social anxiety disorder, obsessive-compulsive behavior, and the owner of an incontinent Chihuahua. Now if I could just sprout a couple of zits and contract a stubborn case of gonorrhea, I would have a nicely balanced palette of woe.

The entire box of chocolates I had gobbled down would probably help with the zits, but of course, you need to have sex to contract gonorrhea. The chances of that happening any time soon seemed fairly grim.

Pedro gave me a sympathetic lick on the ear as if he knew what I was thinking, and we were both sound asleep two minutes later.

I dreamed of Jerry. No surprise there.

Christ only knows what Pedro dreamed of. Pooping probably.

Chapter Two

MY CELL phone jangled on the nightstand. It was Jerry. For a second I wondered if I was still dreaming.

I blinked myself awake. The morning sun was pouring hot molten lava through the bedroom window. It stabbed its way into my eyeballs like battery acid eating through a couple of grapes. My mouth tasted like beer and wine and chocolate and dog hair. Dog hair, because Pedro's tail was in my mouth. I spit it out. Pedro looked offended for a moment, then rolled over and went back to sleep. A hangover was gnawing at the back of my head like a beaver attacking a tree trunk.

"What are you wearing?" Jerry asked.

I tried to ignore the thumping in my brain. After wiping my tongue on the sheet to scrape off the dog hair, I said, "A gorilla suit."

"Ooh, sexy."

Right. "What do you want, Jerry? I'm in bed with a cute Mexican."

"How *is* Pedro?"

"Pooped on my new chair. I'm considering deportation."

"What a bitch."

"*You're* the bitch, Jerry. What do you want?"

"Stanley wants to move the party up a day."

"You mean to *today*?"

"Well. Yeah. It is Saturday, after all. Is that a problem?"

"*Is that a problem?*"

"Whoa. That sounds like a yes."

And suddenly there they were, closing in all over again; every symptom of SAD known to man. This time it started with cramps in the crotch area. If it wasn't SAD, then either my period was starting or my bladder had just exploded like a water balloon. I was hoping for the second option since I was all out of feminine napkins and I faint at the sight of blood.

I fought to keep my anger under control. Something new for me. "Stanley's just doing this to screw with my head, Jerry. Or his brother's head. He's got a mean streak in him a mile wide, and you're too stupid to see it. Probably having the time of his life, jerking all the puppet strings and making everybody dance. Well, I'm not coming today. I can't. I have other plans. Important plans. Things that can't be put off." My voice kept getting higher and higher so I decided to stop talking before I levitated off the bed and banged my head on the ceiling.

"Like what?" He sounded understandably skeptical. The last time I blew off an event because of previous plans, the plans included a hastily arranged root canal and two crowns, and Jerry knew it.

"I'll be busy drinking your gift." *Again,* I failed to add.

"It's only a few friends, Tom. I don't know why you get so freaked out."

"Stanley *says* it's a few friends. For all I know he's invited the first thirty pages of the phone book just to make me feel uncomfortable."

"That's silly."

"Is it? Remember the time he told me to come on over and share some leftovers? No company, he said. No reason to worry, he said. *There were eight people there, Jerry. And I didn't know any of them.*"

"They popped in unannounced. It wasn't—"

"Unannounced my ass. Eight people don't just pop into someone's house unannounced. They came from Scottsdale, Arizona, for Christ's sake. *In two cars.* It's an eight-hour drive. It was an ambush, plain and simple. Stanley's a dick, Jerry. You're married to a dick. And he's not a pretty dick, either. He's a *diseased* dick."

My heart was thumping and clamoring around inside my chest like a squirrel trying to get out of a cardboard box. I figured if I didn't get off the phone soon I'd be in an operating room somewhere having my chest splayed open with a hacksaw and my heart yanked out in a last-ditch effort to slow it down before it fucking exploded.

"How could you cheat on me with that dick, Jerry? *And why is he moving up the party?*"

Jerry spoke around a yawn. "How many times have we been through this? I needed more in a relationship than what you were willing to offer, Tom. Geez, getting you out of the house was like pulling teeth, and when you did deign to go out, there were so many ground rules I practically had to take my laptop with me to keep track of them. We were great in bed, Tom, but that's not living. That's fucking. I needed outside stimulation. I'm a social being. I needed to socialize."

"You needed to cheat."

"Call it what you will."

Pedro still had his eyes closed but I could hear him growling deep in his throat. Even he was getting mad, God love him. Loyalty wasn't *completely* dead in the world.

"And the party?" I asked, clipping my syllables like a grumpy florist snipping stems. I already knew the battle was lost, but I wasn't about to admit defeat with grace.

"Thanks for the coffee, hon," Jerry muttered, obviously to someone other than myself.

"*Is he there?*" I ranted. "*Is Stanley there? Put the son of a bitch on!*"

From a distance a happy voice lilted through the line as if wafting up from the bottom of a well. "Hi, Tom! Good mo-o-orning! Don't worry, it'll be fun! Frank will be there in a couple of hours. Thought you two might like to get to know each other before the party starts!"

My heart immediately stopped thumping. The squirrel must have died. I sat straight up in bed and hissed, *"What did he say?"*

For the first time, Jerry sounded a little uncomfortable. "Well, see, Stanley thought it would be easier for you guys, since you're both a little shy—Jesus, *there's* an understatement—to maybe meet each other before the party starts. That way you can come to the party together and you won't be so rattled about meeting everybody alone."

"What do you mean, 'meeting everybody'? Don't I know these people? And what did the dick mean when he said, 'He'll be there in a couple of hours'? Did he mean here? Is his brother coming here? To my apartment? Uninvited?"

"He *was* invited. Stanley invited him. I mean, *we* invited him."

My toes were cold and my ear was twitching again. The squirrel in my chest lurched back to life, stomping around like Bigfoot, kicking ribs and uprooting organs. One unhappy rodent. "Stanley talked you into this, didn't he? *You* knew it was a bad idea sending his brother over here. *You* knew I'd be upset. But since that's what Stanley wanted, you decided to let him get away with it. It was easier than arguing, right? You're such a wuss, Jerry. God, I can't believe I ever loved you."

"You still love me."

"Not now I don't!"

Jerry tsked. "Double negative."

"Fuck you! What time is he coming? Never mind. It doesn't matter. I won't be here. I'm moving."

Jerry laughed. "He'll be there at four. Party's at eight. I'm sure the two of you will get along just swell. Oh, and one other thing. You might want to lock Pedro in the bedroom. Frank's allergic to dog hair."

"What? What?"

I heard Stanley chuckling in the background as Jerry hung up the phone. The dick.

I WAS out of bed and scrubbing the toilet bowl before my cell phone had stopped sliding down the hallway like a hockey puck. It was sliding down the hallway because that's where I flung it. I ruin more phones that way.

God, Jerry was infuriating. Stanley was *beyond* infuriating.

There I was in my tighty-whities with my morning hard-on still poking up and a toilet brush in one hand and a can of Comet in the other. Pedro was looking worried and feigning sleep as he squinted at me from the bed through slitted eyes, like maybe I was going to toss him a rag and order him to start cleaning the windows or something.

The apartment was already spotless. I knew that. Aside from the occasional mound of Chihuahua poop, the apartment was *always* spotless. So don't ask me why I was scrubbing the toilet. I don't know why I was scrubbing the toilet. It's just what I do.

During my five years with Jerry, he never once scrubbed the toilet bowl. When I confronted him with that fact, he said he couldn't scrub the toilet bowl because I was always in the way, scrubbing it myself. If *he* wanted to scrub it, he'd have to go *through* me to *do* it. Please. It's not like I was *always* scrubbing the toilet bowl. Sometimes I scrubbed the kitchen sink.

Five years ago, I met Jerry at the Brass Rail on a night when, unlike the evening before, I had actually dredged up the courage to sneak my way past the gauntlet of horny gay guys hovering around the front door. Inside, Jerry was leaning against the wall, drink in hand, with his shirt unbuttoned all the way down to his navel, checking out the bar as if it were his own private domain. I had never seen him before in my life. Lord, he was sexy. Trim, black-haired, tall. And green-eyed. It was the eyes that made me fall in love with him. I have a thing for green eyes. Some people like ice cream. I like men with green eyes.

On my seventh cocktail, I found the courage to approach him. Before my eighth cocktail, Jerry and I were in my car heading for the next five years of our lives.

I think he thought my shyness was cute and charming at first. But after a few years, it wasn't so cute and charming anymore. Too much upkeep on his part. Too many evenings spent at home because I was too nervous, too insecure, too *frightened* to step outside the front door and confront people.

It's not like I just sat back and accepted the fact I was fucking nuts. I tried group therapy. Too many strangers judging me. I tried one-on-one therapy with a shrink, but it was too expensive. Plus, I was pretty sure the shrink was judging me. I tried a free experimental study with the University of San Diego, where I was introduced to Xanax and the magical world of impotence. Didn't care for that much. The cure seemed worse than the problem. Plus, the Ethiopian janitor who was always mopping the hallway when I arrived for my evening session seemed to be judging me as I headed for the university's Lunatic Department. One night I was pretty sure I even heard him snicker.

So here I was, single, resigned to my fate, twenty-seven years old, cleaning my bathroom with a boner that was still poking out like a tent pole, nervous because I was about to meet someone who was (supposedly) cute, (apparently) gay, (probably) a nice person, and (most assuredly) just as screwed-up as I was. You'd think I'd be thrilled to death, but no-o-o-o. Not me. I've spent my whole life looking gift horses in the mouth. Not likely to stop now.

After the toilet bowl, I scrubbed the sink, bleached the tub, emptied the hamper, threw the clothes in the washing machine, dusted all the picture frames throughout the apartment, also the tops of all the light bulbs, then I hunkered down and dusted everything else with lemony furniture polish until I could hardly breathe for the fumes, vacuumed (twice), fluffed up the throw pillows, watered the plants and wiped their leaves, changed the sheets on the bed in my room *and* the guest room, realigned the throw rugs using everything but a yardstick and a carpenter's plane to get them straight, shook out the doggy bed, flapped the curtains a bit in case they were dusty too, then I headed for the kitchen and attacked it like G.I. Joe hitting Omaha Beach. That took another hour.

When I was finished, the apartment looked absolutely pristine and my hard-on was long gone.

One job left. I washed the dog. Pedro's least favorite thing in the whole wide world. He paid me back by peeing on the couch. No sulky silences for him. Revenge, that was his motto.

I spent another ten minutes scrubbing the couch then blowing it dry with my blow-dryer.

After one last glare in Pedro's direction, I jumped in the shower, did the ablutions thing, jumped back out, dried off, threw on a pair of my rattiest, most comfortable sweatpants, and went to my desk where I sat down to write a note. "Dear Frank. Sorry I missed you. Even sorrier your brother's a dick." I taped the note to the front door, slammed and relocked the door, went to the kitchen to build myself a ham, beef, tomato, lettuce, potato chip, pickle and mayo sandwich on rye, ate it standing at the sink so I wouldn't make crumbs, polishing it off in nothing flat while Pedro stood below begging for scraps and intermittently humping my leg, then I stood there for five minutes rescrubbing the sink. I went to the door, tore off the note, wadded it up and threw it in the wastebasket. Then I pulled it from the wastebasket, smoothed it out, read it again, sighed, and wadded it up once more and threw it back in.

Then I collapsed on the sofa because I was so damned tired I couldn't see straight but had to jump back up because the sofa was still damp where I had cleaned the dog pee from it earlier. So glaring once more at Pedro, who was busy licking his nuts and not giving two hoots that I was glaring at him, not that he ever did, I dropped into my new chair, the one Pedro had pooped on the night before, and settled in to think about what I was going to do.

I thought about it so long that I fell asleep sitting there half naked in nothing but my scruffy, baggy sweatpants, and I only woke up when the doorbell rang.

Holy Mother of God! It couldn't be four o'clock! It was. Four o'clock to the minute. Apparently time passes at a different clip for insane people. Funny I hadn't figured that out earlier.

Not knowing what else to do, I unlocked the front door, took a deep breath, and yanked it open.

The young man standing on my doorstep looking nervous and fidgeting around was not only gorgeous, but it took me all of two seconds to realize he had green eyes. Green eyes surrounded by long black lashes. My bête noire. Oh Lord.

Neither of us said a word. He eyed my bare tummy and drooping sweatpants while I stood there lost in those fabulous green eyes.

It wasn't until I began to think that one of us should be saying *something*, that I noticed the suitcase in his hand.

Green eyes or not, I didn't much care for the look of *that*.

WE BOTH said "Hi" at the same time. Then we both stopped and apologized at the same time for interrupting each other. I was reminded of Chandler Bing on *Friends*. "Could this *be* any more uncomfortable?"

I'll say one thing for Frank Wells. He. Is. Beautiful. Perhaps a little shorter that I like, but put together very, very nicely. Black hair flopping around on his forehead. Olive skin. Fuzzy arms. And a really sweet face, with a tiny cleft in the chin and one dimple on his right cheek. There was no physical resemblance at all to his brother, the dick. That was a nice bonus.

And those eyes. The irises were as green as the gleam of sunlight through a young leaf. The black lashes surrounding them were thick and long and dark as kohl. The whites were so healthy and clear as to seem tinged with blue.

It took me a minute to pull back from the shock of those light green eyes, and to stop admiring them long enough to see the discomfort and the *fear* that was lurking in their depths. Good grief. The guy was scared to death. The only word I could think of to describe how Frank Wells looked as he stood there on my doorstep was—lost. The guy looked lost. He was still staring at my bare stomach, but he didn't seem to be staring with any sense of interest. He wasn't cruising. There were no lascivious thoughts going on inside his head, dammit, or at least I didn't think there were. My bare tummy and sagging sweatpants were only a place for him to direct those perfect eyes to avoid looking me in the face. I *hoped* he liked what he saw, but there was certainly no hint of it in his manner.

I understood the lost look on Frank Wells's face instinctively. I knew exactly what that aversion of the eyes signified. I have known myself to do the same thing a million times, to look everywhere but at the face of the person in front of me, to be absolutely incapable of doing anything else. It's not just a matter of fear, but the result of a deeply imbedded doubt in one's own self-worth. I also understood instinctively that Frank's discomfort at our meeting was greater than any discomfort I had ever labored under in similar circumstances, and that his opinion of himself was lower than my opinion of myself had *ever* been. This guy's anxiety problems made mine look positively inconsequential. I whined and railed and kowtowed to SAD. Frank Wells truly *suffered* from it. The simple fact that he had brought himself to my doorstep was an incredible act of courage on his part. That much I knew for a fact. And it had only taken a second for me to realize it.

The man was an open book. With a really nice cover.

Suddenly, it was very, very important to me to put the guy at ease. It actually hurt me to see him so damned uncomfortable. My mothering instinct took over before I even knew I had one.

I reached out and grasped his hand. In his surprise, he dropped the suitcase from the other hand. When it hit the landing, it sounded heavy, like maybe everything the kid had packed up and hauled away from Indiana was squeezed into that one beat-up old piece of Samsonite luggage.

Before he could reach for it, I scooped it up, swallowing a grunt when I did—the damn thing must have weighed fifty pounds—and pulled Frank and his worldly possessions through the door, not unlike the proverbial spider and the poor innocent fly.

A look of surprise shot across the young man's face as I dragged him into my living room, and then that look of surprise twisted itself into a bewildered grin, when he looked down to see Pedro humping his leg, something I rather wished I had thought of first.

Frank Wells bent down and kindly wagged a finger in Pedro's humping face as if to say, "Now, now, mustn't do that."

Only then did I remember the guy was allergic to dogs. Oh, well. Too late to do anything about it now. If he started sneezing I'd give him a hanky.

To my amazement, Pedro released Frank's leg, looked up into his face with what can only be described as a shamefaced moue—rather like a child with his hand caught in the cookie jar—then gave his tail an apologetic little shake. And he did all this while still humping the empty air. It always took a while for Pedro's motor to die down.

I watched, still amazed, as Pedro gave Frank's fingertips a friendly lick, then leaped straight up into Frank's arms as if the two were long-lost buddies.

If I had been the one to say "Now, now, mustn't do that," Pedro would have pooped in my cornflakes.

Frank clutched Pedro to his chest, gave him a kiss on the top of his little apple-shaped head, then shot a glance in my direction. His shyness returned in a heartbeat.

"Fucking dog," was all I could think to say, and Frank smiled, flashing teeth that were so white it made me want to lick them. He gave Pedro another peck on the head, and my heart did a little skitter to see those perfect lips pucker up in a kiss. I tried my damnedest not to imagine that kiss directed to the head of my pecker. God, I'm a horrible person.

Frank was wearing a battered Van Halen T-shirt which must have been older than he was and a pair of black Levi's that had faded to sepia. The knees were out, and the flash of skin I glimpsed through the knee holes was just as brown and fuzzy as the kid's arms, which sported some very nice biceps, I noticed. Not that Frank Wells was muscle-*bound.* He was actually kind of a little guy, but very, very cute and very, very well constructed.

I love cute little fuzzy guys with muscles. Just saying.

I was still holding the suitcase. Frank looked at it, then looked at me. His voice was as soft and warm as flannel. "Sorry. I checked out of the hotel so I had to bring the bag with me. Don't worry, I'm not moving in or anything."

Shit, I thought. *Why not?* But the words I chose to *speak* were, "I wasn't worried."

"Oh." He looked embarrassed again. He snuggled his face into Pedro's neck and looked around the apartment. I could feel his discomfort growing once more.

Simply knowing Frank's SAD was worse than mine wasn't enough to make my own case of SAD fall by the wayside. It came thundering back like a herd of buffalo stomping through a chandelier store. Maybe not as debilitating as Frank's, but just as nerve-wrenching nevertheless.

"Um, sit down, Frank. Oh wait. Formalities first." I stuck out my hand. "I'm Tom Morgan. It's nice to meet you."

Frank blushed, his ears turning bright red as he juggled Pedro around in an attempt to stick out his hand without dropping my dog on its head. "Frank Wells," he said. "Nice to meet you too."

When we shook hands, his fingers were as cold as mine. Again, I could feel the sweat forming at my hairline, one of those preliminary symptoms that usually heralds a full-fledged attack of jitters. I forced myself to ignore it. No easy feat. "Sit down, Frank. Make yourself comfortable. That piece of crap mongrel you're holding is called Pedro. Don't be surprised if he poops in your shirt pocket. He has sneaky bowels."

Frank hoisted Pedro up in front of his face and looked him dead in the eyes. "You wouldn't do that, would you, short stuff?"

Pedro licked his nose. Lucky mutt.

While Frank sat rather stiffly on the edge of the sofa (well away from the wet spot, by good fortune), I headed to the fridge for beers, figuring a little alcohol could only improve the situation. I snagged a T-shirt from the back of a chair as I went and found myself hoping that Frank Wells would be inordinately disappointed when I slipped it over my head and covered up my naked chest.

Chapter Three

I PIDDLED around in the kitchen trying to decide whether to serve the beer in bottles *à la butch*, or in crystal stemware *à la fruitcup*. I finally deciding that *butch* was the way to go. Not because I *was* butch by any long stretch of the imagination, although I thought Frank had the potential to be, but because I knew that we were both so nervous we would be tipping over stemware left and right like two lumberjacks mowing down an old growth forest, and those crystal glasses cost me thirty bucks a pop. I can be insane and still be frugal, for heaven's sake. I do work at a bank, after all.

Slyly glancing back through my kitchen door into the living room, I managed to sneak a closer look at my ex-lover's new lover's younger brother, Frank Wells. It dawned on me that perhaps Frank's scruffy style of dress, with his outdated Van Halen T-shirt and his rumpled, raggedy jeans, was maybe a wee bit more than the casual fashion statement it seemed to be. Looking at his shoes, especially, and my mother always told me that to truly judge a man you have to study his shoes. (This was a bit of advice my mother should have known was a lie since my own father, who by all accounts was a very snappy dresser, had turned out to be the schmuck of the century, taking a powder as he did halfway between my conception and my birth, never to be seen again). So, playing by my mother's rule book, I was quick to note that Frank's Reeboks were in the same sad condition as the old Reeboks I wore to paint in. Maybe even a little shabbier than my old Reeboks. In other words, I would rather have died a lingering death a million times over than wear those shoes to meet anyone for the first time. Especially a *gay* someone. We all know how snooty and judgmental gays can be.

I didn't think Frank Wells could be one of those people who honestly don't care about their appearance. People who don't care about their appearance have a much too healthy outlook on life to ever suffer from social anxiety disorder. People who don't care about their appearance are actually *normal*, for goodness sake. Well. Compared to people like me. Who aren't. Normal.

Suddenly, being a bit of a snoot myself, I found myself wondering what other articles of sartorial splendor lay hidden inside that battered suitcase Frank was hauling around. Admittedly, for all I knew there could have been two or three Armani suits in there, but I didn't think so. I had known Frank Wells for all of two minutes and I have to say I already felt I *knew* him pretty well. We had a common denominator, Frank and I, and that common denominator spoke worlds about a person's psyche. SAD does not jump on the backs of normal people. It simply doesn't.

No. Somewhere deep inside, Frank Wells was just as damaged as I was. And I already found myself liking the guy all the more because of it. Birds of a feather, and all that.

Frank was starting to look like he was thinking of maybe making a run for the front door and jumping ship if I didn't show up pretty soon, so I thumbtacked what I hoped was an Emily Post smile to my face and sauntered back into the living room, beers in hand, mouth going a mile a minute.

Sometimes to keep social anxiety disorder at bay, you just have to talk its hind legs off.

"So how long have you been in town, Frank? San Diego must be quite a change from what you're used to. Pigs and chickens and stuff, right? I mean you came from a farm, right? Indiana, was it? That must be a great way to grow up, although it didn't make your brother any more likable. The guy's a miserable putz, but then I'm sure you're aware of that. Stole my lover right out from under me, the son of a bitch."

By the time Frank reached out to take one of the proffered beers from my hand he was beginning to look a little shell-shocked. My tirades sometimes have that effect on people. Never slows me down, though. I just keep right on talking. Suicidally, sometimes.

"Not that I'm calling your mother a bitch, you understand. When I call your brother a *son* of a bitch, I'm just using the term colloquially. At least I *think* it's colloquially. I mean, well hell, Frank, you know what I mean." I could feel sweat popping out on my forehead. Uh-oh. "What hotel were you staying at? Probably pretty expensive, huh? I'm surprised you aren't staying with your asshole brother and my asshole ex. I'll bet Stanley didn't offer to put you up though, did he? No. He wouldn't. God, I hate that guy. So I understand you're twenty-four. How's that working out for you? I'm twenty-seven, you know. Well, almost twenty-seven and a half, or I will be in six months."

My mouth ran down at about the same time Frank finished pouring his entire beer down his throat, all in three glugs. He was probably hoping for a quick death from alcohol poisoning, or at least the good fortune to drown himself in it, but I think I would need to be serving something a little stronger and a little deeper than beer for that to take place, much to Frank's disappointment, I'm sure.

I was about to start talking again, I couldn't help myself, but Pedro growled at me so I flipped my mouth shut like a mailbox lid and let a blessed silence descend upon the room. Chihuahuas aren't so dumb.

One thing about talking yourself into a hole, when you do finally shut up, you at least stop settling deeper.

I could see Frank trying to work up the courage to speak. What a pair, I thought. He can't talk and I can't shut up.

Pedro did three quick turns in Frank's lap, finally found a comfortable position, and settled in for a nap, after giving me one last look that seemed to say "behave yourself." Frank rested his hand protectively across Pedro's back. He may not have bonded with me yet, but Frank had quickly become friends with my dog. Probably a good sign.

"No, he didn't offer," was all Frank said.

"Stanley?" I asked.

Frank nodded sadly. "Yeah. You were right, what you said earlier."

"What'd I say?"

"You said Stanley was a dick."

"Did I? Did I say that?" God, I'm such an ass. Of course I said it. I say it every five minutes to anybody who will listen.

Frank nodded and looked rather sadly at his empty beer bottle. I understood that look completely. Standing over him, I tipped my own beer down my throat, then did an about-face and sashayed off to the kitchen for a couple more. I figured Frank and I had some serious drinking to do if we were ever to actually settle into a normal conversation. SAD people don't just have conversations, you know. They don't just *chat*. Ever. Normal people can casually spill their guts. SAD people eviscerate themselves in an attempt to *look* casual as they are spilling their guts. For SAD people, nothing is without pain.

Thus the alcohol.

Plus we actually had a party to attend later. God knows, that would require even *more* alcohol. For *both* of us.

Yep. If I was any sort of judge, things were shaping up to be a pretty drunken Saturday all around. Should prove interesting.

FRANK and I were well into our third round of beers, and we had hardly spoken six words to each other during the last two. Pedro was still snoring away in Frank's lap. He had a little drool dribbling out onto Frank's crotch, which put me in mind of other body fluids, and that thought made me squirm around in my seat. God, I'm a slut. Of course, I'm a *non-practicing* slut, too shy to be anything else, unlike Jerry and Stanley who practice being a slut every chance they get, apparently, since they had practiced *me* right out of a relationship. That's not to say that I wouldn't *mind* being a practicing slut if I were built for it, but unfortunately I'm not. All my sluttiness pretty much goes on inside my head. To derail this train of thought from dragging me any further into the doldrums, I said, "I thought you were allergic to dogs, Frank."

Frank looked down fondly at his crotch. (Not unlike the way I was looking at it.) "I am," he said. "Pedro seems to be an exception. Maybe it's the short hair. Or the fact that he's so little. Plus he smells like he just had a bath."

Pedro growled in his sleep at the word "bath" and we both grinned.

I figured the beers must be working their magic. Those were the most words I had heard Frank string together since I dragged him through my front door. I liked the sound of his voice.

"I like the sound of your voice," I said, surprising myself. Lord, the beers must be working on me too.

Frank blinked and his ears turned red again, but he seemed pleased. "Thanks."

Frank still looked like he was sitting on eggshells. "Kick your shoes off," I told him. "We have a few hours to kill before the party. Might as well relax."

Little worry lines immediately popped up between Frank's fabulously green eyes. His ears got redder. I wondered if they were going to burst into flames.

Frank cleared his throat like a nervous rabbi about to deliver a scathing sermon to two thousand pissed-off Nazis with bazookas. Other than myself, I have never in my life seen anyone look so uncomfortable as Frank did at that moment. Frank's voice was so soft that I actually had to lean forward and stop guzzling beer to hear the words coming out of his mouth. "I don't think I can go to the party, Tom. I'm not ready for that much confrontation. I-I have some issues with shyness."

I realized then that Frank did not know that I knew about his little problem. And if he thought I didn't know about *his* problem, then perhaps he didn't know about *mine*.

"Frank, Jerry told me about your issues with shyness. You suffer from social anxiety disorder. So do I."

"You do?"

"Jesus, Frank, why do you think Jerry and the dick sent you over here?"

"I thought they just didn't want me over *there*."

"Hmm," I said. "There might be a bit of truth in that too."

Frank was eyeing me like maybe he thought I was pulling his leg. Not that I wouldn't mind.

"You?" he asked again, pushing his hair away from his forehead so as to look at me a little closer. "But you're not shy."

This was too much even for me. "Good grief, Frank. Pull your head out of your ass. Haven't you noticed that you and I are about as conversational as a couple of pumpkins sitting in a cornfield?"

(I was in Indiana once. I know they have pumpkins sitting in cornfields, although I think they pronounce them "punkins," and I know those pumpkins or punkins or whatever the hell they are don't do a whole lot of talking, although now that I think about it, maybe they talk their little stems off when no farmers or gay tourists are around, so maybe they really *do* talk more than Frank and I, in which case my little *bon mot* was actually misapplied. Isn't it funny how I can jabber on forever inside my head over such inconsequential things as pumpkins and cornfields when what I really wanted to say was this…)

"I used to think I was the shyest person in the world, Frank. I now know that is not the case. *You* are the shyest person in the world. I can't tell you how relieved that makes me."

Frank looked like I had punched him in the gut. Suddenly his eyes were those of a trapped animal. He gently slid Pedro off his lap, eliciting a couple of growls, and pushed himself up from the sofa. "I think I'd better go. Thanks for the beers. I just remembered something I really need to be doing."

He glanced around for his suitcase, spotted it, and went for it like a drowning man heading for a life jacket.

But I beat him to it, scooping the suitcase off the floor and holding it behind my back.

"Come on, Frank. Sit down. I wasn't trying to make fun of you. What I said is true. I *do* suffer from shyness just like you. That's the only reason Jerry and Stanley sent you over here. They thought we would both be more comfortable going to the party if we didn't have to go alone. Misery loves company and all that, you know? In their own clumsy fashion, the dick and the asshole were trying to be nice."

Yeah, right. I was amazed I could say that with a straight face.

Frank was looking more uncomfortable by the minute. He couldn't leave because I was holding his suitcase with all his worldly possessions in it and he was too nice a guy to simply knock my lights out and grab the suitcase and run. Besides, the poor guy really had nowhere to go. And no way to *get* there even if he did have somewhere to go. He wasn't driving. He must have come in a cab.

"Did you cab it here?" I asked.

Frank looked down at his shoe tops. "Couldn't afford a cab. I took the bus."

My apartment was about a mile from the bus stop. Jeez, the poor guy schlepped that suitcase all the way across town just because his brother the dick was too selfish and too lazy to pick him up and drive him over here. I was getting madder at Jerry and Stanley with every passing minute.

"Frank, sit down. Please. We need to talk, okay? We need to get past all this shyness bullshit and just *talk*. I'm going to put your suitcase right here by the door, then I'm going to get us a couple more beers. After I say what I have to say, I won't stop you if you still want to go. Okay? Is that a deal? Will you stick around long enough to just hear me out? Huh?"

Frank nodded, dragging his eyes up from his shoe tops to center them on my face. I could see the effort it took him to do that one simple thing. God, his eyes were so green. And leery. "Okay," he said. "I'll wait."

He didn't sound like he was too thrilled about the idea, so I kept a close eye on him while I hurried off to the kitchen to pluck a couple more beers from the fridge. And all the time I was keeping that close eye on my houseguest through the kitchen door, I was wondering just what the hell I was going to say to make him feel more at ease.

At that very moment, it dawned on me that I didn't want him to leave, because I really, really liked Frank Wells.

Good Lord, I thought. For the first time in two years, Jerry wasn't in my head at all. He must have fallen out through my mouth the first time my jaw gaped open at the sight of Frank.

Well, wasn't *that* an unexpected turn of events! Even for an insane person.

I found myself almost smiling as I popped the tops on two new beers and headed back to the living room, snagging a humongous bag of chips along the way, just in case Frank hadn't eaten.

I swallowed my "almost" smile fast enough when I saw the look on Frank's face. Apparently in the time it had taken me to scuttle off to the kitchen and convince myself I had a blossoming case of the hots for Frank Wells, Frank had dredged up the intestinal fortitude to get good and pissed off.

Golly. Believe it or not, that made him even sexier.

Chapter Four

"I'M NOT hungry," Frank snapped.

"So don't eat," I snapped back. "Who said these chips were for you, anyway? Maybe they're for me. Maybe they're for Pedro. Who the hell said they were for you?"

Going into alpha-male hyperdrive, I tore the bag open a smidgeon too forcefully and chips flew everywhere. The last time I saw Pedro move so fast was when I dropped two pounds of hamburger on the kitchen floor while making meatballs. He was all over those chips like black on a bowling ball. Frank scooped him off the floor before he could eat more than a pound or two, and once again he shook his finger in Pedro's face. "No! Bad dog! No!"

This time Pedro took that flapping digit as an insult and bit it. Frank yelped, stuck his wounded finger in his mouth, and dropped Pedro like a sack of laundry. Pedro scooped up another mouthful of chips while the opportunity presented itself, after which he took a moment to hike up his back leg and pee all over Frank's foot as a sort of *coup de grace*. He then sauntered off with his curly tail arched across his back, looking for all the world like a little general who has just won the war and damn well knew it.

Frank shook his head and grinned, watching Pedro stalk off. Then he looked down at his dripping tennis shoe and his grin widened. He turned to me, plucked one of the beers from my hand, and clinked his bottle against mine.

"Cheers," he said. He didn't seem to be pissed off any longer.

"Is your whole family nuts, Frank, or just you and your brother?"

"You need to train your dog, Tom. Those salty chips are bad for him. He isn't housebroken very well either, in case you hadn't noticed. And since you ask, my whole family is nuts, except for my brother, Stanley. Stanley is beyond nuts. Stanley's an asshole. But I think you already know that."

Then he looked down at his sodden sneaker again, and for the first time, I witnessed the young man laugh. Freely. Without the restraints of SAD holding him back.

That laugh was a beautiful thing to watch. I got so lost in enjoying it that it took me a minute to realize my dog had just peed on this guy's foot and maybe I should do something to atone for that breach of etiquette.

I dropped to my knees in front of Frank and his laughter died so fast I thought he must have swallowed his tongue. I looked up and saw him gazing down at me wide-eyed, as I kneeled there in front of him. It was obvious what he thought I was going to do. And if I had only consumed a few more beers on this fine afternoon I might have done it. As it was, I merely said, "Don't worry. I'm not going for your crotch. Maybe later, if you're good."

Frank opened his mouth to speak but nothing came out. I took that as a good sign.

Trying to ignore the proximity of my face to Frank's fly, I untied his shoes and slipped them off his feet, one at a time, rather like the prince doing his foot-sizing thing with Cinderella's glass slipper, only backward. I handled Frank's beat-up old Reeboks like they were glass too. Very gingerly. But that was only because they were covered with dog pee. I wasn't afraid I would hurt them or anything. They looked like he had trudged the Appalachian Trail wearing them. In both directions. In the mud. About the only thing that could have made those shoes look worse would have been running them through a garbage disposal.

"I'm going to clean these for you, Frank. It's the least I can do."

When I realized Pedro had sprayed one of Frank's socks too, I gently gripped his ankles one by one and tugged his socks off as well. His hand came out to rest itself on my shoulder so he wouldn't lose his balance. I liked the feel of that hand there. I liked it a lot. I also enjoyed the sight of his bare feet smack in front of my face. They were lovely feet. Tan and sinewy with little tufts of black hair over the big toes. I got a glimpse of fuzzy ankles too. I love fuzzy ankles.

Frank's embarrassment seemed to swoop back in like a raucous flock of sea gulls dive-bombing a dead fish. "You don't have to do that. It's okay. Really."

"Too late." I grinned, hauling myself to my feet, holding out the reeking shoes and socks like a fistful of Emmy awards. "I'll just toss these in the washer. They'll be clean and dry by the time we have to go to the party."

Just mentioning the party was like throwing water on a campfire. Frank looked worried all over again in the space of a heartbeat. He also looked like he wanted to say something.

"What?" I asked, sensing his hesitation.

He hemmed and hawed around for a moment, then finally came out with it. "As long as you're washing those, can you throw in a few other things too?" He glanced at his battered suitcase still standing by the front door. "I've been in town three days, and well—"

I was so thrilled we were being friendly with each other that I would have been happy to do anything he wanted. While washing his clothes wasn't exactly what I really had in mind, it seemed like a promising place to start.

"Hell," I said. "Slip everything off. I'll wash it all. Won't take but a few minutes."

Frank laughed again. This time I think he was laughing at the hopeful look on my face, thinking maybe my houseguest was about to strip down to his underpants and even possibly *beyond*. But apparently that would have been another feat that would require more than three beers to accomplish.

"No, there's just a few things. Where's the washer?"

Frank grabbed his suitcase and followed me down the hall to where my stackable washer and dryer stood in an out-of-the-way corner like a stocky sneak thief trying to look inconspicuous. I dropped in the shoes and socks. After first removing a shower bag filled with personal hygiene crap and a couple of manila envelopes stuffed with God knows what, Frank hefted the suitcase up and tipped everything else he owned in after the shoes.

"I guess you're not big on sorting," I commented.

To which Frank said, "It's a waste of time. Just set that sucker on *fumigate*. Everything will come out fine."

"Are you sure you're gay?" I asked. I never knew a gay person in my life who didn't know how to properly sort laundry. Or make a bed.

Frank looked surprised. "Who said I was gay?"

Oops. "Your brother. I'm sorry. You mean you're not?" That would explain a lot, I thought.

Frank took a couple of beats to think it over, then shrugged. "No. I am. I just didn't know Stanley had told you."

"Did you know *I* was gay?" I asked.

Frank laughed again. This time there wasn't much charity in it. "Yeah, although I think I would have figured it out pretty quick anyway. That little comment about my crotch was pretty much a dead giveaway. Plus you're not exactly lumberjack material."

If he hadn't been so damned right, I would have been offended.

TWO beers later we were feeling very little pain, although I did see Frank keeping a nervous eye on the clock. It was obvious that he wasn't looking forward to the goddamn party any more than I was. The dryer rumbled comfortably in the background while Pedro snored from the back of the couch where he was perched like a sleeping parrot. All was forgiven apparently. In Pedro's mind at least. And Frank's too, I guess, since he had his arm draped along the back of the sofa with

Pedro's chin resting on the back of his hand. They were friends again. All was right with the world.

Frank and I weren't bumping heads so much either. Our two cases of social anxiety disorder seemed to have found a demilitarized zone where we could pretty much be ourselves with less danger of our shared psychoses reaching out to slap us mute. On a social level, I had not talked this much with anyone in months. Frank seemed to be enjoying himself too.

God bless booze.

"So what are you going to do as far as making a living goes?" I asked, downing the last dregs of my fifth beer and seriously considering going for a sixth. "Do you have any job prospects lined up?"

Frank looked over to study Pedro's face instead of my own. Maybe SAD wasn't totally at bay after all. "I thought I'd stay with Stanley until I get on my feet. He's my brother, after all. Surely he wouldn't begrudge me that much help. I don't know how his partner will feel about it though."

I did. Jerry would take one look at Frank and be all for the idea. Then one day Stanley would come home from work and find Jerry's tongue in Frank's ass and that would be the end of a beautiful relationship. Frank and Jerry would both be out on their ears and I would be jealous that Jerry's tongue got to where I wanted mine to go first.

None of this needed to be said, however. Sometimes even I know when to shut up. I was curious though. "So what did you think of Jerry when you met him?"

Frank shrugged. "Haven't met him. Haven't seen Stanley yet either. I've been waiting for an invitation, but it must have got lost in the mail." He rolled his beautiful green eyes. "Maybe I'm an idiot for expecting any help from Stanley at all. Or Jerry either, for that matter. If not, I guess I can always hike my way back home. Dad will be glad to see me, at any rate. It's not like I'm unwanted *everywhere* in the world."

Frank forced up a chuckle, as if to make light of that last statement, but I thought I detected a hint of sadness in it too. And maybe even a hint of truth.

Frank seemed to feel the need to explain himself further. "It's not like I *want* to be a nuisance to Stanley and Jerry, but the way money is I don't have much choice. Surely Stanley will understand that."

I tried to swallow my anger at knowing Frank had been in town for three days and still not seen his brother. Lord, Stanley and Jerry really were dicks. Dicks of the lowest caliber. It seemed to me that Frank was beginning to suspect as much himself. Gads, the guy must be a nervous wreck having no money, no longer a place to stay, and suffering from a debilitating case of shyness on top of everything else. I couldn't even *imagine* what I would do under those circumstances, although tossing a Molotov cocktail through Stanley and Jerry's front window seemed like a reasonable first step.

I didn't bother asking Frank why he had decided to leave the farm. It was pretty obvious. A gay man living in rural Indiana probably has very few options for socializing with anyone not wearing a John Deere hat and overalls. While those two articles of clothing can be sexy as hell if that's *all* a man is wearing, in Indiana most farmers also seem to be wearing pig poop and days-old sweat and harbor a very high grudge against anyone who enjoys flirting with members of their own sex. Frank *had* to leave Indiana or sooner or later he would have been stomped into the mud behind someone's barn after offending some yahoo's sense of propriety. He knew it and I knew it.

Life isn't easy for gay people. Never is. Never was.

"So you get along okay with Stanley then," I said. "I mean, you don't hate each other or anything?"

Frank looked down at his bare feet, gazed back through the hallway door toward the sound of the dryer thumping away in the distance, peered up at the ceiling, then over at Pedro. Everywhere but at me. "We're not what you'd call close. But still I think he'll help me out. I don't see why he shouldn't." Frank didn't sound convinced, and knowing Stanley as well as I did, I thought Frank had good reason to be unconvinced.

I mulled it over. "So I guess it all hinges on what happens at the party tonight. Whether he takes you in or throws you out or ignores you completely and lets you die miserable and alone on the cold, hard streets of San Diego."

Frank did a vaudevillian eye roll while spitting up a community-theater-caliber groan. "Thanks, Tom. Now I can relax and enjoy the party. And here I was worried I might not be comfortable."

I clucked my tongue in sympathy. "Another beer, Frank?"

"Hell, yes."

It was getting dark out, so on the way to the kitchen I flipped on a lamp. I popped open two beers, and as an afterthought threw together a couple of ham sandwiches to go with them. For Frank, a lot truly did hinge on how things went at the party tonight, so I knew I would never forgive myself if I sent him in there drunk as a skunk and incoherently slobbering all over the place.

While my own trepidation about attending the party was still hammering away in the back of my mind and periodically causing me a heart palpitation or two, I was more than aware of the fact that having Frank there to worry about was a godsend for me. It took my mind off my own insecurities, and let me worry about someone else's insecurities for a change. And let's face it, the worst that could happen to me at Jerry's little soiree was that I would make a complete fool of myself and be forever humiliated. In Frank's case, the possible consequences were considerably more dire. The rest of his life might actually be affected. And I liked Frank. I didn't want to see him hurt. Or embarrassed. Or humbled into hightailing it back home to Indiana like a chastised puppy.

Frank's lovely bare feet were propped on my coffee table (they really were very attractive feet), so I plopped both sandwiches and his beer on the table beside them and perched myself on my new chair across the way while Pedro eyed the sandwiches like maybe they were meant for him.

"You've mentioned your dad, Frank. Is your mother still alive too?"

Frank studied my face for a brief moment, then his shyness got the better of him and he looked away to grab a sandwich. Between mouthfuls he said, "She died a long time ago. Dad never remarried." A look of concern crossed Frank's face. Almost a look of guilt. "Dad's going to have a rough time running the farm without my help. There's a lot of work involved even though it's a pretty small operation. Livestock, mostly. A couple hundred acres of cropland too, but Dad leases that out."

"He can't be very old, your dad. Surely he'll be okay."

Frank was digging into his sandwich like it was the first thing he had eaten all day. I felt a stab of concern. Lord, maybe it really *was* the first thing he had eaten all day.

"Dad's not well, actually. He won't talk about it, but it's pretty obvious. I probably shouldn't have left. But even he told me I should. Get it out of your system, he told me. See a little bit of the world, go visit your brother in sunny California, then come back here and milk the cows." Frank laughed at that. "Dad's a nice guy. I hope he's okay."

Pedro leaped down from the back of the sofa and bumped Frank's arm with his head. He wasn't particularly subtle about it either. Frank merely gazed down at him, frowned, and said, "No. Go back to sleep. Good dogs don't beg."

Pedro thought about that for a second, heaved up a sigh and flew back to the top of the sofa where he curled back up into a discontented ball, still eyeing the sandwich, but no longer with any sense of hope of partaking in it. He didn't even pee on Frank's arm in retaliation. I was impressed.

I glanced at the clock. It was almost seven. My heart gave a nervous lurch inside my chest. Party time was drawing near. At that very moment the dryer buzzed, and Frank polished off the second sandwich.

"Do you want to clean up before the party?" I asked. "You can shower here if you want."

Frank glanced at me as if wondering whether I had any ulterior motives buried in that offer, but apparently the determined look of angelic innocence I quickly plastered across my face put him at ease.

"Maybe I should," he said, hauling himself to his feet. "I'll get my clothes from the dryer too."

As an afterthought, he added, "I hope I'm not being too much of a pest. If I am, just say so."

I smiled my most charming smile. "You're not a pest at all. Go get cleaned up."

In the hallway, he turned and very sweetly said, "Thanks, Tom. I don't think I could face this party on my own. I'm glad you'll be there with me."

"Ditto," I said, and meant it. I could see by the relieved expression on Frank's face that he knew I was being sincere. That shared moment of understanding seemed to bring us together in full. It put us on the same team. Us against them. I liked that feeling. Frank seemed to like it too. With one last bashful smile, he turned and headed down the hall in search of the bathroom. I let him find it on his own. I had other things to think about.

I WAS almost dressed when I heard Frank come out of the bathroom. I went to see if he had found everything all right and ran into him headfirst. Literally. Almost knocking him off his feet.

"Jesus, I'm sorry."

Frank blushed all the way from the soles of his feet to the top of his head. "That's okay, Tom. You almost knocked me naked, though."

It was then that I noticed what he was wearing. Or what he *wasn't* wearing. Which was pretty much everything. Or nothing. Depending on how you looked at it.

He was dripping wet and he had a towel tucked low around his waist. He was frantically scrambling to retuck it after our head-on collision jarred it loose. Just my luck, he succeeded in resecuring the towel before it slid to the floor. I've never been so disappointed in my life.

My eyes were immediately riveted to a tiny trail of dark hair that wandered south from Frank's belly button and disappeared just above a promising bulge in that damn towel. The rest of Frank's chest was hairless, well-defined but not pushy about it. His broad brown areolas looked out at the world with an air of superiority, as well they might, they were so tempting, with their tiny little nipples perfectly centered in each one. His legs were the kind of legs I dream about when I'm having *those* kinds of dreams. Strong and hairy. And just by looking at Frank's legs, I could imagine how they would feel against my face, how his skin would taste against my tongue. That skin was the warm, delicate color of coffee with too much cream, the kind of brown that comes from the gene pool, not the sun. One day on a California beach and Frank would probably be as brown as a filbert, sporting a darker tan than I could acquire all year.

He blushed again at the way I was looking at him, and this time when he blushed, I blushed right back. It was an awkward moment.

"I'm sorry," I stammered. "Didn't mean to stare. Or knock you naked."

"You didn't?"

"Well, maybe I did."

Frank laughed, and only then did I see the fresh beer in his hand. By the slight pinkish cast to his eyes, I suspected Frank had helped himself to a *couple* of brews since I went to get dressed. Maybe he was more freaked out about the party than he appeared. I know I was.

He gave me a hopeful look. God, he was cute. "We could skip the party and stay here," he said.

Was he flirting? I didn't think so. I think he just really, really didn't want to go to the party. It was obviously going to be up to me to keep Frank's eye on the big picture.

"You need a place to stay, remember? If you want to start a new life in San Diego, Stanley is going to have to help you get it started.

You're going to have to suck up to him a little. Stanley likes being sucked up to. Most dicks do. Slight pun intended." It took every ounce of willpower I possessed not to take another gander at his crotch when I said it.

"O-oka-ay," he moaned like a five-year-old being told to put the Snickers bag away until after dinner. "Can we have another beer before we go?"

"Heck, yes," I said. "As many as you want." And that went for me too. The closer it came to party time, the antsier I was becoming. I had already suffered three coronary infarctions while I was getting dressed. At least I think they were coronary infarctions. I suppose they might have been small gas explosions brought on by all the beer. Or maybe my hormones were popping like popcorn from having a damn-near-naked man in my apartment for the first time since God knew when.

Frank bent down and scooped an armful of hot clothes out of the dryer. When he turned his back to me, I saw another one of my all-time favorite male anatomy goodies—a little tuft of hair just above the crack of Frank's ass.

God, when *was* the last time I had partaken of sex with someone other than myself? Couldn't be as long as it felt, could it?

I stood there imagining how that little tuft of hair would tickle my nose while my tongue slid between Frank's butt cheeks, and it was all I could do not to rip that towel off, drop to my knees, and make a complete fool of myself smack in front of the Kenmore stackable. Before I could decide whether I cared about making a fool of myself or not, Frank said, "Ta-ta," and galloped back to the bathroom dribbling laundry along the way.

Just as he reached the bathroom door, the towel accidentally slid to the floor (finally), and I was blessed with the sight of the most beautiful heinie I had seen in many a long year. Fuzzy, round, and scrumptious.

This time it was definitely a coronary infarction I felt.

"Oops," Frank said, and closed the door giggling, dragging the towel in behind him with his foot. Then he poked his head back out and said, "Were you going to bring me another beer, then?"

"You betcha," I practically sang out. "Anything you want!"

I didn't realize until later that the sight of Frank's ass had all but obliterated any fear I had about the upcoming party. Jeez, could the severity of social anxiety disorder actually be mitigated by the sufferer getting a glimpse of a fine male posterior every once in a while? Seemed a bit farfetched. Still, the world of medical miracles had often hinged on odd coincidences. The discovery of penicillin sprang to mind. This might be just one more example.

I headed for the kitchen and the cold beer. One more for him and one more for me should just about do it. I didn't know about Frank, but I was getting into dangerous territory with all this drinking. I had been known to sing entire Gilbert and Sullivan librettos after six glasses of Scotch. Unbidden. At dinner. In a crowded restaurant. With breadsticks in my ears. God knows what I would do after a dozen beers.

I liked Frank a lot. I didn't even mind waiting on him hand and foot. And I was beginning to like him drunk even more than I liked him sober. If I didn't drink myself into a *complete* blackout, this might prove to be a rather enjoyable evening after all.

A few minutes later, Frank and I were downing fresh beers, him on one side of the bathroom door, me on the other. I could hear him in there humming a Beatles tune off-key and periodically grumbling about something or other. I was running a clothes brush over my new slacks trying to remove all traces of Pedro and belting out the tit willow song from *The Mikado*.

I checked myself in the bedroom mirror. Brand-new button-down Arrow shirt, lightly starched, but not stiff, long sleeves rakishly turned back twice to expose my forearms. New front-pleated black trousers with a slim mahogany belt, and an almost-new pair of oxblood penny loafers with actual pennies in the slots just for the hell of it that perfectly matched the belt. I thought I looked pretty good. As soon as Frank vacated the bathroom, I'd add a little gel to my hair to get that casual spiky look going on, gargle a quick slug of high-octane mouthwash to make my breath pretty, and I'd be ready to party.

And the very moment I thought that thought, I knew I wasn't ready at all. I broke into a cold sweat, swallowed back a swarm of butterflies that were trying to fly up my throat, and my fingertips went numb. Wondering just how many strangers Stanley had purposely invited to this goddamn party just to freak me out, I felt my legs turn to Jell-O and my left ear started twitching again. Suddenly my clothes were all wrong and my haircut looked stupid. I discovered a zit on the end of my nose, saw thirty pounds of fat hanging off my ass that hadn't been there two seconds before, and I was pretty sure my breath smelled like a sick possum had crawled down my throat and died. Then I felt the flu coming on.

Before I could decide to dive under the bed, Frank came strolling out of the bathroom with his hair still wet and a half-empty beer bottle stuck in his pants pocket like a Luger. He was humming "Norwegian Wood" and looked remarkably calm and confident for a person with SAD who was about to attend a party with God knows how many strangers present. That look didn't last long, however. The minute he saw the terror on my face, his confidence shattered like one of those crystal snow globes dropped out of a thirty-story window onto a concrete sidewalk.

"Oh crap," he said, and his face went gray.

I almost forgot my terror when I checked out Frank's attire. The jeans he had on were new and stiff and the deepest, darkest blue I had ever seen on an article of clothing. Even running them through a washer and dryer hadn't toned down their color or softened them up. They must have been made of aluminum. He looked like he had stuffed his legs down a couple of stovepipes and he walked like a cowboy who had just climbed down off his horse after three weeks in the saddle. Bowlegged? You could have driven a MINI Cooper between his knees. His shirt was a tee with a tiny hole just over the left tit and a picture of a petticoated Donna Reed on the front. In a dialogue bubble above her head, Miss Reed announced, "Dinner's ready!" I wondered if Frank even knew who Donna Reed was. I was afraid to see what was on the back. Frank's shoes were the same battered tennis shoes he had worn earlier, clean now, after being hosed down by Pedro and run through the washer, but still looking pretty beat-up for a social engagement. The only concession he had made to formal attire was the black socks he wore under his tennies. It was a good thing Frank was beautiful. It made his total lack of style almost charming.

Almost.

I brushed aside my own terror long enough to supplement Frank's. "Um, how would you feel about me doing a little damage control on your outfit? Not that you don't look great, but—"

He looked down at himself as if he just now for the very first time noticed there was a body standing there underneath his head. "Too dressy?" he asked, crestfallen. I hoped he was kidding.

"Not for a hoedown," I said.

I dragged him into my bedroom and told him to kick off his shoes. He was like a child, doing everything I told him to do. Fear is a great tranquilizer, apparently. I tossed him a pair of black dress shoes. His basket was so tempting in those tight-ass blue jeans that no one would look at his shoes anyway.

"They're too big," he whined after trying one on, so I threw him an extra pair of socks.

When the shoes were in place and Frank seemed reasonably comfortable with them poking out the bottom of his cast-iron pant legs, I ventured another suggestion. "Let's try for a slightly dressier top, okay?"

"But this is my best shirt," Frank joked with a straight face. At least I think he was joking. God, I hoped so.

"Well, let's just see how *this* looks. Take that thing off."

I drained another four ounces from my beer bottle while Frank pulled his Donna Reed T-shirt over his head and threw it on the bed. His freshly showered body smelled like heaven. I stared at his perfect chest so long that he finally stuck a hand on one hip and cocked his head to the side as if to say "Ye-e-s?"

My hands were trembling as I handed him a cashmere V-neck sweater in pale yellow. I figured the yellow would look great against his skin, and my hands were trembling because I was getting a boner seeing Frank standing there in my bedroom half-dressed smelling like an angel. He was too busy worrying about how he looked to take any notice of my boner. That was either a good or a bad thing, depending on how you looked at it.

There wasn't much I could do about the boner at the moment, since boners pretty much have a mind of their own, but I was pleased to note that the sweater really did look great on Frank. He pushed the sleeves up to his elbows, exposing his hairy forearms, then shook the damp hair away from his eyes. "Well?" he asked. "Am I fit for human consumption?"

"God, yes," I said. "I mean, hell, yes. I mean yes."

He surveyed himself in the mirror for all of two seconds, then turned to look me up and down. "So we're really going then, are we?"

"Guess so," I said. "You nervous?"

"Nope. You?"

"Not a bit."

We were both lying through our teeth. We were scared to death.

"One more beer before we go?" I asked, hopefully.

"One or two beers sounds great," Frank said, cleverly augmenting my suggestion with an extra serving of alcohol. I thought I detected a slight tremor in his voice. It seemed to counterpoint the tremor in mine. What a pair of cowards we were.

God, SAD sucks.

Frank, on the other hand, dress sense or no dress sense, was just one small notch below wonderful.

Thankfully, I was too drunk and too nervous to fully comprehend the ramifications of that thought.

Chapter Five

GIGGLING like a couple of third-graders, we toppled out of the cab in front of Jerry and Stanley's rented condo. I couldn't help but notice, for the umpteenth time, that Frank was a hell of a good-looking man. Even slobberingly drunk he was a looker. He didn't seem to share any of the symptoms of his brother's assholeiness, either, and God help me, I've always been attracted to nice men. "Nice" to me is just as much a turn-on as "handsome." Maybe even *more* of a turn-on. I also couldn't help noticing that Frank looked better in my yellow cashmere sweater than I *ever* had. That was a turn-on too. Yes siree.

We took one look at Jerry and Stanley's front door and the smiles fled our faces like fleas jumping off a dying dog. There seemed to be an incredible number of voices laughing and babbling and chattering behind that door. Sounded like a big flapping flock of geese. Gazing around, we saw that there also seemed to be an inordinate number of automobiles parked on the street for a neighborhood where all the condos had underground parking. Just how many guests did Stanley really invite? I wondered. This didn't look like the first thirty pages of the phone book. This looked like maybe all the way up to J or K. How many people could Stanley possibly know? And if they knew him, why the hell would they accept an invitation to a party thrown by such a dick? Maybe they came for Jerry's sake. That at least made sense.

"You're mumbling," Frank said.

"No, I'm not."

"Yes, you are. Munk and drumbling. I mean drunk and mumbling."

"God, Frank, shut up."

"Let's go back to your place and have another beer, what d'ya say, Tom? I'll buy."

"You don't have any money. How are you going to buy? And what about Stanley? You need your brother's help. God help you, but you do. And let me just be the first to say, rotsaruck."

"You speak Japanese. I'm impressed."

"Frank, *please* shut up. You really want to go back to my place?"

"With all my heart and soul," Frank said, gazing at his brother's front door with absolute terror splattered all over his face.

"Me, too," I said, and at that very moment our cab drove away. We were stuck.

I was about to say I didn't really mind walking twenty miles if Frank didn't, when that damned door popped open and I saw Jerry beckoning to us to come on in.

"Damn," I said.

"Damn," Frank echoed.

"Damn," Jerry called out. "Where the hell you been? We were getting worried about you two."

I'll bet. "Car trouble," I said. "Had to take a cab at the last minute."

Jerry looked us over. "Good thing. You're both so drunk you can barely stand up. Stanley's going to love this."

"Oh, is *he* here?" Frank asked.

And we looked at each other and started giggling again. Frank pulled two beer bottles out from under his sweater and handed me one. They were warm from being stuck down his pants for the past twenty minutes. Lucky beer bottles. I wondered if Frank's pecker was suffering from hypothermia, and if it was, if there was anything I could do to warm it up again. We popped open the beers and plopped down on the curb with a couple of satisfied grunts.

"We'll be in as soon as we're finished," I said over my shoulder.

"Yeah," Frank echoed. "As foon as we're sinished."

"Fine," Jerry growled, and slammed the door.

It was a lovely night to be sitting on a curb drinking warm beer with a handsome farmer from Indiana. If it hadn't been for that blasted party hanging over our heads like a frigging vulture, I would have been enjoying myself immensely.

Frank and I gulped our beers faster than we should have and when we stood up we had to hold onto each other until we found our equilibrium. Obviously, Frank wasn't any better at drinking than I was.

"Oh hell," I said. "Let's get this over with."

Frank seemed to have been smacked on the head with a sober stick all of a sudden. "Stay with me, okay, Tom?"

I leaned in and kissed his cheek before I even realized what I was doing. Frank didn't seem to mind. He was probably too scared to notice. I wasn't. I remembered the feel of his cheek against mine and the way his neck smelled all warm and fragrant for the rest of the night. It's what kept me going.

"I won't leave your side," I said. "I promise, Frank."

And hand in hand, like a hammered Hansel and Gretel approaching the big bad witch's cottage, we stumbled up to my ex's front door and softly knocked.

The door swung open. What had sounded from the curb like a gabbling flock of geese now became the raucous roar of a hundred or more revelers, each and every one laughing and jabbering as they clutched a drink with one hand and someone else's ass with the other, or so it seemed. The crowd was predominantly gay male, with just a smattering of lesbians strewn about for texture. Terrified, we were pulled into this tempest of sound and color and frantically cheerful humanity and immediately lost sight of each other. Like two doomed sinners sucked blindly through the gates of hell, Frank and I suddenly found ourselves facing our greatest fear *alone*. Christ. And after all our preparation too.

Isn't that just the way it always ends up?

NOW, SAD, in an unfunny way, is a funny thing. You can sometimes kill it dead with alcohol, as Frank and I were trying to do on this particular night, but the general consensus is that one should not let that particular form of treatment become a habit. Otherwise one would be drunk *all* the time, and that would, of course, lead to a whole *new* set of problems. So on the whole, it is the considered opinion of most medical experts that it is better to suffer from SAD than be a raging, slobbering, pee-down-your-pant-leg alcoholic.

SAD is also funny, in the same unfunny way, because it doesn't always affect everyone in an identical manner. Some who suffer from it may only be affected when trying to *eat* in front of other people. Or having to *speak* in front of other people. Or—and this is the most common manifestation of social anxiety disorder—when the sufferer is thrown into any social situation with any group of people, be it large, small, or in-between. Casual or formal. Once there, he is bombarded with the fear that he will be judged by those around him, or ridiculed, or totally ostracized and shipped off to Siberia for some unfathomable reason or other.

In my case, and probably Frank's, it basically boiled down to the fear of being humiliated and made to feel unworthy in *any* sort of social situation, be it eating, speaking, mingling, or just standing around looking stupid with anywhere from one person to a thousand.

Sounds like shyness, you say. Well, yes and no. The main difference between simple shyness and a thundering case of social anxiety is that the shy person is able to function. He may not be comfortable doing it, but he can hide his shyness well enough not to stand out in a crowd. He does not suffer the physical symptoms that a person with SAD suffers.

He does not, in effect, turn into a blob of quivering, quaking Jell-O and pass out flat on the floor. Or, if gay, slap his hand to his forehead and swoon like Aunt Pittypat in *Gone with the Wind*. Usually, he doesn't feel compelled to drink himself silly either. Like Frank and I.

And now that Frank and I had finally arrived at the dreaded PARTY (every time the word PARTY entered my head, I heard maniacal laughter booming from the wings like in some cheesy horror flick), I was forced to accept the fact that all the drinking we had done had not helped at all. It fact, it made things worse. Now I was not only worried about being judged a moron by the people around me, but with the room spinning the way it was, I was also worried about falling flat on my face even *before* I passed out from fear.

I nervously poked my way through this jabbering tossed salad of humanity looking for Frank, but all I saw were strangers, with maybe a few recognizable acquaintances scattered about like croutons. A few people said hello as I passed but I blithely ignored them. All I could think about was rescuing Frank. I had no idea how he could have slipped from my grasp so quickly or what horrors were being visited upon him by this uncaring mob of strangers.

Someone stuck a drink in my hand, and I sipped it while I searched. Then someone else took hold of my elbow, and I turned to see Jerry's face three inches from my own.

"I'd offer you a drink," he said, shouting to be heard above the crowd, "but I see you already have one. Maybe that should be your last, what do you think? And what the hell is going on with you and Stanley's brother? You looked awfully cozy out there on the street, drinking and schmoozing and cuddling in front of the neighbors."

"Thanks," I grumped. "A slut offering lessons in moderation and morality. Love it. Where'd he go? Where's Frank?"

"Stanley is introducing him around."

"I'll bet. Why hasn't Frank been invited over here before now? He's been in town for three days."

Jerry looked uncomfortable. "Yeah, well, you know how it is. Stanley and I were busy with work, and what with one thing and another—"

"Oh please. The poor guy's broke and alone and far away from home, and you two left him to dangle in the wind for *three days*. He had to use up all his money for a hotel room just because you guys couldn't be bothered to put him up for a couple of nights. I can believe it from Stanley, he's such a dick, but I thought *you* were nicer than that."

"I *am* nice."

"No, you're not. You're a Stanley-in-training. Pretty soon you'll be a full-fledged dick yourself, which is one step up from slut. You can have another party to celebrate the promotion. *Where's Frank?*"

I was trembling I was so mad. Or maybe I was trembling because I was throwing a hissy fit at my ex-lover while surrounded by a bunch of strangers who didn't know me from Adam but who were hanging onto every word I sputtered like I was the Dalai Lama throwing a tantrum at the UN. Who knows? The only one *not* hanging onto my every word was Jerry, who had walked away shaking his head. I always hated it when he did that. It wasn't until that moment that I realized I had left his birthday present in the cab. Oh well. I'd rather the cabbie drank it anyway.

"*Where the hell is Frank?*" I screamed at Jerry's retreating back. The secret to throwing a good hissy fit is to mean it. Sincerity. That's the key to a good hissy fit. And ignoring any audience you might inadvertently acquire.

Out of the corner of my eye, I saw a jubilant Stanley tugging a horrified Frank through the crowd like a pull toy. Frank's eyes were as big as dinner plates, but not in a good way, not like he was having the time of his life or anything. But Stanley obviously was.

"What's all the hubbub?" Stanley asked, all grins and forced camaraderie, winking at a guest here and there as if letting them in on the joke, all the while heading straight for me. "And what's all the yelling about? Oh, hello, Tom."

Stanley was a handsome guy, dammit. I had to admit that. But likeable? No. I've seen spores that were more congenial. He wasn't *nice* handsome like Frank, either. He was more *bad boy* handsome. Like Satan in a clingy pair of slacks and a tight shirt, with his barbed tail flopping around behind his head. Sleek and sexy, but apt to bite, like a cranky Doberman. That was Stanley. And tonight I noticed a smear of white powder on the tip of his nose. Coke. Uh-oh. Everybody on this side of the Mississippi knew what an ass Stanley became when he snorted cocaine. No wonder Jerry was looking a little out of sorts.

Stanley looked me up and down and gave his head a sad little shake. He turned to face the roomful of partiers who were watching every move we made like the leery opening night audience of the latest Broadway flop, thrilled to be in on the disaster but appalled they had actually paid good money to attend. Knowing grins were passing back and forth among the crowd as they eyed me and eyed Frank and hung on Stanley's every word as if to say, "Good old Stanley. What a card."

Frank cast a humiliated glance in my direction as Stanley dragged him around to face the crowd.

"Everybody, this is my brother Frank! Fresh off the farm in Indiana! Let's give him a rousing cheer, what'dya say?"

There were a few choruses of "Hello!" and "Hey, farm boy!" and somebody off in the back of the crowd yelled "Where the hell'd you get those pants, Frank?"

Frank's face turned so red he looked like a stoplight. He looked at nothing but the floor even while Stanley held his arm up over his head like he had just won the Heavyweight Crown. If there had been a hole in that floor, I knew Frank would have happily done an Alice in Wonderland and dived through it without a moment's hesitation. And I would have dived in after him.

"If anybody needs any yard work done or chickens plucked or pigs castrated, then Frank's your man!" Stanley boomed out. "Looking for work is good old Frank. Wants to live in the big city like his favorite big brother. Ain't that sweet?"

I seemed to sense a couple of tics of sympathy for Frank in the crowd now. But there was still plenty of laughter there too. Laughter at Frank's expense. And that pissed me off mightily.

"Gotta warn you, though," Stanley blathered on, sniffing now and then to keep the drugs up inside his nose where they belonged. "Bro seems to have a bit of a drinking problem. So I wouldn't give him the keys to the house or anything. But as long as he's just trimming the verge or mucking out the stables he should be reliable enough."

There were a couple of sympathetic grumbles in the crowd now, and even Jerry seemed to think Stanley had gone far enough. He pulled Frank's arm out of Stanley's hand and led him back to me. I heard him muttering apologies to Frank as he dragged him along.

But Stanley wasn't finished yet. Now he came after me.

"You all know Tom," Stanley announced, grandly sweeping his arms in my direction like Vanna White introducing the letter R to a rapt world. "I hope you'll all try to make him feel welcome. He's afraid of crowds, you know. Scared poopless of being the center of attention is poor old Tom. Maybe nonentities always feel that way. Who knows? Anyway, let's try to make him feel like a normal person, okay? And try not to mention the fact that he's plastered. He'll sober up eventually. I think."

My eyes met Frank's. We gazed at each other and something clicked between us. We turned back to Stanley and gave him an appraising stare, like he was a new exhibit at the zoo. Maybe a two-headed anteater just discovered on the Argentinean pampas. I turned back to Frank with a questioning look, and with an evil little smile and a wink, Frank nodded. We were obviously sharing the same wicked thought. And that thought was a doozy.

Together we walked up to Stanley and with no hesitation whatsoever, both our fists shot out at the same moment. Mine caught Stanley just below the right eye. Frank's made contact smack with the bridge of Stanley's drug-packed nose. Stanley went down in midsentence like a head-shot deer. Coke snot flew everywhere.

Jerry let out an unmanly scream, embarrassing really, and flung himself over Stanley's prone body. He tried to revive Stanley by kissing

Stanley's forehead ten or twelve times. When that didn't work, he gave Stanley's cheek a dainty slap. Stanley moaned but he didn't look like he'd be waking up any time soon.

"Slap him harder," Frank suggested, biting back a giggle.

"Much harder," I agreed with a grin. I hadn't had this much fun since I won two thousand bucks on the lottery. (Of course, immediately after that I flew off to Vegas where I managed to turn my two thousand bucks into ninety-five cents in less than three hours, but that's another story.)

The sympathetic noises from the party crowd were meant for Stanley now. Not Frank. In fact, Frank and I seemed to be pretty unpopular all of a sudden. Not that we cared. We were finally having fun. It was about time, too. Up until the moment Stanley's head hit the floor, the party had been a real drag.

When Jerry shot dirty looks in our direction, I was appalled to see tears in his eyes. Geez, what a wuss. He was making Aunt Pittypatt look butch.

Frank snuggled up next to me happy as a clam as we looked down at poor Stanley who was sprawled out on the floor, arms and legs akimbo, with his nose dribbling blood and cocaine and his eye turning black even as a near-hysterical Jerry slapped him progressively harder and harder, first on one cheek, then on the other, in an attempt to wake him up. It was a lovely sight to see.

"You were worried about me," Frank said, ignoring the hostile murmurings of the crowd around us, centering all his attention on Jerry bitch-slapping the tar out of Stanley in a vain attempt to bring him round.

I nodded. "Yeah."

"So you were trying to rescue me."

I nodded again. "Yeah. I guess."

"Like a white knight."

"Well, more like a drunken banker."

"Still—"

Frank stuck his hand down my back pocket in a proprietary sort of way and left it there.

After that, SAD or no SAD, Frank and I found the party rather enjoyable. While Stanley lay snoozing and moaning and looking pathetic on the living room floor, Frank and I mixed and mingled and had another drink. Jerry had sprung for a disc jockey, so Frank and I were just about to partake of a slow dance together when Stanley woke up. Embarrassed, he staggered up off the floor, wiped the snot and blood off his face with his shirtsleeve, and with a nasty glint in his eyes, beckoned for us to follow him.

I didn't figure Frank and I were about to be awarded a coffeemaker as the door prize for being named the evening's Most Congenial Houseguests and I was right.

Stanley held a cold compress to his nose that somebody had handed him and he none too politely escorted us to the front door after he screamed at Jerry to call us a cab. Between threats of legal action and a possible change of wills, as if Stanley really had a will, and as if he would have really left Frank anything in it if he had, he pulled Frank aside with a growl just before he tossed us out on our ears.

"What the hell are you doing in California, Frank? Be honest. What do you want from me?"

Frank still had his hand in my back pocket so I was close enough to see the whites of his eyes when he answered. "I just need a little help getting on my feet. Maybe a place to stay until I find a job and get some money set aside."

Stanley snarled like a rat. "Yeah, right. That sounds like a euphemism for 'permanent houseguest'. Or maybe 'sponge' is a better word."

Jerry joined us, shuffling his feet and looking uncomfortable as hell. "We've got room," he said, trying to ease the tension. "We could put him up for a couple of weeks in the spare bedroom."

Stanley all but snapped his head off. "Stay out of this, Jerry. This is between me and my brother. Did you call the fucking cab?"

Jerry gave me a shamefaced look and turned away to stare at the street. "Yeah, I called it," he mumbled.

Stanley checked his compress to see if he was still bleeding. There was a meanness in his eyes I had never seen there before, although I had always suspected he had it in him. "What I'll do, Frank, is give you the money to get the hell back home. That's what I'll do. A one-way bus ticket to Indianapolis. Take it or leave it."

Frank opened his mouth to answer (God knows what he was going to say), but I didn't give him a chance. "Frank doesn't need your money," I said. "And he's staying."

Stanley spun on me like a striking rattlesnake. "What was that, Tom?"

"I said he's staying."

Stanley laughed but there wasn't much humor in it. "And how's he going to manage that? Sleep under an overpass with the rest of the bums?"

Frank's eyes traveled to me, then to Stanley, then back to me. He looked like he was at Wimbledon, trying to figure out the game from the cheap seats.

"Tom, I—" Frank began.

Never taking my eyes off Stanley, I held my hand up, cutting Frank off. "He'll be staying with me."

Stanley smirked. "He will?"

Frank blinked. "I will?"

Jerry jumped like someone had poked a knitting needle in his butt. He spun around to face us. "Say what?"

I detected a glimmer of jealousy in those two tiny words that I found highly amusing.

"What about money?" Stanley asked, ignoring Jerry. Ignoring Frank too, for that matter. All his attention was now centered on me.

"I'll help him find a job," I said.

"You will?" Frank asked, a bemused smile twisting the corners of his mouth, offering a glimpse of those incredibly white teeth which I still wanted to lick.

"I will," I said. "Happily."

Stanley tenderly patted his sore eye. I was sorry I wouldn't be around to see the surprised look on his face when he checked a mirror and saw how black and puffy that eye was getting. His nose was getting bigger too, swelling up like a fat beefsteak tomato. Stanley wouldn't be too happy about that either, but I thought it was pretty funny. He was starting to look like W. C. Fields. Not exactly a looker in *anybody's* book. I figured good old Stanley wouldn't be snorting any foreign substances up *that* nose for a while. Too tender. Stanley flung the old bloody compress into the hedge beside the front door and spat a little blood onto the sidewalk, trying to look butch but not quite carrying it off, since butch people don't usually look so damned beat-up.

"Fine," he snarled. "Jerry and I wash our hands of both of you."

"Now wait a minute—" Jerry started.

"Shut up, Jerry." Stanley glowered at Jerry like maybe he was ready to throw him out too. He turned his mean little eyes to Frank and me while Jerry stood there looking horrified and helpless.

And before Jerry could say another word, Stanley slammed the door in our faces with a nasty grin.

Can't say I was surprised.

The only thing surprising to me was that Frank's hand was still firmly ensconced in my back pocket. It seemed to have found a home there. And I was pretty sure that in my eagerness to piss off Stanley, I had also committed to letting the rest of Frank move in too. Into my apartment. Into my life. Good God. What had I done?

I didn't say two words on the long cab ride home.

Neither did Frank, since he was cuddled up beside me with his head on my shoulder, sound asleep. Or passed out. Whichever.

Just before he drowsed off to sleep he had muttered, "I really like you, Tom."

"I really like you too," I muttered back, just loud enough so the driver wouldn't hear, but Frank's eyes were already closed. I didn't know if Frank heard me or not.

Having nothing better to do as the cab wended its way through the empty late-night streets toward home and hearth, I leaned in to kiss the top of Frank's head. He was softly snoring. He'd never know. I left my lips in his hair and breathed in his fragrance as I thought things over.

By the time the cab pulled up in front of my apartment building twenty minutes later, I had come to two fairly astounding conclusions.

Number one. I was more than happy to let Frank Wells move into my life.

And number two. I was hopelessly smitten with the man, which pretty well explained number one.

And all it took was a twenty-minute cab ride.

This from a guy who once obsessed for three hours about which condiments to put on a hamburger.

IF I still harbored any misgivings about Frank moving in, they didn't last more than fifteen seconds after we walked in the front door. Frank came to me while I was still locking the door. As Pedro humped my ankle in his customary Chihuahua howdy, Frank sweetly cupped my face in his hands and pressed his lips to mine ever so gently. If he was still drunk, it didn't show. His eyes were clear, the irises as bright and green as sunlight sifting through a forest canopy. From behind those thick black lashes of his, he watched me intently as our lips came together.

At the feel of Frank's warm mouth on mine, I closed my eyes and savored the taste of him. His hands slowly slid away from my face, rested briefly on each side of my neck, and then he wrapped his strong, fuzzy arms around my back and pulled me close.

With his lips still on mine, he mumbled, "Thank you."

All I could do was nod. My heart was doing somersaults inside my chest, but not a SAD somersault. This was a *good* somersault. The kind I hadn't felt since what's-his-name moved away. It actually took me a minute to place the name. Jerry. Since Jerry moved away. I smiled in the middle of Frank's kiss and he smiled in return.

"What?" he asked softly, breaking the kiss to slide his lips across my cheek.

"Nothing. I just forgot my ex's name."

"Good," Frank said. Our mouths came together again. His hips were pressed tightly to mine. I was hard. So was Frank. I could feel it. I was beginning to tremble.

My tongue shot out and licked his front teeth. "There," I said, leaning back to look in his eyes, gauging his reaction. "Got that out of the way. I've been wanting to lick those choppers since you first walked through my door."

"Strange," he said. "I've been wanting to do this." And he slammed his mouth down on mine. His lips opened wide to encompass my own, and his tongue dove in, Greg Louganis style, sort of a half gainer with a big wet twist. When our tongues slammed into each other, I could really taste him. I actually thought I might do one of those Aunt Pittypat swoons for a second. God, he was sexy. Frank tugged my shirttail out of my pants and burrowed his hands underneath. He ran his hot palms along my ribcage, stroking the fine hair on my stomach, sliding around to my back, outlining my shoulder blades with his fingertips. Everywhere he touched, I burned.

He was still wearing my yellow sweater. I yanked it over his head so fast I almost tore our noses off. "Ouch," we both said, and laughed.

My lips slid away from his mouth to kiss the dimple in his chin. Then his throat. I ran my tongue over the topography of his Adam's apple, all sharp and hard and bobbing up and down when he swallowed. He seemed to be swallowing a lot. But then, so was I. I kicked off my shoes, scooted Pedro out of the way with my foot, and slid my lips down Frank's chest, brushing first one nipple with my tongue, then the other. His chest was warm and smooth and felt like heaven. He smelled of my soap. I liked that. I could hear his heart beating a syncopated rhythm in counterpoint to my own, slightly off-kilter, like two drummers pounding out different beats at the same time.

He stroked my face, gently easing me downward. Coaxing, not pushing. I clutched his ass and pulled his stomach into my face, breathing in his smell. God, his skin was so hot. He held me there. I kissed his belly button, then nibbled at the little cluster of hair that trailed from his belly button downward. Frank was hunched over kissing the top of my head. His belt buckle was cold and sharp against my chin, and I reached up to undo it and get it out of the way. I could feel him kicking his shoes off while I worked at the belt. His legs were shaking. I really liked that.

I was fully on my knees now, and Pedro was getting into the act, first humping my thigh, then hopping around while his humper was still going to tackle the back of Frank's ankle. He'd work on Frank's ankle for a while, then hump his way back to me. He was starting to snort and pant. Pedro, I mean. Not Frank.

"I don't do three-ways," Frank finally said. "Can we move this into the bedroom?"

"Are you talking to me or the dog?" I asked.

"The dog," he said.

I stopped what I was doing and looked up into Frank's face. He grinned at my sour expression. "Kidding," he said. "Just kidding. I was talking to you. Duh."

"Thank God," I said. "I was about to tear up your lease."

"I don't have a lease."

"That's right. You might want to keep that in mind the next time you toy with my sensibilities. *Pedro, stop humping!*"

"Does *he* have a lease?"

I was pressing my cheek against something long and hard that was stashed under Frank's zipper. I couldn't imagine what it was but I was damned tootin' going to find out. "Pedro doesn't need a lease. It's his apartment. He only allows me to stay because I buy the groceries and let him sleep between my legs when the weather is cold."

"Oh, God, I think I'm going to come."

"Really?"

"Naw. Just thinking about sleeping between your legs."

"Don't scare me, Frank."

"Uh-oh," Frank said. "I feel a bout of shyness coming on."

"You've gotta be kidding. Your dick is pressed against my cheek and it's as hard as a rock. That is your dick, isn't it?"

"Well, it's not a howitzer."

"So it won't go off, then?"

"Oh, it'll go off when it's ready."

"Are you really feeling shy?" During this whole conversation I had not once stopped nibbling at the crotch of Frank's jeans. I was like a hog rooting for truffles.

He tried to give me a lackadaisical shrug, but he was trembling so hard it was a pretty sorry attempt. "The shy feeling's passed. Now I'm just horny."

"Oh good," I said, and meant it.

With that, I slid Frank's zipper down and out sprang the most beautiful cock I'd ever seen. I tugged his jeans down to his knees and what do you know. No underwear.

I licked a drop of moisture from the tip of his dick and Frank gasped. Then he said, "Oh shit!" And before I could move, his sperm shot over my head and landed in my hair. He pressed his crotch into my face, and again his sperm shot out, smearing my cheek, my nose, my lips. I licked it away and took his cock into my mouth to finish the job.

Frank's come tasted sweet and hot and scrumptious. His whole body was trembling like a tree in a windstorm as I sucked the last delicious drops from him. His pubic hair smelled clean and warm against my face. The hair on his legs tickled my cheeks. His balls lay heavy against my chin.

"Oh God," I said.

"Oh, no you don't," Frank said.

He roughly pushed me away from his dick and slammed me down onto the floor on my back, practically driving the air out of my lungs. He peeled my pants off and flung them across the room before I knew what was happening.

Pressing me flat to the floor with a hand to my chest, he circled my cock with his other hand and slowly stroked it, drawing back the foreskin as I lifted my head to watch him. With every light in the apartment blazing, I saw it all at high res. So did Frank. He smiled and said, "Beautiful," before slipping it between his lips. Two seconds later, I came. My back arched and Frank rode me like a bronco as I came and came and came. Jesus, I couldn't seem to stop.

With my cock still in his mouth, he looked up to see how I was feeling about the whole thing. He stroked my stomach, caressed my balls, and slowly, oh so slowly continued to suck me dry as he explored my body for the very first time with his wandering hands. He seemed to like what he was finding.

Then he laughed. Still licking and tasting my dick as if there was nothing else in the world he would rather be doing. He casually pulled the remaining clothes from our bodies with one hand while caressing my chest with the other.

Finally, he gave my cock a last lingering kiss and stretched out beside me on the floor. Once again, Frank cupped my face in his hands and pressed his lips to mine, leaving them there for the longest time, as if absorbing and committing to memory every heart-pounding moment we had just shared together. I could taste my come on his mouth and I knew he could taste his own on mine. It was not the first time I had experienced that with a lover, but it was the first time I had experienced it with Frank. And his innate sweetness and the gentle, open-eyed way he made love, made that kiss, without a doubt, the most erotic kiss I had ever experienced in my life.

When the kiss finally ended and he pressed his face into my neck to cuddle, I whispered into his hair, "Lord, Frank."

His lips moved against my throat. "It's been a while."

"For me too."

"Don't talk," he said. "Let's just hold each other."

And so we did, lying there on the foyer floor. Pedro finally stopped humping and curled up beside us. He was asleep in no time. Sex always did wear him out. His or anybody else's. Frank and I fell asleep maybe an hour later, still wrapped in each other's arms. We hadn't spoken another word, but our hands never seemed to rest as we lazily explored each other's bodies, stroking, caressing. Snuggling. Just before I dozed off for good, I pulled an afghan from the recliner and covered us up. Frank plucked two throw pillows from the sofa to stick under our heads. We slept until dawn, spooning on the foyer floor.

When I opened my eyes, Frank and Pedro were gone. Maybe they eloped.

Five minutes later, I was having a panic attack, complicated by the worst hangover I'd suffered in years. And through it all, I *still* had a smile on my face.

Talk about mixed signals.

Chapter Six

FRANK came through the front door with a Sunday paper under his arm. He was dragging a pissed-off Pedro along behind him, tethered and grumbling at the end of his leash. Frank looked happy and bright-eyed, his cheeks rosy from the morning air. Pedro looked like he would gladly disembowel the first human who even *remotely* tried to cheer him up. Pedro *hated* morning air.

I was standing naked at the kitchen sink with an aspirin bottle in one hand, an inflated paper bag in the other, and a hard-on.

Frank took in the hard-on first. In fact, maybe that's *all* he took in.

"Somebody's up," he said. "In more ways than one."

I stuck the paper bag over my mouth and took a couple of deep breaths, wide-eyed, watching Frank. I continued to breathe into the bag even when Frank dropped to his knees in front of me and took my cock in his mouth.

"Panic attack?" he asked around my dick.

I nodded. The paper bag crackled as it ballooned in and out. I closed my eyes at the sensation of Frank's mouth encircling my cock and when I did, the aspirins fell out of my hand and rolled across the floor. I dropped the paper bag and clutched the sides of his head.

Forming actual words was the hardest thing I had ever done in my life. "Please, God, take your clothes off."

"Don't call me God," he said, looking up at me with those incredible green eyes, his words slurred because his mouth was full of my throbbing pecker. "Call me Frank. Please. And before I take my clothes off, I want to show you this."

He pulled a sheet of paper from his shirt pocket and waved it over his head directly in my face. "Blood test," he said, still mumbling around my dick. "Took it three weeks ago. I'm clean. Thought you should know."

With my cock still in his mouth, I was doing my damnedest to concentrate on that sheet of paper with the long list of numbers and medical abbreviations on it, but it wasn't easy. I had no idea what most of those figures meant anyway. They were a mystery. But one figure caught my eye.

"Uh-oh, Frank. This doesn't look good."

Frank spat out my dick and looked up at me with the biggest eyes I had ever seen. He might as well have had the word *terror* tattooed across his forehead in purple ink.

"What? What?"

I smiled down at him. "Your blood sugar's a little high."

He laughed. "Christ, Tom, you scared me to death. The blood sugar is high because I was nervous going in and ate a box of donuts on the way. Anything else you want to bitch about?"

"No. I have one of these too, you know. Took it two months ago. And since you're the first person I've been with since, I guess that means we're safe."

"Oh goodie," he said. "That means I can do anything I want."

I flapped a finger in his face. "As long as you say please first."

"Whatever," he mumbled, rolling his eyes.

And since he was still on his knees in front of me, without missing a beat, he took my rigid cock back into his mouth and began shedding his clothes, piece by piece. By the time he was naked, I had to make him stop doing what he was doing, or there would have been a rerun of the previous night's experiment in premature ejaculation.

I gently eased myself from his mouth, but he gripped my ass and held me in place while he burrowed his nose under my testicles. He smiled when he took first one testicle into his mouth, then he freed it to go after the other. He tried to put them both in his mouth, but they wouldn't fit. Jesus. Could this guy do *anything* that didn't make me want to come?

I pulled him to his feet and dragged him down the hall to the bedroom, stopping only long enough to free Pedro from his leash. At the bedroom door, I none too gently pushed Frank inside, noticing happily when I did that his pecker was sticking straight up and bouncing around in front of him like a divining rod. It was all I could do take my eyes off it long enough to ease Pedro away from the bedroom door with my bare foot, which he tried to bite out of sheer petulance, before slamming the door in his little Chihuahua face. I wanted no interruptions this time.

Idly stroking his own cock, which was erotic as hell, don't think it wasn't, Frank stood at the edge of the bed, watching me, wondering maybe what I was going to do next. What I did was grab his shoulders, spin him around, and throw him facedown on the bed. I dropped to my knees and leaning over the foot of the bed, played my hands along the back of Frank's gorgeous hairy legs. Slowly, I splayed them apart. Admiring. Kneading. His calf muscles were tense and hard and perfectly delineated. He was trembling again. Every square inch of him.

I ran my lips from his ankles upward, first along one leg, then along the other, savoring the heat of his skin and the sensation of his leg hair scraping my face. When I reached the point where those two fabulous legs came together, I spread Frank's fuzzy ass cheeks and dove right in. I gently circled his puckered opening with my tongue, tasting, experimenting, wondering how Frank was feeling about it. But judging by the amount of shaking he was doing, and the occasional gasp that issued from his throat, and the way he lifted his trembling ass to meet me halfway, I figured he wasn't getting offended or anything, so I plowed right ahead.

By the way, in case you're wondering, that little patch of hair at the base of Frank's spine really did tickle my nose when my tongue was up his ass, just as I suspected it would.

God, he was the sexiest man I had ever known. Just being in his orbit made me feel sexy as hell too. Even flat on his stomach with his ass in my face, Frank was perfect. Maybe *especially* flat on his stomach with his ass in my face, Frank was perfect.

When I flipped him over onto his back and he aimed his iron cock in my direction, begging for me to take it into my mouth, he was even better. I was more than happy to do exactly what he wanted me to do, but I had a couple of other things I wanted to do first. And I took my sweet time doing them. First, I set about licking his balls. They were fat and tight and heavy, he was so excited. They were hairy too. Just like his legs. Just like his ass. Only Frank's chest was smooth. As smooth and hot as sun-warmed glass. His nipples were hard little rocks perched in the middle of broad, brown areolas. I stroked Frank's stomach while I licked his nuts, going from one to the other, like a kid with two all-day suckers who doesn't know which one he likes the best.

Frank had flung his arm over his face, blocking out the light, blocking out everything but the sensation of my lips on his balls. When I headed north and nibbled the base of his cock, it lurched in my hand. Frank gasped, then laughed. Then he raised his hips, pleading for me to get to where I was going.

Still, I didn't hurry. I licked along the shaft of his cock, and there was considerable licking to be done. Frank's dick wasn't exactly small. It wasn't as big as mine, but I haven't seen too many that were. Frank's dick was cut and perfectly formed. The head of it was shaped like a mini-muffin, overriding its paper cup. The slit was dribbling moisture like a leaky faucet, and I periodically stopped what I was doing and lapped it away as I worked my way farther north.

When I finally popped the head of Frank's dick into my mouth, Frank started trembling again. When I pushed my head down over it to the very root, to where his pubic hair was flush against my face, his hips shot upward and I almost gagged. But it was a happy gag.

Never letting his cock leave my mouth, Frank wiggled around until he was facing the other way. Once there, he buried his face in *my* crotch. Licking. Lapping. Even when I'm fully aroused, my foreskin needs to be pulled back. Frank found the mechanics of it fascinating—sliding the foreskin back, releasing it, sliding it back again. I wondered if he had ever had sex with an uncircumcised man before. He was like a kid with a new toy, and believe me, I was more than happy to be the center of his attention.

He finally decided to get down to brass tacks and slid his warm lips over my dick while his hands stroked my body, from my stomach to my back to my legs. Frank's own legs were wrapped tightly around my shoulders. It didn't take long to figure out that Frank and I both loved to sixty-nine. We had easy access to all our favorite body parts that way and neither of us was shy about exploring. We might not be much at socializing, but by God, stick a dick in our faces and we could rumble with the best of them.

I was getting really close to coming, and by the way his hips were involuntarily lunging and shuddering, I suspected Frank was too.

I pulled back to watch my hand stroke his dick, occasionally sipping away the precome that kept forming at the tip. Frank decided he would do the same thing, and we lay there stroking each other, faces and dicks at eye level, working our way toward the big finale.

Frank was so breathless he could hardly speak. "I'm gonna come in a minute."

I kept slowly stroking. "Me too."

"I wanna watch you when you come," Frank said.

"I wanna watch you too."

Then he said, "Uuuuhhh! Don't stop, Tom! Don't stop!"

I slowed down but I didn't stop. I stroked his hard cock from the head to the base, periodically licking away the precome, just because it tasted so damned good, and all the while smiling at the way Frank was shaking.

While I worked on him, he worked on me. Long slow strokes. Occasional kisses at the tip, lapping away the liquid seeping from my dick with his hot tongue, but always with his eye out for that one irreversible moment when there was no turning back. And I reached that moment a second later.

So did Frank.

With a monumental shudder, he arched his back and filled my hand with gouts of hot semen. He cried out as I continued to stroke his shooting cock. His come was going everywhere. In my face, across his stomach, dribbling down my arm. I pressed my smiling face to his balls and watched him shoot. Lordy. It was like the Fourth of July.

I was so wrapped up in what he was doing I almost didn't see my own ejaculation looming. But Frank saw it and he was ready when it came. He continued to slowly pump me, lingering his fingers around the head of my dick with every upward stroke, teasing me there until I was ready to scream. When I finally came, it was with such force that I wasn't the only one who gasped. Frank gasped too. He pressed his lips into the base of my cock so he could feel the surging semen gushing upward as it fought its way out into the morning air.

I looked down at him as he watched me come, and his face was covered with my juices. He licked them away from his mouth, then circled those hot lips around my dick one last time, as if to lay claim to those final spurting drops. I felt him draw them from me, like milk through a straw.

I gave a last shudder and fell back, my face still buried in Frank's crotch.

Talk about funky. We were both splattered with come. It was everywhere. We looked at each other and laughed. Then we wiggled around until we could get our lips together and we gave each other a hot, slippery, come-y kiss.

Before we could dry out and stick together like a couple of Post-it Notes, I dragged us off to the shower. There we shared our first bath. And it was wonderful. We soaped each other down, dried each other off, and wrapped ourselves in a couple of terry robes I pulled out of the closet. Then we headed to the kitchen for breakfast.

It was our first day as roomies, and I was already happy as a clam over the way things were turning out. I hoped Frank was too, and considering the way he always ejaculated when I wanted him to, I could only assume he was.

Pedro was still pissed, grumbling around the apartment like he was in the first stages of rabies or something, but a little flattery, an ass rub, and a couple of doggie biscuits set things right.

After breakfast, Frank and I lounged around on the sofa, finishing our coffee, occasionally peeking under each other's bathrobes simply because we couldn't seem to stay away, and digging through the Sunday paper, looking for employment opportunities. For Frank, of course, not Pedro.

Pedro was pretty much unemployable. Hell, even I knew that.

THERE were times that morning when Frank and I still became shy with each other. Admittedly, we hadn't known each other very long, but still, one would think that two incredible bouts of hot sex would alleviate the tension a bit. And it did. A bit. Just not completely.

While Frank studied the want ads and sipped his coffee, I worked my way up to asking the question that had been bothering me, the question that had thrown me into a panic attack five minutes after waking up that morning on the living room floor. I had to build up to it, though. It wasn't an easy question to ask.

"I'm glad you're staying, Frank. Don't worry. We'll find you a job."

"I don't know what I would have done without you, Tom. You were so right about my brother. What the hell is wrong with him, anyway? Why is he so damned mean?"

I waved away all talk of Stanley. I had other things on my mind.

"Here it is, Frank," I said, taking a deep breath. "Here's what I need to know."

Frank stopped what he was doing and gave me his full attention. Geez, the guy was just so damned *nice*. And those green eyes! And that hair! And that body! And—Christ, I almost forgot what I was going to say.

"What are we going to be?" I finally asked, nervous as hell. I shouldn't have been asking this particular question at all. I knew that. I was probably about to scare the guy off. But it couldn't be helped. I *had* to ask. I wanted to know before I fell any harder for Frank. I had already worked my way up to what would be a hell of a heartache if things didn't pan out. I didn't want to let myself get buried any further in this avalanche of feelings I was experiencing. I had enough emotional problems going on. I didn't need a broken heart to contend with on top of everything else. Hell, I wasn't even over Jerry yet. Well, maybe I was. Last night seemed to have pretty well fixed *that* problem. "We'll be living under the same roof, Frank, but what is our day-to-day relationship going to be? Are we roomies with sexual benefits, or just roomies? Are we working our way toward something more? You have to know I'm crazy about you already. How do you feel about me? Don't answer that. No, wait. Tell me. No, don't. Shit."

That went pretty well, I thought, up until the end of my speech, at least. Sort of fell apart there. But at least I avoided the L word. That was my main objective. Nothing scares off a prospective suitor like the indiscriminate use of the L word.

Frank laughed at my stammering finale, which wasn't the response I was looking for. But he was laughing in a *nice* way. He probably didn't know *how* to laugh any other way. We were sitting cross-legged on the sofa in our bathrobes facing each other with the Sunday paper scattered all over ourselves and half the room. He set his coffee cup aside, swept the paper from our laps, and leaning forward, lay his hands on my bare ankles. He gently stroked my calves as he spoke. While I had gone to great lengths not to say that one little word that begins with the letter L, Frank apparently saw no reason to avoid it at all.

"I love being with you, Tom. I'm not very experienced, you know. Sexually, I mean. And I've never been in love. Can you believe that? I'm twenty-four and I've never been in love. There's not a lot of opportunity for gay love growing up on a tiny farm in Indiana."

"You certainly seem to know what to do," I said, skirting my way around the L word even now, although Frank was the one who said it first, not me. "I mean, sexually you seem to know what to do." Sheesh. Talk about an understatement.

"With you, I do," he said. "With you, I don't seem to have a governor. You know what a governor is? It's an engine part on a tractor that keeps it from going too fast. For safety. But with you I don't have one. I just go assholing along doing whatever the hell I want. Full speed ahead and damn the torpedoes." He laughed. "And it's usually because you're doing it all before I am, so I just happily follow along. Plus, I really like your torpedo."

He lifted my foot and placed a kiss on the tip of my big toe. That toe had never been kissed in its life. I wondered if it was smart enough to know what had just happened. Would it lord it over the other toes now that it had been singled out and kissed by Frank Wells, or was it just a fucking toe and didn't know *what* the hell was going on? Like me.

I also wondered if there was some sort of antipsychotic medication I could take that would make me stop thinking these weird-ass thoughts or was I pretty well stuck with them for the rest of my frigging life?

Frank's incredibly green eyes homed in on my face. It was like there was nothing else in the room he wanted to look at but me. My heart gave a funny little thump and I knew I had just fallen a little bit more in love. Oops. L word.

"Tom," Frank went on, "I don't think I can live with you if we decide to just be roommates. Sleeping in separate bedrooms and all? I'd go crazy. Watching you. Wanting you. Can't we go on like we're going? I'm beginning to understand what maybe falling in love is like. And I don't want to stop understanding it. And I don't want to fall in love with anybody else, either. I want to fall in love with you. All the way. I already love your body. I already love your humongous cock. I love the way you make me feel. I love the way I think I make you feel. I love the way you come. I love the way *I* come when I'm watching *you* come. That's love already, isn't it? I'm already in love with you, aren't I, Tom? Huh? Say something."

Tears gathered in my eyes and my throat closed up. "Can't. Too choked up." I barely got the words out before Frank fell into my arms. We hugged as tightly as two people can possibly hug without going through some sort of surgical cloning procedure. Then we hugged each other again.

He pulled away long enough to look me square in the eyes again. "I'll get a job. Don't worry. I'm not asking for charity, staying here. I can't pay you anything right now, but I will. You'll see. I'm a hard worker, Tom. I may be shy, but I can work. I actually *like* working. I'll be pulling my weight in no time. I promise. So if you can be a little forgiving about the money right now, what do you say about all the other stuff? What do you say about me maybe being in love with you already? Is that what you want too? Please say it is. Please say you want me in the same way I want you."

I was so happy and so stunned and at such a loss for exactly the right words to say that I was almost glad the phone chose that precise moment to ring. But I couldn't let Frank hang around wondering what my answer would be. If he was going to be so damned nice all the time, and so damned honest, then I would have to learn to be nice and honest too. After all, I really was nuts about the guy. If we were going to be an item, the least I could do was drag myself up to his level.

I grabbed a fistful of his bathrobe and pulled him to me. Our lips came together as if they were meant to be nowhere else, and when they got to where they were going they felt right at home. "I'm in love with you already, Frank. I loved you the minute you cold-cocked your brother. No, that's not true. I loved you the minute I almost knocked your towel off in the hallway. No, wait, I loved you the very second I saw that little patch of hair over the crack of your ass. No wait—"

The phone was still ringing.

Frank stuck his tongue down my throat to shut me up. He looked happy doing it. And that made me happy. This was going to be fun. I felt like a dead elephant had just rolled off my chest. I had said the L word and the sky hadn't fallen in. Frank was still here. And as far as I could tell he was in love with me just as much as I was in love with him. And after only two days! Were we nuts?

Now that I had finally said the L word, I couldn't seem to *stop* saying it. Even inside my head. L. L. L. What a wonderful word.

Then I thought about all the things that could go wrong. He could cheat. I could cheat. He could really be lazy and never work a day of his life. I could lose my job. Or get shot in the head in a bank robbery. Or Pedro could get fleas.

I picked up the phone just so I'd stop thinking.

IT WAS Jerry.

"What do *you* want?" I asked.

I mouthed the word *J-e-r-r-y* to Frank, who rolled his pretty green eyes and went back to the paper. He didn't even look threatened. What a guy.

Jerry was using his cheesy, chipper, consoling voice. The one he always used after he did something stupid. Like cheat. Or throw me out of his house. "So have you sent Frank packing?" he asked.

I knew right away that I was going to enjoy the hell out of this conversation. In fact, I would probably remember it fondly for years.

"Nope," I said. "Frank's still here."

"For how long?"

"Forever, I hope."

"You mean—"

"Yep. I mean."

Jerry actually spluttered. I love it when exes splutter. "But you just *met* the guy!"

"Yes, I did."

"You're too weird for a committed relationship!"

"Yes, I am. So is Frank. We're perfect for each other."

"He's too young for you."

"Oh please."

"He doesn't even have a job."

"We're working on that."

"Look, Tom, don't do this. I'm sorry about last night."

"This isn't about last night."

"Yes it is. Stanley's sorry about last night too."

"Yeah, I got the flowers."

"Huh?"

"A joke."

"Oh." Jerry lowered his voice conspiratorially. "Stanley's in the bathroom, but listen, I've been thinking. Maybe this whole me and Stanley thing isn't working out. I don't like the fact that he's messing around with drugs again."

"Oh. Is Stanley on drugs? I thought that was kabuki makeup he had smeared all over his nose last night. I thought maybe he had been cast as Madame Butterfly to open the San Diego opera season and he was just showing off his stage persona for me and the other guests. You mean that was drugs? Drugs, like in coke? Not like coke The Real Thing, but coke the shit people snort up their noses to fuck their brains up even more than they're already fucked up? That kind of coke? Well, I'm just full-blown astounded. I thought Stanley was on the fast track to sainthood. That's going to pretty much blow his chance for *that*, don't you think? And the Nobel Prize for world peace will probably go right out the window too. Drugs! Well, I'll be!"

"Come on, Tom. What do you think? Let's have dinner tonight. I've missed you."

I thought about that, but not in the way Jerry was hoping I would think about it. "Let me get this straight, Jerry. First you're married to me, but then you go off and cheat with Stanley, after which you quickly decide you like him better than me and dump me to move in with him, but now you're saying you want to meet up with me and cheat on

Stanley because you've taken it into your head to dump Stanley and move in with *me* again."

"Wow," Frank whispered around his coffee cup. "Nice sentence structure."

Jerry stammered, "Uh—"

"Well said, dickhead."

"See?" Jerry said. "See? You're just mad about last night. Trust me, Tom, I really think we should get togeth—"

I hung up the phone. Softly. Calmly. Like an adult. Tee-hee.

Frank was smiling. "You enjoyed that, didn't you," he said.

I smiled back. "More than you'll ever know."

Frank was just about to start on the *New York Times* crossword puzzle when I plucked the paper and pencil from his hand and pulled him off the sofa.

"Get dressed," I said. "We're going shopping."

Frank looked surprised. "Shopping for what?"

"Clothes. You can't go on job interviews with those tight-ass blue jeans you wore last night. I won't let you. We're going to set the farm boy aside and make a city slicker out of you. Externally, anyway. Internally, I would appreciate you staying exactly the way you are. Okay?"

He shrugged. "Okay. But I'm broke. I couldn't buy a bagel."

"Don't worry about that. We'll figure something out."

"Which means you intend to spring for everything."

"Right. That's what lovers do."

"Lovers," Frank said, walking into my arms. "I like the sound of that."

My heart gave a little lurch of happiness when his arms slid around me. "Me too, Frank. I like it a lot."

He kissed my neck. "Can we at least keep track of the money you spend so I can pay you back as soon as I have a paycheck coming in?"

"If you insist," I said.

"I do." Frank cleared his throat. "And when we get home, we're going to have a long talk about training your dog."

"If you insist," I said, this time with considerable doubt in my voice. I had tried to train Pedro before. It was a lot like teaching a goldfish to tap dance. In other words—good luck.

Frank beetled his brows. "I *do* insist."

And we both gazed down at Pedro, who was looking guilty as hell for some reason.

"Too late," I said.

"Crap," Frank groaned.

"Yep," I said. "That's what that look means. Crap. Help me find it, will you? Usually if we follow our noses—"

Frank waggled an admonitory finger in Pedro's face. "Bad dog! Bad dog!"

Pedro yawned and dragged his ass around in a circle on the carpet. Either he was bored and his hemorrhoids were itching, or he was bored and making a statement. I figured it was the latter.

Thus our first day as a family began.

Chapter Seven

IT'S FUNNY how quickly a person's life can change.

Frank and I slid without a hitch into the new dynamics of our exploding relationship. It was clear from the get-go that we profoundly *liked* each other. But there was love there too. A lot of it. And our love grew stronger with every passing day. But the *liking* was even more important. Frank and I both agreed on that. It was the liking that gave our relationship a solid base, for with liking came a host of secondary goodies. Respect for each other. An honest desire to please. The willingness to give up a bit of what one wants so that the other person can have a say in what *he* wants. To be able to equally share in the choices we made, choices that would affect us both, either individually or as a unit.

The sexual draw we felt for each other was nothing short of cataclysmic. I mean cataclysmic in a good way. A simple look could pass between us, and we were both immediately aroused. The *hunger* I felt for Frank was astonishing. At the oddest times, I would find myself suddenly weak in the knees, longing for the feel of him. It could happen anywhere—while standing in line at the grocery store, or sitting behind my desk at work, or in the middle of pumping gas, or watching the evening news. A dozen times a day I would find myself aching to see the come explode from his body, to taste it, to smell it, to feel its liquid heat on my skin and on my lips. To watch it spurt from his body and see him gasp and shudder and writhe when it did. It's a wonder we got *anything* done during those first few weeks together, for as often as I longed for Frank, he also longed for me. And when one of us longed, the other reciprocated. Gladly.

I can honestly say the happiest moments of my twenty-seven years on this planet were spent in Frank's fuzzy, naked arms during those first incredible weeks the two of us shared as a couple. Geez Louise, love is grand.

Money, or Frank's lack of it, quickly proved to be a non-issue. Frank found work on the second day of his job search at one of the nurseries in town. He loved tending the plants. Plant-tending is a perfect job for someone with social anxiety disorder. One never feels inferior around a plant. If he does, then he has a much more serious problem going on than SAD. Flat-out insanity springs to mind. While Frank might still feel uncomfortable around his fellow employees at the nursery, his shyness was alleviated by the fact he was doing something he enjoyed, and something he knew quite a bit about, having been raised on a farm and all.

I ceded my car to Frank because the nursery was miles away from the apartment while my bank was only a short bus ride downtown. I was so happy to be able to do something for Frank to help ease him into his new life that the act of giving up my car did not even seem a sacrifice to me. It tickled me pink to think I could rescue him from a daily two-hour bus ride to and from work. And it was good for me too. On nice days I now walked to work. Since almost every day in San Diego is nice, I quickly shed three pounds. And as everyone knows, losing weight is almost *always* a good thing.

Frank and I joined a support group for people with social anxiety disorder. In fact, we joined two support groups. Unfortunately, we never made it to the first meeting of either group because on both occasions we chickened out at the front door and went for cheeseburgers instead.

Not once during the beginning weeks of our relationship did we even *consider* going to a bar for drinks. Even stone-cold sober, we were perfectly content to be in each other's company. Just the two of us.

I mean three.

Pedro must not be forgotten. And in truth, Pedro was sometimes the only jarring note in our otherwise idyllic existence. It drove Frank nuts that Pedro was not everything he wished him to be. He quickly came to love Pedro, but he did not love the occasional smelly accident or the constant begging or the periodic attempt by Pedro to remove a finger or two from the hand that fed him.

Chihuahuas are notoriously cranky. It's a simple fact of nature. But Frank didn't like it, so he did everything in his power to change the natural order.

And Pedro fought him every step of the way.

Frank enrolled Pedro in obedience courses being held at a dog-bathing spa not far from the apartment. On the first day of the course, heralded as a "meet and greet" for the students to get to know each other, Frank and I clipped a leash to a freshly scrubbed and exceedingly pissed off Pedro (he knew something was up) and set off to begin his new life in academia. Frank and I were so nervous, what with all the other dog owners hovering around the front door mingling and sharing pet stories with their tethered pets looking all happy and excited too, that Pedro must have picked up on our anxiety and took it as a sign that we were in danger. His instinct for protection kicked in. Yes, even Chihuahuas have one, especially where their masters are concerned. He went into full battle mode, growling at six pet owners, snapping at a pretty little Pomeranian who just wanted to get laid, nipping two instructors who tried to intercede, and damn near emasculating a Russian wolfhound when Pedro latched onto his nuts with his sharp little teeth and refused to let go. Pedro wreaked such havoc that we were firmly, and not very politely, evicted from the premises before the first class ever began. Hell, we didn't even get to the free tea and cookies and doggy treats.

Frank was steamed for all of five minutes, then he started laughing. Then I started laughing. By the time we were back at the apartment, Pedro was laughing too, prancing and frolicking and nipping (playfully) at our pant legs. He knew he had won. And so did we. Even Frank had to admit it.

NEEDLESS to say, obedience school was never mentioned again. Pedro certainly never brought it up, and neither did Frank. Secretly though, I began a more concerted effort to teach Pedro a few of the most fundamental rules that applied to living with humans. Like not pooping everywhere he took a fancy to poop. And not humping every ankle that came looming onto his horizon. I knew I had been a bad influence on Pedro, letting him get the upper hand (or upper paw) in our relationship, and I tried to atone for my sins. With minimal success, I'm afraid. Pedro was simply too set in his ways. Old dog, new tricks. That sort of thing. And secretly, I still thought of Pedro's shortcomings as part of his charm. Thank God most dog owners know better.

One day I walked in on Frank having a spirited conversation on the phone. He was all smiles, and I have to say, when I walked into the room his smiles grew even wider, God love him. I ask you, is there anything greater in the world than having your man light up when you walk into a room? Even being told "you look skinny in those jeans" doesn't hold a candle to it. I was overcome with a sudden urge for two-peckered sex, but Frank had other ideas.

"Here he is now," Frank said into the phone. "I'll let *you* tell him."

Who is it? I mouthed. Frank just shrugged and handed me the phone.

"Hello?" I ventured into the mouthpiece, wondering at Frank's mysterious little grin.

"Hello, young man!" A booming voice sang out. "I hear you've taken my boy under your wing!"

"Uh—"

"This is Frankie's dad. You can call me Joseph. Or Joe. I don't care. Pretty near everybody calls me one or the other. I just wanted to let you know that I appreciate you helping Frank get settled in. He ain't never been in a big city before, so I'm glad you two found each other. Otherwise he'd probably be sleeping in the bus station. He tells me you've got a dog. Got four myself. Wonderful things, dogs. You'll never have a better friend than your dog. Remember that, son."

I looked down at Pedro who was sniffing around the floor lamp looking for a place to pee. He had just hiked up his hind leg in preparation for the first salvo when Frank saw what I was looking at, gasped, and scooped Pedro into the air. He grabbed his leash and a plastic poop bag and ran out the front door with Pedro under his arm before Pedro knew what the hell was happening.

Frank's father apparently didn't know what was happening either. "What's the matter, boy? Cat got your tongue? You still there? Hello? Hello?"

"Mr. Wells," I said. "I mean Joseph. I mean Joe. It's a pleasure to meet you, sir. I've heard a lot about you. And I'm more than happy to be helping Frank-*ie* out. He's a great guy." And hot in bed. But that didn't need to be said, so I left it out. "Did he tell you he's found a job already?"

"Yes, he did, Tom. That is your name, isn't it? Tom? And he told me you were loaning him your car to get to work in too. That's a fine thing to do for another human being. I kinda had to choke back a tear when Frankie told me that. You're a good man, Tom. A good man and a good friend to my boy. The true measure of a man is what he does for others, not what he does for himself, and you measure up just fine, Tom. I'll never forget it. Neither will Frankie."

It was obvious that Frank's dad was the sort of person who tells you exactly how he feels and unapologetically makes no bones about wearing his heart on his sleeve. I respect people like that. You always know exactly where you stand with them, and there is nothing underhanded about the things they say. Their words can be taken at face value. Someone like Stanley the dick could tell you how wonderful you are, and you know all along that what he is actually *thinking* is pretty much the polar opposite of the syrupy crap pouring out of his mouth.

Frank's dad seemed to divine my thoughts. "Guess Frankie's big brother didn't have time to help him out. Too bad about that, but Stanley's always been a selfish shit. Even when he was little he used to hog all the candy. Poor Frankie hardly ever got any. Probably why he's got such pretty teeth. Sometimes people are just born assholes, Tom. No rhyme or reason to it. It's just the way it is. I hate to admit it, but Stanley's one of them."

I bit back a laugh and made a mental note to never try to pull the wool over Joseph Wells's eyes. Obviously Indiana farmers know bullshit when they see it. Even as it applies to members of their own family. Suffice it to say, it was nice to know that my opinion of Stanley was backed by a competent authority. The man's father, no less.

"These phone calls cost money, son, so I'm going to let you go. It's been a real pleasure talking to you."

"It's been a pleasure for me too. And don't worry about the cost next time. You call collect any time you want. We'd both love to hear from you."

"We'll see. We'll see. Anyway, give Frankie a hug for me. And thanks again for everything you've done."

"If you'll just hold on a second, Frank will be right back. He's walking the dog. I'm sure he'd like to say good-bye."

"No, son, that's okay. Time is money, especially where Ma Bell is concerned, or whoever the hell is running the phone company these days. You just tell Frankie what I said, and don't forget the phone works both ways. I'd love to hear from you boys too, any time you feel like talking."

"Okay, sir. We'll call. I promise."

"Bye then. I gotta run. A farm don't operate itself, you know." And Joseph Wells softly hung up the phone, but not before I heard the sound of coughing. A lot of coughing. I remembered what Frank had told me about his dad being unwell. I hoped it was nothing serious. I really liked the guy.

I headed out the front door in search of my new lover and my ill-trained dog. I wanted to tell Frank right away everything his father and I had talked about. And then I wanted to get Frank back inside and take another stab at that two-peckered sex idea I had entertained earlier.

IT WAS during the second week of Frank's new job at the nursery that Jerry called me at the bank just before noon and asked me to meet him for lunch. I hadn't heard a peep from the guy since the morning after the party. In truth, I had all but forgotten that Jerry existed at all. I wondered if he would be crushed if I told him that. I snickered at the thought, then decided I was being mean. Besides, why should I tell him how happy I was when he'd *see* how happy I was the minute we got together anyway? My obvious happiness would probably be *more* than enough to crush the fucker. Then I decided *that* was mean too, so I straightened my wimple and promised myself I would play nicely. After all, it wasn't Jerry's fault I ended up with the good brother, while he ended up with Stanley. Oh, wait a minute. Yes it was. The slut.

I straightened my wimple *again* and walked out of the bank at one minute after twelve, adjusting my tie and making myself presentable.

Jerry was waiting by the ATM, leaning against the rail. He shot me a chipper little grin when he spotted me. I offered him a bland smile and a limp wave in return, striving for the impression that I wasn't all that excited to see him again and was really only here out of some unavoidable sense of duty. It worked. Jerry deflated like a leaky balloon. Poor guy. He had no idea what I was about to do to his ego. There is nothing worse than seeing a happy ex. Nothing. Believe me, I know.

On the flip side of the coin, there's nothing more satisfying than seeing a *miserable* ex. It's a boon to one's ego to learn that the bastard really did wind up being sorry he dumped you, just like you screamed that he would as he walked out the door. And at the moment, Jerry was looking pretty darned sorry indeed.

I gave him a sympathetic pout. "Are things that bad with you and Stanley, then?"

Jerry tried to look astonished but he didn't carry it off very well. Then he tried to look smug, but that just seemed pathetic, and he knew it. Finally, he bit the bullet and said, "There is no more 'you and Stanley'. I mean me and Stanley. He dumped me and split. Didn't even pay his half of the rent before he left."

"Gee," I couldn't help saying. "Just like you did to me."

Jerry appeared stricken by my words. "I'm sorry, Tom. I really am. I was such an ass."

He sounded sincere. He even looked sincere. It took me about three seconds to realize, my God in heaven, he *was* sincere.

He was talking to me but he was looking at his shoes. A little trick he must have learned from me during one of my SAD attacks. Even in Jerry's quieter moments, he rarely muttered. But he was muttering now. "I'm sorry I hurt you, Tom. I shouldn't have done it. It was wrong of me."

Suddenly I was the one feeling uncomfortable. I don't know what I had expected from Jerry but it wasn't sincerity. And it sure as hell wasn't remorse. I gave him an awkward pat on the back. We were walking down the street by this time, heading for the cafe on the corner. It was one of the few restaurants I felt comfortable eating in, thanks to the high booths that prevented the other diners from watching me chew. Pretty much a SAD requirement, as I've mentioned earlier. Jerry knew all this. That's why he didn't question where we were going. He had been around the block enough times with me and my idiosyncrasies to know that if we were going to have lunch, it was going to be in this cafe or nowhere.

"Wrong or not," I told him, "our breakup is water under the bridge. It's old news, Jerry. I don't hold any grudges and I hope you don't either. We both survived. That's what counts. Life goes on." Two weeks ago I was crying in my beer over the guy. Then I spend a few rapturous hours with my face in Frank's crotch and I change my tune completely. Fickle, huh?

Jerry waited until we were seated in the cafe. Happily, we were ushered into my favorite booth. The one by the window. Out of habit, I immediately commandeered the seat that left me facing *away* from the rest of the restaurant. Another SAD requirement. Jerry knew the rules, so he was content taking the other seat, even though it put his back to the window and gave me the view. It was no great loss on his part, since the view consisted solely of a homeless man sitting on a bus bench cleaning his grungy toenails with a pocket knife.

When we were situated, Jerry peered over his menu to study my face. He let the conversation pick up where it had left off out in the street.

"It looks like *your* life is proceeding nicely. Still with Frank, I guess."

There might have been a hint of snippiness in the statement, but Jerry hid it pretty well. I realized he was fishing for information. I wondered if he was going to ask me to take him back. I hoped not. I didn't want to hurt him. He seemed hurt enough already, thanks to that dick Stanley.

"Still with Frank," I said, nodding, making a concerted effort not to jump up and do a jig. No need to rub it in his face that I was happy and he was not. I could tell by the bruised look in his eyes that he was more than aware of the fact. "He's working now," I went on. "Things are going great. He's a wonderful guy. I hope you can get to know him."

I told myself to shut up. I was gloating. It was just so hard to talk about Frank without rattling on and on and on and—

"I want you back," Jerry said. "I still love you, Tom, and I want you back." He reached out to grasp my hand. It startled me. I jerked away and tipped over the saltshaker. Jerry looked stunned that I had pulled away from him like that. He carefully righted the saltshaker, brushed the salt off the table, then rested his hands in his lap.

"I'm sorry," I said. "You surprised me is all."

"S'okay," he said. But he didn't try to touch me again. He seemed to have learned his lesson. And he seemed to have finally accepted where he stood in the grand order of things.

"Maybe this wasn't such a good idea," he said. "I don't want to come between you and Frank. Well, I *do*, but I don't think it's going to happen." He looked me squarely in the eye. "It's not, is it? Going to happen?"

Sadly, for him, I said, "No, Jerry, it's not. I'm sorry."

Whatever Jerry was about to say was left unsaid, because that was the moment the waitress came to take our orders. The rest of our lunch date was pretty much just a matter of eating and passing generic pleasantries back and forth. He did not try to take my hand again. He did not tell me he loved me again. He did not ask me to take him back again. The only request he made of me was to "pass the ketchup."

When we parted ways, Jerry said good-bye with his hands in his trouser pockets, as if he didn't trust himself not to reach out to me again. I told him to take care of himself, he said the same to me, and then I watched him walk away. His shoulders were hunched as if he were walking into a rainstorm, but it was a clear and sunny California day. He was like the cartoon guy with the little black cloud hanging over his head wherever he goes. I couldn't help wondering if I would ever see Jerry again, and that thought saddened me.

Funny. I hadn't expected sweet revenge to taste so bitter.

I headed back to the bank, depressed by the way things had turned out and longing for the day to end.

I needed to see Frank again. I *ached* to see him. To feel his arms around me and hear him tell me what a wonderful person I am while I pressed my face to his neck and breathed in his heavenly scent.

More than anything, I needed to convince myself I had picked the right man to share my life with.

As if I didn't already know.

Chapter Eight

TIME has a way of getting away from us when we're happy. It also has a way of pushing our problems into the background. Frank and I were so nuts about each other, and so content in our new life together, that we actually found social anxiety playing a very small part in our existence.

I got into the habit of phoning Frank's dad at least once or twice a week, and my friendship with the man grew exponentially. He did not speak to me of his illness, which was growing harder and harder for Joe to disguise as the weeks went by, but he told me many things about Frank. The 4-H hog that won Frank a blue ribbon at the county fair when the boy was eleven. The fact that Frank once had an epileptic seizure after driving a John Deere tractor for eight hours straight, an event not altogether unheard of because of the particular blatting sound that a John Deere engine makes and the way that sound sometimes affects the human brain. All news to me, of course, being a city boy. I had never heard the blat of a John Deere tractor in my life. And didn't want to.

Joe had many great stories about Frank growing up, but he never once mentioned Stanley. I figured there was a deep wound there for him. One that he simply tried to avoid. And certainly one he did not wish to share with me. That suited me just fine. Stanley's treatment of Frank had left me with a permanent hatred for the guy, a hatred even stronger than the one I already felt for him after he broke up my relationship with Jerry.

Mr. Wells never once mentioned his illness to me, but I detected a weakening in his voice as time passed. And the coughing increased. It was a racking, heavy cough that sometimes seemed to take him by surprise. When it did, he would often feign a household emergency just to get off the phone. His favorite was "My beans are burning, gotta run." Then a spate of coughing and a gentle click of the receiver as he softly severed our connection.

On our three-month anniversary, Frank brought home dinner after work. Pizza and wine. It was Friday night and neither of us had to work the next day, so after we polished off the wine and pretty much slaughtered two entire pizzas, I ran out for another bottle of burgundy while Frank walked Pedro around the block a couple of times.

Pedro's housebreaking lessons were coming along nicely, thank you very much. He had us trained to take him out whenever he was in the mood for a walk by simply glancing at the front door, looking wistfully uncomfortable, and tucking his tail between his legs. Worked like a charm. Neither Frank nor I had walked so much in our lives. The problem, however, was that when Pedro wanted a walk, that was exactly what he wanted. A *walk*. Nothing more. So after touring the neighborhood and tormenting a few dogs and maybe sniffing around a few bushes and barking at a couple of cats and humping a fencepost or two, which he always seemed to enjoy, don't ask me why, we would return home and Pedro would then pee or poop pretty much wherever the hell he wanted. Under the table. On top of the sofa. Behind the television. Just like he always had.

Frank and I, by this time, would simply clean up the mess and think no more about it. It never occurred to us to wonder why we bothered with the walk in the first place. And Pedro certainly wasn't going to enlighten us. He enjoyed his constitutionals way too much to jeopardize them by being forthright, even if he *could* have explained things to us in a language we could understand.

Pedro was undoubtedly chuckling into his Alpo about how easy humans are to train. And he would have been right. He had us trained very, very well and it had hardly taken any time at all.

Back home, Frank and I settled into the second bottle of wine and I could tell something was bothering him. He had been quiet all evening. Not one to beat around the bush, I forced it out of him.

"It's Pop," Frank finally admitted. "He sounds so weak on the phone now. I think he's getting sicker."

"I know," I said. "Still no clues as to what's wrong with him, huh?"

"No idea," Frank sighed. "If he knows, he's not talking. But it entails a lot of coughing. Dad used to be a smoker, you know. Hope it's not what I think it is."

I shuddered. "Cancer?" It's what I had feared all along but was too afraid to mention.

"Yeah. Lung cancer, maybe. God, I hope not. But do you think he'll talk to me about it? Nope. All he talks about is how wonderful you are. He won't hear about me coming home either. He knows I'm happy here."

My heart skidded to a stop inside my chest. "You told him you wanted to come home?"

I was sitting on the couch and Frank was sprawled out beside me on his back with his head in my lap. He reached up to stroke my cheek. "Not for good, Tom. Just to help him out for a while."

"If you go," I said, "then I'm coming with you."

Frank jumped up and grabbed my shoulders. "Are you serious? You'd go back with me? I'd probably lose my job, you know. I haven't been at the nursery long enough to rate a vacation."

"There are other jobs," I said.

"Yeah," he said. "For me. What about you?"

"I don't think Moony would fire me for asking for a few weeks off. I'll just tell him it's an emergency. Do you think your dad would mind if I tagged along?"

Frank smiled and settled back down with his head in my lap again. "He's always telling me he'd like to meet you. I think he knows we're an item. We've never talked about it, but Dad's not dumb. He might be a little bewildered, wondering why his two sons both ended up gay, but he's not dumb."

"Maybe you should call Stanley," I said. "Tell him what's going on."

"Stanley doesn't care about anybody but Stanley. He never even calls home to see how Dad's doing."

"Well, if your dad's sick—"

"Forget it. I'm not calling Stanley. Besides, I have no idea where he is and unless I'm sorely mistaken, neither do you. And even if I *did* know, I wouldn't call him."

And that was that.

Idly, Frank flipped over onto his stomach and began unbuttoning my shirt. Stroking my chest. Pressing his lips to my belly, licking the fluff of hair around my belly button. Nothing hurried, just sort of finding something to do while thinking things through. My dick wasn't being so lackadaisical about the sudden interest in my anatomy however, and I could tell Frank could feel it poking him in the chin through my trousers by the little smile that made his dimple deepen.

He scooched up and sucked on my nipple. Gently at first, then with a little more enthusiasm. Nipping me with his perfect teeth. Breathing his hot breath on my chest. It smelled like pepperoni, his breath. I knew because I had my eyes closed, happily absorbing every new sensation as it came along, and the homey smell of pepperoni was one of them. Pepperoni and male arousal. I could smell them both. Yum.

Frank was still talking. I don't know how he did it. I couldn't have put twelve coherent words together, I was suddenly so turned-on.

"I think we should go, Tom. Dad's been good to me and he's all alone. I don't want him to lose the farm. God knows what might happen if he gets really sick and there is no one there to help him. If he goes to the hospital, what happens to all the animals? Who's going to feed them?"

I gasped when his hand came to rest on my closed fly and he gave it a little squeeze. Lordy, I wanted that thing open. I could almost hear Tom Junior dragging a tin cup up and down the inside of my zipper, screaming for his freedom. "How many animals are you talking about?" I asked, breathless.

"Quite a few," Frank said with my nipple still in his mouth. His hands were sliding along my rib cage. Not tickling. Stroking.

Now *my* hands were beginning to move too. I had burrowed one of them under the back of Frank's shirt and found the little patch of hair over his ass. I loved that spot. It was my favorite spot in all the world. Almost. I twiddled the hair there and once in a while I would dip my forefinger into the crack of his ass for a little external massaging. Nothing invasive. Just reconnoitering the terrain. Judging by the way Frank's butt was moving around, he seemed to enjoy my reconnoitering. Or reconoodling, as he called it.

Frank pressed his lips to mine and worked his tongue inside my mouth. Even that didn't stop him from talking. "What about Pedro?"

"Hmm," I said, both in response to the question and in response to the heavenly taste of Frank's kiss. "We'll have to take him with us. We'll drive. Cheaper than flying. What d'you think?"

"I think I want to get naked," Frank said. And less than a minute later, he was. And so was I.

Apparently Frank wasn't in the mood to waste time. He slid his tongue under my foreskin. Tasting. Discovering. He kept at it until my dick was standing at full attention, throbbing with my heartbeat, banging against his lips like a battering ram testing the castle gate. Geez. And I thought I was hard *before*.

"You ever measure this thing?" Frank asked with a smile, his gorgeous green eyes looking up at me even while my dick still prodded that beautiful mouth, begging to be let in. "It's the biggest dick I've ever seen. Even in porno."

I was having trouble talking. I usually *did* have trouble talking when someone's tongue was burrowing around under my foreskin like a gopher.

"Is it?" I gasped. For some reason it always embarrassed me when people commented on the size of my equipment. Funny that would embarrass me when a tongue circumnavigating the head of my dick didn't. But hey, that's just me.

Frank was still on the sofa beside me, still sprawled out on his stomach and naked as a jaybird. While he worked on my dick, I gently kneaded his beautiful ass. I worked my fingers down between his legs to caress his balls from behind. Being a polite fellow, Frank opened his legs to provide me easier access. Dickwise, as in *my* dick, he had apparently decided to get down to brass tacks. He stopped fooling around with my foreskin and slid it out of the way as he took me deep into his mouth. It was Tom Junior's favorite place to be. Frank always seemed to like it there too. I savored every sensation as he drew me in. Every moment, every movement. The caress of his lips and every flick of his tongue. Frank always sucked dick like he meant it. You could tell he was having a good time. And needless to say, so was I.

I leaned over to kiss Frank's broad shoulder. His skin tasted hot and salty. I trailed my tongue down his spine, reaching out with both hands now to stroke his butt, lightly brushing my fingertips over the hair there, savoring the heat of the man, the plush softness of his perfect ass. His hot body was giving off the scent of desire now. He was excited. I could smell it on him. I could smell it on myself.

I closed my eyes. His mouth was like velvet around my dick. His tongue stabbed into my slit as if seeking a place to hide. My legs started shaking, just like they always did when he did that. I could feel him smile around me. He had noticed the shaking too.

"You're dripping," he said. "I can taste you."

"I want to taste you too," I said.

"Okay," Frank mumbled, and without letting my dick slide from between his lips, he rolled onto his side, facing the back of the couch, exposing himself to me. I slid down sideways until my face was in his crotch.

My fingers circled his cock. He was already dripping, just like me. I slid my thumb across the slit of his dick and smeared the liquid around. Frank arched his hips, aching for me to keep doing it. Not to stop. Not ever to stop. All that humping he had been doing on the sofa cushion while he sucked my dick seemed to have taken its toll. I got the distinct impression that Frank was about three heartbeats away from shooting.

I held his cock in my fist and slowly stroked it until another drop of precome glistened at the tip. This time I brought my lips down and sucked it away.

Again Frank arched his hips, and I took him into my mouth as far as he would go.

He sighed happily. And so did I.

Without further ado, while my mouth was still on him, he came.

A second later, I followed suit. Boy, Frank was good.

We held each other as our heartbeats gently slowed. Our mouths stayed exactly where they were. Our hands continued caressing all the places they liked to caress. And all the while, I had never felt more loved and more satisfied in all my life. Small wonder I was smiling.

Finally, we let our cocks slide away from each other's lips. Still, mine lay heavily against Frank's cheek. Lingering there. Resting. A hot lump of flesh. Drained, but still very much alive. Frank looked up across the expanse of my flat stomach, damp with perspiration, and his eyes were the greenest I had ever seen them.

He smiled at me and I smiled back. He looked so happy there with my softening dick pressed against the side of his face, I thought my heart would burst.

"Whenever you want to go," I said, "we'll go. Just let me arrange it at work."

He kissed my stomach. "Thank you, Tom. I love you, you know."

"I love you too," I said, pulling him close. "We'll take care of your dad. Just don't worry."

"Um, Tom, do you think you're ready to tackle farm life? I mean, well, being raised in the city and all—"

I honest to God guffawed, and I don't guffaw often. Most gay people don't. "Don't you worry about me," I said. "How hard can farm life be? I'll just follow your lead and do what you do, so don't waste another minute worrying about *that*. Plus, it will only be for a couple of weeks. Okay? I'll be fine. Just fine."

Frank nodded. He closed his eyes, and since we were still in the sixty-nine position, he pressed his face into my stomach. I couldn't see, since my vision was pretty well taken up with Frank's crotch, but it felt like he was grinning. He lay there so long, with his face pressed into my stomach, that I thought he had fallen asleep. But then he kissed my belly button, and I knew he was just thinking things over.

I hugged Frank's thighs, while his pillow of dark pubic hair tickled my face. The air around us was scented with the smell of sex and pizza and two satiated men who just happened to be very much in love. I closed my eyes and thought things over too. I had some money set aside. Quite a bit, in fact. I could manage it. If Moony wouldn't give me time off from work, then I'd quit. Fuck him. Frank came first.

Frank would always come first. It was a matter of priorities. What else is love about, if not priorities?

And sex. Lots and lots of sex.

JERRY was apoplectic when I told him. "You're not going! I won't have it! You can't just throw your career away like this! What the hell is wrong with you, Tom? Have you had a nervous breakdown or something? Is this kid a fucking witch? Did he put a spell on you?"

I grinned. Since we were on the phone, Jerry couldn't see the grin, so I wasn't being cruel. Well, maybe I was. Just a little. "That would be a warlock, I think. And yes, Frank has put a spell on me. It's called love. Ever hear of it? And don't be such a drama queen. I'm not throwing my career away. I'm simply taking an unscheduled vacation." At least I hoped Moony would see it that way.

For the past three months, Jerry had been calling every couple of days or so, as if he was afraid to let go. Telling me how much he missed me. Telling me how much he wanted me back. Hoping against hope that I'd had a knockdown drag-out fight with Frank and he might find an opening to squeeze himself back into my life. He was always desperate to find out what Frank and I had been up to, even though it drove him crazy when he did. This time he got more information than he bargained for, and he wasn't happy about it.

"And what about Pedro? You can't just drag him across state lines. He's half mine, unless you've forgotten."

That pissed me off. "Then you're a deadbeat dad! I haven't seen you feeding him or taking him to the vet or cleaning up his messes lately! You relinquished all rights to Pedro when you stopped caring for him. So don't talk to me about Pedro, you cheating little shit. Just don't!"

"Oh, so now we're back to the cheating, huh? Don't you think that proves you still love me, Tom? My God, you can't have a conversation with me or with anybody else for that matter without bringing up the fact that I once cheated on you."

"Well, gee whiz. Sorry. But when my lover takes his pecker somewhere else for servicing, packs up and leaves without so much as an apology and moves in with a home-wrecking poophead named Stanley, leaving me in the lurch with apartment rent, vet bills, and that damned credit card we jointly used, then yes, I'm going to bring it up now and then! If you don't want people bringing shit like that up, *then don't fucking do those fucking things in the first fucking place!*"

I felt a hand at the back of my neck. It was Frank. Trying to calm me. Trying to head off the aneurism that was about to explode somewhere down around my analytic converter, or whatever that human organ is called that pumps out the neurotransmitters responsible for making a person throw a fucking snit.

"Hang up the phone," he whispered. "It's not worth it."

I glanced at my watch. It was almost time to leave for work anyway.

I did some yoga breathing to calm myself down, then said into the phone clearly, concisely, and without malice, "Good-bye, Jerry. Have a nice life."

Jerry stammered, "But—but—but—"

And I hung up the phone. I allowed myself two seconds to feel sad about what I had just done to Jerry, not that he didn't deserve it, then turned and gave Frank a grateful kiss for always seeming to be there when I needed him most.

Now off to work, and my confrontation with Mr. Moonhouse.

Hopefully, that confrontation would be a little less traumatic.

IT WASN'T. In fact, it was considerably worse.

Mr. Moonhouse was in a foul mood when I walked into the bank. I didn't know why. Maybe his wife had refused to give him a blow job that morning. Or maybe she *had* given him a blow job but was forced to interrupt and water the petunias before he could make his customary deposit. Bankers are funny about that sort of thing. Deposits and all. Or maybe Moony owned a Chihuahua. Sometimes that was enough to throw a person's day off. Believe me, I know.

Whatever the reason, when I asked for a minute of Moony's time, he looked at me like I was asking for a loan. Bankers are funny about *that* sort of thing *too*, don't think they aren't.

I couldn't help noticing that Moony was looking a tad unkempt this morning. It was as if he had run out the door on his way to work without checking a few things first. For instance, half of his shirt was untucked. Plus, he needed to clean his horn-rimmed glasses. They were filthy. And to top it all off, two cowlicks were poking out of the left side of his head like a couple of weeds and a booger was dangling from his nose. A big one. I couldn't take my eyes off that booger. It was like—magnetic. Every time he breathed in or out, the damn thing fluttered. It was hard to talk to the man, what with that dangling shirttail, those funky glasses and flapping cowlicks, and that frigging fluttering booger.

I had to put my own problems on hold long enough to ask him what was wrong. Hell, anybody would. "Mr. Moonhouse, are you okay? You look a little—flustered."

"I got a call about you at my house this morning, son. Just a few minutes ago, in fact."

"About *me*?" That couldn't be good. It did, however, explain why he had been staring at me so strangely since I walked into the bank. Sort of a cross between "sympathetically appalled" and "unintentionally irked" with a smidgeon of "regrettable sexual curiosity" thrown in to confuse the issue.

Uncharacteristically, Moony stepped forward and slipped an arm around my shoulder. With his other hand he patted my forearm. I got the distinct impression he had been wanting to lay his hands on me for a very long time. For a host of reasons. His breath smelled of Twinkies. Breakfast of champions.

"I'm so sorry, dear boy. I had no idea you were going through such a crisis at home. Gambling, is it? Liquor? Hookers? Male prostitutes, maybe?"

Moony had a twinkle in his eye when he mentioned male prostitutes that made me think quite possibly that maybe it wasn't only Mrs. Moony's throat he had been hosing down, but at the moment that was neither here nor there. I was getting irritated.

I shook his arm off. "What the heck are you talking about?"

He put the arm right back where it had been and pulled me close. "It's okay, Tom. Can I call you Tom?"

"You just did."

"Yes, well, let's not be snippy. That won't help."

"Help with what?"

"Help with our little crisis, son."

"And just what crisis might that be, pray tell?" I was past being astounded. I was even past being irritated. I had moved right along to really, really mad. Furious, in fact. "Spit it out, Moony. What's the problem?"

He tsked. "Mr. Moonhouse is my name. You know that. But I understand you're upset so we'll let that little breach of protocol slide for the moment. Tell me, son, is there anything you'd like to tell me?"

"Like what?"

"Well, for instance, maybe you would like to explain why you are about to quit your position at this bank without any formal notice after putting in three long and happy years here. We're a family, Tom. You don't just quit a family. You give them a heads-up. You give them a little *warning*."

"I'm not quitting."

"You're not?"

"No. Who said I was?"

Here he stumbled. "Well, the call was anonymous."

"Anonymous, huh?" Jerry. What a putz. "I suppose he told you I'd been embezzling funds too, this anonymous caller of yours. Or snatching ballpoint pens and calendars out of the storeroom and toilet paper out of the bathroom and selling it all on eBay. What were his accusations precisely? That I had been stashing rolls of quarters down the crotch of my pants every night and walking out the door with them?"

"Well, son, there usually *is* a sizable bulge down there—"

"Yes, and it's all me, as you undoubtedly know, since you're looking at it all the time."

He jumped as if he had been zapped with a cattle prod. "How dare you accuse me of such a thing! I'm a happily married man."

"Yeah, well, so am I."

He gave me a sympathetic cluck. "Yes, so I hear. And I also hear that the person you've got yourself mixed up with is the person who is leading you down the road to disaster. What do you have to say to that?"

"I have a couple of things to say to that. One, you shouldn't believe everything you hear from total strangers, and two, if you say one more word about my lover that isn't positively *steeped* in respect and admiration, I'm going to rip your tie off and strangle you with it."

Moony blinked. At least I *think* he blinked. Those glasses really were funky. "Wait a minute. Did you say you weren't quitting?"

"That's what I said."

"Then what did you want to see me about?"

"I need some time off. Just three weeks or so. A family emergency."

"A family emergency."

"Yeah, that's all it is. I'm not embezzling or quitting or any of those other things. I just need a little time off."

"Time off."

Okay. Now I was getting mad again. "Is there an echo in here? Yes. Time off."

I could hear the wheels turning inside Moony's unkempt head as he thought things over. Golly, I'd had no idea he was so enthralled with my work. Or maybe it was just my basket he was enthralled with. But for whatever reason, it certainly seemed that Moony liked having me around and had been thrown into quite a dither thinking I might actually leave. That's when it hit me. Jeez, this was a perfect time to ask for a raise.

I was just about to do exactly that, when Moony cleared his throat, took a gander at the ceiling, looked down at the toes of his shoes and gave a little buff to one of them on the back of his other pant leg, like that was really going to help his appearance any. Then he said the last thing I expected him to say.

"I'm sorry, son. You're fired. Please clean out your desk."

I was so dumbfounded, I actually said, "But what about my raise?"

Moony chose to ignore that. "I'm sorry, Tom, but our employees must he held to the highest fiduciary and personal standards. And clearly, you have some problems that need to be dealt with before you can be deemed trustworthy enough to remain with us here at the bank. I'll give you a glowing recommendation to help you find a new position elsewhere. It's the least I can do."

Yeah, the very least. But what did I expect? I did threaten to strangle him, after all. That's not something you often see on a quarterly evaluation sheet.

He took a final glance at my crotch, pulled the booger out of his nose, looked at it with surprise, then turned and walked away.

In the matter of clearing out my desk, I did Moony one better. Or two better. I also cleared out my savings and checking accounts. He watched in horror as the teller issued me a check for $42,000 and change and told me she would miss our little chats over coffee.

I could never remember *having* a chat with her over coffee, but I told her to have a nice day anyway, stuffed my cashier's check into my pocket, picked up my cardboard box of desk crap, set the box back down, gave Moony the finger while adjusting my crotch for his benefit, then picked the box back up and regally strolled from the bank whistling a merry tune from *Pirates of Penzance*. I gave every impression of having taken a leisurely tour of the premises on my royal outing only to ultimately find the establishment wanting. Just like a queen, huh?

I crossed the street to our rival bank and opened a checking account, throwing in all my money, except for a couple of grand which I thought I might need for the upcoming road trip to Indiana. Back on the street, I took a final glance at my old bank and breathed in a healthy gulp of morning air. Turning my back on the last three years of my life, I hopped on the bus, since Frank still had the car, and headed home. And while I headed home, I cogitated.

Three months ago I had a job but no Frank. Now, I had Frank but no job. It didn't take me long to figure out which scenario I liked best.

Jobs were everywhere. Men too, but not like Frank. Even being suddenly thrust among the ranks of the unemployed, I couldn't find a whole lot to complain about.

Oddly, I couldn't scrape up much anger at Jerry for setting the wheels in motion for *getting* me fired. In fact, I forgave him completely. Now I was free to help Frank take care of his dad. That topped everything else that was on my plate at the moment. Should I tell Jerry his nefarious plan had backfired? Naw. Let him think he had ruined my life forever, getting me canned and all. It was something he could ponder and regret and feel ashamed about in his old age, never knowing he had actually done me a favor. Can I be a bitch, or what?

Thank heavens I'd had some money in the bank to fall back on. That made all the cogitating and all the figuring and all the snide forgiving considerably less stressful. Even I was smart enough to admit that.

And just to reassure me that *everything* in life doesn't change at the drop of a hat, back at the apartment God had arranged for Pedro to take a poop on the ottoman.

What a guy. Is God *thorough*, or what?

FRANK and I paid our little old lady neighbor, Miss Wiggins, who also happened to be the apartment manager, two months' rent in advance. We put our houseplants into her care too, which seemed to bring home to her the fact that we were really leaving, so she cried over us and told us to hurry back and to be sure to keep our eyes peeled because the world was positively *packed* with serial killers waiting to pounce on unsuspecting travelers (she'd seen it on *60 Minutes*). We put a hold on the newspaper, phoned the utility company to give them a heads-up we'd be out of town, then loaded the car with everything we thought we might need on the trip, which was a depressing amount of stuff. We practically made ourselves sick polishing off two gallons of milk so it wouldn't spoil in the fridge while we were gone, packed up Pedro's toys, his doggie bed, an industrial-sized squirt bottle filled with spray cleaner, and a dozen rolls of paper towels in case Pedro decided to poop his way across country, and we were on the road by nightfall, worn out before we ever left town.

Taking turns behind the wheel, and driving nonstop, it took us three days to reach the Indiana state line. It also took five and a half tanks of gas, eighteen drive-thru orders of cheeseburgers and fries, six blow jobs (just to keep the driver awake, you know, plus the passenger has to do *something* to stave off boredom), a box and a half of doggie chews, most of the paper towels, and about a quart of spray cleaner to clean off the back seat, which we did exactly twenty-nine times. I counted. Poop? Don't even ask.

And when he wasn't pooping, Pedro barked. He barked the whole way.

We rolled up to Joseph Wells's front gate, unbathed, unshaved, and bleary-eyed with fatigue at the very crack of a rose-red Indiana dawn. Our ears were stuffed with wads of paper towels because Pedro was *still* barking. There was a trail of weary steam dribbling out from under the hood of the Toyota and something in the motor was pecking like a woodpecker. The oil light was flashing as I switched off the ignition. Not a good sign. I figured I had killed my car, and if Pedro didn't shut up pretty soon he was going to be next.

I looked over at Frank and his face was beaming. I took a moment to appreciate how butch he looked with three days growth of black stubble peppering his face; then he leaned across the seat, gave me a quick kiss on the lips, and practically *sprang* from the car. I don't know how he did it. I could barely move. My ass seemed to have bonded to the seat cushion.

Frank's dad was already up when we pulled in the front gate. He was milking the cows, or so Frank said, since he could see a light burning in the barn. Can you believe it? Milking the cows? At five in the morning? Off in the distance, I could see a guy waving at us from the barn door. He had a bucket in his hand.

Golly, I thought, rural America is just like it's played in the movies. This should be fun.

Then, like a bolt of lightning zapping me in the head from on high, I experienced my first full-blown panic attack about what I was getting myself into here. I grabbed an empty potato chip bag off the floorboard and started breathing into it. In. Out. In. Out. What in God's name was I thinking? Milking cows at five in the morning? Slopping hogs? Pulling on hip boots and wading through a gelatinous parfait of animal poop before breakfast every day? Frank was right. I *am* a city boy. A city boy through and through. I don't like animal poop. Pedro notwithstanding. There's a world of difference between a cute little pile of Chihuahua droppings and the quantity of waste material that squirts out of the back end of a six hundred-pound cow. And I have a low threshold for nausea. I could lap up semen all day, if Frank's the supplier, but one spoonful of mayonnaise makes me barf. Go figure.

"That's not Pop," Frank said, sticking his head back through the car window. I could hear the worry in his voice. "That guy in the barn door. That's not Pop."

Frank took off with Pedro hot on his heels. They were both running for the barn while I was still groaning and cussing and trying to peel my cramped foot off the gas pedal and scoot my atrophied ass off the car seat. I had several potential disasters running around inside my head simultaneously. I was worried about Frank's dad, afraid I was crippled for life since my legs didn't seem to be working and my ass felt like a lump of lead, upset because Frank was concerned about the stranger in the barn, sorry I had maybe murdered my car by driving it nonstop for three days, still a little bit panicked about being unemployed, and fearful that Pedro would get eaten by a hog or some other cantankerous farm animal before I could limp my way across the barnyard to protect him.

Suddenly, social anxiety disorder was the least of my problems.

And what was that sound I heard in the distance? Chickens? That's what it sounded like. Chickens. Lots and lots of chickens. This was not good. Unless they've been plucked and breaded and run through a deep fryer, I hate chickens. I don't even like canaries. Little beady eyes. Feathers. Pointy, clackety toenails. Who gives a shit if they can sing? They freak me out. I didn't even want to *think* about what I would do among an entire herd of chickens.

But more important than all these other disastrous scenarios I found myself conjuring up, there was one that stood out above all the rest. That was this: Just why the hell was Frank now hugging that guy in the barn door if it wasn't his dad, and why did the guy suddenly look so young and handsome and brawny and why, oh why, did the guy's hands seem to be inching pretty damn close to Frank's ass?

That got my blood pumping, don't think it didn't. I was out of the car and shuffling my way toward the barn on my numb-ass legs before the cock crowed.

So to speak.

Chapter Nine

I TOOK a detour on my way to the barn to rescue Pedro from a face-off with a pack of wild dogs, or maybe they lived there: I didn't know, and Pedro obviously didn't care *where* they lived, he just wanted to kick some ass after being trapped inside a moving vehicle for three days. He didn't care how big the dogs were. Or how *many* there were, for that matter. Chihuahuas are kind of stupid that way. Anyway, by the time I scooped him up and made my way to the barn door, Frank was gone. The hugger with the wandering hands was still standing there, watching me approach.

I hated the guy at first glance. To begin with, he was younger than me. It's easy to hate people who are younger than you. Everyone does it, whether they admit it or not. Secondly, the guy was handsome enough to turn heads in the dark. Blond hair, pale blue eyes, a creamy complexion with rosy cheeks that any woman in the world would happily kill for. He had a buffed-up body that was stuffed very nicely into a pair of faded jeans and a green Dickies work shirt with the sleeves torn off. The guy's arms were bulging with muscles and smothered in blond hair and his biceps rolled around like croquet balls when he moved. They were yummy. If I didn't already hate the guy, I would have found those biceps very, very appealing.

He stuck his hand out. The one not holding the bucket. "So here's the lucky fella."

I didn't know what he meant by that, but it didn't sound too threatening so I took the hand he offered and gave it a cautious shake.

Cautious, because I wasn't sure where that hand had been. On a cow's nipple, I presumed. Or more than one. I was pretty sure that cows had several. The guy *was* holding a bucket of milk, after all, and standing in a barn door. I vaguely wondered if there was anything like a bottle of hand sanitizer lying around the place.

I was just curious and jealous and pissed off enough at the way this total stranger had hugged Frank two minutes earlier (it certainly looked like they had been in each other's arms before) that my fears of social contact were pretty well obliterated. I tried to ignore a blob of excrement that had somehow managed to adhere to the tip of my ninety-dollar penny loafer as I wended my way across the barnyard. I wasn't sure what manner of livestock the excrement exuded from, and I wasn't sure I wanted to know. Poop is poop, no matter how you slice it. With a concerted effort, I tore my mind away from my damned shoe and pointedly asked, "Um. Who might you be?"

His grip on my hand tightened, but in a friendly way. "Jeff Moody. You're Tom, right? Frank told me all about you."

"He did?" I asked, sounding stupid even to myself.

"Yeah. Over the phone. He talks about you a lot."

Apparently these two had been in communication with each other and I hadn't even known it. Suddenly, an errant glob of poop on my shoe didn't seem like such a big deal. It was funny that Frank had never mentioned he had a hunky friend back in Indiana, or that they spoke on the phone on a regular basis, or that the guy looked as good as he did in a pair of faded blue jeans. And judging by the outline of a fine-looking dick etched beneath the worn denim covering his crotch, he was the type of guy who never wears underwear either. Seemed to me, Frank should have mentioned these things. Perhaps not about the dick, but the other stuff would have been good to know.

Moody took it upon himself to fill in the silent, echoing, cavernous hole I had left in the conversation while I pondered these revelations. "I'd like to hate your guts, Tom, but I just can't bring myself to do it. You've been a good friend to Frank, and more than a friend, I guess, but I can't hold it against you. I *won't* hold it against you. Especially now. Frank's going to need you more than ever."

"Why's that?" I asked, still sounding stupid.

"To help him take care of the farm, of course. It's only a one-man job for Joe, but for anybody else it'd take two. Nobody works as hard as Joe does. Nobody would *want* to." Moody leaned in close. I caught a whiff of spearmint gum. Smelled nice. "Don't you know what I'm talking about? You look a little lost."

"Huh?" Apparently I was getting stupider by the minute.

I jumped when Moody slapped himself in the forehead hard enough to kill a cat. I could actually hear his brain ricocheting around inside his brainpan from the impact. "Well, no, I guess you *don't* know," he said, more to himself than to me. "How the hell could you? It's Frank's dad. He took a turn for the worse last night. That's why I'm here. He called and asked me to help him out by milking his cows this morning. Joe loves to milk his cows. Talks to them like they're people. I knew that if he needed help doing *that*, then he was in pretty bad shape. And he was. I wanted to call an ambulance when I got here, but he wouldn't let me. I hadn't seen Joe for a few weeks. You could have knocked me over with a feather when I got a good look at him this morning. He must have lost thirty pounds. I'm no doctor, but it looks like cancer to me. Has Frank told you anything about that?"

I shook my head. "Frank knew something was up, but he wasn't sure what. His dad wouldn't talk to him about it. Frank suspected though. And yeah, he thinks it's cancer too. Lung cancer maybe. Where's his dad now? Where'd Frank go?"

"Joe's laid up in his bed. I'm not even sure he can walk, Tom. He's awful weak. I sent Frank off to see him." Moody set the milk bucket aside and wiped his hands on the sides of his shirt. "Come on. I'll take you to them."

A cow mooed from somewhere inside the barn. Moody poked his head back through the door, and yelled, "Hold your apple butter, Mary Lou! I'll get back to you in a minute!"

"Mary Lou?" I asked.

Moody chuckled. "Yeah, that Joe's a card. All his cows got names. And most of the pigs. Even a few chickens, I think. The ones he hasn't eaten anyway."

I didn't know what to say to that. "What about Stanley?" I asked, as we took off for the house. I still had Pedro tucked under my arm, and he wasn't happy. He wanted to explore. Or pick another fight. Or poop. "Has anybody called him? Somebody should tell Stanley about his dad, don't you think?"

Moody grunted. "No, I *don't* think. Stanley's about as useless as tits on a bull. He never helped his dad when Joe was well. I seriously doubt if he'd do much better when the poor guy's sick. Forget about Stanley. He's an asshole. And I'm not talking out of school. Joe would tell you the same thing."

I stifled a laugh. "He already did. More than once."

"Well, there you go."

As much as I hated to admit it, I was beginning to like Jeff Moody a little. Of course, that might only last as long as I was left in the dark as to what sort of relationship he had shared with Frank. If it was the down and dirty kind of relationship, the kind Frank had with me, then Moody's likeability quotient would probably suffer real fast. I didn't think I could be quite as magnanimous when it came to Frank's old love life as Moody seemed to be with Frank's new one. Meaning me.

I followed him through a squeaky, crooked gate that led into a grassless backyard. There was a shed that looked like it was about to topple over, an old well with a pump handle sticking out of it, and a clothesline that stretched from a huge maple tree all the way across the yard to an upright board nailed to the side of a fence post. The only thing hanging on the clothesline was a single work glove. I saw the other glove lying in the dirt where it had landed after blowing off the line. Trying not to look totally useless, I picked it up and clipped it to the line with another clothespin that just happened to be hanging there. It took a bit of juggling to do all that without dropping Pedro on his head.

"That dog ever walk?" Moody asked. "Or do you carry him around everywhere you go like a purse?"

"Purse," I said. And that was the end of that. Sometimes people ask too many questions. Pedro licked my chin. I guess he agreed.

The two-story farmhouse was in need of a coat of paint, but it looked solid and respectable nevertheless. It seemed to have been haphazardly added onto a few times over the years. A room here. A porch there. Bay windows stuck out in a couple of places, obviously afterthoughts. A brick chimney, not quite true, climbed up one side of the house. There were a couple of bricks missing at the top, making it look like a chipped, tobacco-stained tooth. The house was all odd angles and had obviously withstood more summers and winters than I had ever seen. It meandered around the yard like a drunk. But it was a happy drunk. Homey and self-satisfied. An old tractor tire, seven feet across, lay in the yard by the back step. It was painted white and filled with petunias, offering up a splash of color to the otherwise bland surroundings of dead grass and unpainted homestead.

The screen door squeaked and twanged when Moody held it open for me. I ducked my head and walked inside. Moody followed.

The house was what I call man-clean. Things were neat and tidy enough at first glance, but it could probably have used a good scrubbing in the corners and in a few out of the way places, those places a woman (or a guy with OCD) would be picking at and fussing over but a normal man tends to blithely ignore. Then, in a burst of insight unusual for me, I understood what I was seeing. The house hadn't had a good cleaning since Frank left, and Frank had left three months ago.

The rooms were just becoming light since we were still on the verge of dawn, but a couple of table lamps were lit here and there, casting shadows through doorways and illuminating pictures on the wall. Family pictures. I stopped for a second in front of a grade school snapshot of a really cute kid with no front teeth, a few scattered freckles, and the biggest, greenest eyes I had ever seen. It took me about a second to realize it was Frank at around six years of age, a cutie even then. I was happy to note that his dimples were already in place. A swelling of love for the guy exploded in my chest like a nova.

Moody seemed to understand what I was feeling. He patted my shoulder and urged me on down a dark hallway with a long, battered runner covering the wood floor and muffling our footsteps. At the end of the hall a closed door waited. I heard Frank's voice coming from the other side of the door. And a second voice too. A deeper voice. It sounded like Frank was cajoling and the other voice was having no part of it. The term "bumping heads" sprang to my mind.

Moody motioned me forward, trying to be polite, I guess, offering me first entry. I grasped the doorknob and gingerly pulled open the door as if peeling away a scab.

The voices stopped the minute Moody and I stuck our heads inside.

ALTHOUGH I had never seen Frank's dad before, not even a photograph, I knew immediately that the face I looked at now would not have been the face I would have seen on the man a year earlier. Or maybe even a month earlier. Joseph Wells had been ravaged by his illness. And the ravaging looked sudden. His eyes, as green as Frank's, were too big for his face. And I could see it was a face that had once been handsome. He had the look of someone who laughs easily, or did at one time in his life. But not now. The illness had snatched his laughter away from him as thoroughly as it had snatched away everything else. He looked stunned by the turn of events that had put him in his bed, helpless and weak as a newborn. People like Joe Wells don't handle helplessness well. It's not something they understand. It's not something they have the patience for.

But cancer doesn't ask for understanding or patience. It just demands its pound of flesh. Joseph Wells was in the process of finding that out, and it was a sorrowing thing to watch.

Frank was perched on the edge of his dad's bed. They were holding hands. They both looked over at the sound of the bedroom door opening, and it took some effort for him to do it, but Joe managed to dredge up a smile to welcome us in. When he did, even his teeth looked too big for his face. But the smile was genuine, and it gave me a glimpse of the man Joseph Wells had once been, and it was a man I would have liked. I found myself hoping he knew that.

There were tears sparkling Frank's cheek as he watched me walk into the room with Moody trailing along in my wake. Seeing Frank, Pedro squirmed around in my arms until Frank was forced to reach out and take him from me. He gave the dog a peck on the forehead, then watched as Pedro squirmed out of *his* arms and walked across Joe's chest until man and dog were nose to nose. Joe grinned and Pedro licked the grin. Pedro immediately curled up in the crook of Joe's arm and just lay there, obviously waiting to see what would happen next.

"That's Pedro," Frank said.

Joe nodded. "Figured it wasn't Tom."

Frank laughed, wiped away a couple of tears, and turned to me. "No, Pop. *That's* Tom."

I smiled and stuck out my hand. Joe Wells took it with the hand that wasn't occupied with Pedro and gave it a weak shake. "You're a handsome one," he said. "It's nice to meet you, Tom."

"It's nice to meet you too, sir."

"Joe. Call me Joe." And then he started coughing. Not only did pain light up his eyes when the coughing really took hold, but considerable fear showed up there too. Joe dropped my hand and grabbed for a tissue from the nightstand. Looking embarrassed, he held it to his mouth until the coughing stopped, then dropped the tissue in a wastebasket by the side of the bed. Following his movements with my eyes, I spotted a drop of blood on the used tissue as it lay there among a dozen others. Each and every one of them was stained with blood. By the look of concern on Frank's face, I knew he had seen it too.

When Joe had the coughing fit under control, he took a moment to gather his strength and wipe the tears from his eyes. Then he tried to pick up where we had left off. "He met Samson yet?" he asked Frank, tilting his head at me.

And Frank laughed. "Is that monster still here?"

Joe looked shocked, but I could tell it was just for show. This was clearly a conversation they had had before, and it was clearly one they enjoyed having. Like an inside joke.

"You can't expect me to kill off a member of the family, Frank. Samson's here to stay, by God." Joe turned to me. There was a speck of blood at the corner of his smile which Frank wiped away with another tissue before Joe could stop him. He obviously didn't like being babied. "Tom, you stay away from Samson now, you hear? He'd just as soon kill you as look at you, and that's God's own truth. Ask Jeff there, he'll tell you."

I didn't know who Samson was, but I was beginning to think it was maybe a third brother they kept hidden away. Maybe somebody like that poor banjo player in *Deliverance* who had a few scrambled genes to contend with and maybe a pet axe, and for safety reasons they kept him chained to the back of the barn like a goat.

Moody, standing behind me, spoke with such force that I jumped a foot in the air. "That fucker! I'd kill him myself if I could. Nothing would make me happier."

I couldn't stand the suspense another second. "Who the hell is Samson, and if he's so dangerous why is he still hanging around the place?"

Joe laughed. Frank rolled his eyes. And Moody groaned. "Don't ask," they all said in unison.

Which made me want to ask again, so I did, this time with a little more desperation in my voice, "Come on now, who the hell is—"

"You all run on now," Joe said. "I'm feeling a little tired. Think I'll take me a nap. And don't be hurtin' Samson while I'm out." He chuckled to himself and closed his eyes.

"Wouldn't dream of it," Moody mumbled. "Best go finish the milking, I guess." And with that, he stalked out of the room.

Frank made a shushing motion with his finger to his lip and beckoned me to follow him quietly out the door. We left the room on tiptoe, leaving Pedro where he was, happily tucked away in Joe's arms. Joe looked like he enjoyed having him there. We left the bedroom door ajar behind us, in case Pedro got the urge to roam around and maybe decorate his new surroundings with a pile of Chihuahua poop as a sort of christening ritual.

I followed Frank into the kitchen where he started puttering around at the counter. It took me a minute to figure out he was making a pot of coffee and rustling us up some breakfast. What I really wanted to do was sleep, but breakfast sounded good too.

Frank was the saddest I had ever seen him. I walked up behind him and wrapped my arms around his waist. He turned in my arms and pressed his face to my neck. I stroked his back. "I'm sorry, Frank. I guess your dad looks worse than he did when you left, huh?"

Frank nodded. I felt moisture on my neck. He was softly crying. "Way worse. If I'd known he was going to fail like this, I never would have left."

"It would have happened either way. With you here or with you gone. You can't beat yourself up over it. There's nothing you could have done. Just be glad you're here now. Maybe we can get him to a doctor."

"He doesn't want a doctor. He watched Mom die of cancer, stuck in a hospital with tubes poking out of her, and at the end she was all alone. She died in the middle of the night without a soul around. Pop doesn't want that. He already told me. He wants to die right where he is. In his bed. And I'm going to let him do it. I'm just sorry I dragged you into all this. If you want to go back to San Diego and—"

"I've got nothing to go back to. I intend to stay right here with you. When we go back to San Diego, we'll go back together. Besides, you're going to need my help. Your friend said there's a lot of work needs to be done on the farm what with the animals and all, plus we'll have to see to your dad's needs too. We'll have our hands full. No way you could do it by yourself, Frank. Even if you could, I wouldn't let you. And I imagine Moody has his own farm to run. He can't be coming over here all the time to help us out. We'll manage just fine on our own."

Frank brushed his lips against mine. "Thanks, Tom. I'm glad you're here. I love you, you know."

"I love you too. Now, who the hell is Samson?" What I really wanted to hear about was Jeff Moody, the hunk out in the barn milking the cows with the sizable package tucked away in those skintight blue jeans, but I figured *that* cross-examination would have to wait. I'd start with Samson first and work my way up to Frank's old trick later, if that's what he was. Not that I doubted it for a minute.

Frank laughed. Taking my hand, he dragged me through the house to the back door.

"Come on. I'll introduce you to Samson."

Outside, the sun was just coming up, and I got a better look at the place. It looked like every farm I had ever seen in every movie I had ever watched about life on a farm. The four dogs Pedro had picked a fight with earlier lay sprawled out across the backyard like a flock of sheep. They raised their heads and gawked at us when we came through the back door, hoping for some table scraps maybe. "No, Shep. No, Beau. Frannie, Tige. Sleep now," Frank said, and they lay back down and went back to sleep. I suddenly realized why Frank had been so appalled when he first saw how ill-trained Pedro was. Is. Seems farm dogs are a little more obedient than the standard spoiled Chihuahua. Come to think of it, who isn't?

I didn't know what to expect from this Samson business, but I knew there was one question I needed to ask Frank right away. Otherwise, I was going to have to start breathing into a paper bag again.

"Uh, tell me, Frank. Does your dad have chickens? Please tell me he doesn't have chickens."

Frank looked at me like I had just sprouted a second head. "You got something against chickens?"

"Well, in large groups they kind of freak me out. I don't mind *eating* them, of course, fried, stewed, with dumplings, stuffed in a taco, I don't give a shit how they're cooked, but—"

"You're kidding. You don't like chickens." It wasn't a question. It was a statement.

"Nope." That was a statement too. Mine. And I meant it.

Frank stopped walking, turned to face me, and gripped my shoulders. "Well, then I hate to tell you this, Tom, but yeah he has a few—"

"Oh, I guess that's okay."

"—hundred. He has a few hundred. Nine hundred to be precise. Give or take a few chicken dinners."

I blinked. Nine hundred chickens. Oh God. I guess I was going to need that paper bag after all.

Then Frank managed to knock the chickens right out of my head by saying, "You are so cute. I'm going to get us fed and showered, send Jeff home so we can do a few hours' work around the farm, get the chores caught up and all, and then I'll check in on Pop, see how he's doing, and then, by God, I'm going to get you into my old bedroom and rip your clothes off and monopolize your dick until it explodes. How does that sound?" There was a glimmer in Frank's green eyes that was really, really sexy.

I cleared my throat, trying to ignore the stirring of my dick inside my trousers. "That reminds me. I have a few questions about Jeff Moody too."

"Screw Jeff Moody," Frank said.

"Did you?" I asked. "Screw him?"

And Frank shrugged. "Maybe in another lifetime. Now I've got you."

I grinned. That was exactly what I wanted to hear. Moody be damned. Chickens too. I had a man who loved me. And he had green eyes.

I was just getting all gooshy inside and Tom Junior was creeping down my pant leg in anticipation of things to come when Frank up and broke the spell again.

"But first, ta-da!" he grandly announced like a sideshow barker. "I'd like you to meet Samson!"

We were just rounding the corner of the barn. I could hear Moody somewhere inside grumbling at a cow, telling it through what sounded like clenched teeth to please be so kind as to get off his fucking foot.

I started to giggle at that, but then I saw what Frank was pointing at and my jaw fell open. I wasn't sure, but I thought maybe a couple of fillings fell out.

I swear I had never seen anything like it before in my life.

FRANK had his arms folded across his chest and he was staring at the same thing I was staring at. The only difference was he was looking proud as punch while I was looking thunderstruck and horrified. Frank dropped his head to my shoulder and we sort of leaned into each other. His arm snaked around my waist all lovey-dovey, or it would have been if I hadn't been shocked all the way down to my toes by what the hell was standing there in front of us looking back.

"Pretty impressive, huh?" Frank grinned.

Impressive wasn't the word I was groping for. I think the word was *Holy crap!*

Samson was a pig. A giant pig. "Samson's a pig," I said. "A giant pig." I knew I was stating the obvious, but I sure didn't know what else to say.

Frank chuckled. "Well, to be precise, Samson is a boar. See those tusks?"

I did indeed. Four big-ass fangs sticking out of the creature's mouth pointing off in four different directions like daggers. They must have been six inches long. Just looking at those tusks made my nuts crawl up into my body and cower in fear. Samson was one ugly hog. And he looked mean to boot.

Frank went right on talking as if he was leading a tour group through the frigging White House. "Samson is a Yorkshire hog mix. He weighs, as near as we can figure, about one thousand four hundred pounds. He stands four feet high and is just shy of eight feet long from snout to tail. Take a good long look, Tom. You'll never see another one like him."

Good, I thought. *I never want to.*

Samson stared back at me with his little piggy eyes, and they truly were the only things about him that were little. A rope of drool dangled off one of his tusks like a watch chain. He blessed us with a snort. I think it was pig talk for, "What the fuck are *you* staring at?"

He was in a muddy pen that was big enough to park six or seven cruise ships in. There was a watering trough at one end that looked like a coffin and smack in the middle of the enclosure was the rusted out cab of a '52 Chevy pickup sitting up on its front wheels with the back of its cabin sitting in the mud. The truck's bed was missing. The rubber front tires were missing too. It was sitting on its rims. Maybe Samson had chewed the tires off in some sort of maniacal feeding frenzy. God knows he *looked* crazy enough to have maniacal feeding frenzies. Every five minutes maybe. All the other fences on the farm were made of wood, but the one around Samson's pen was constructed of round iron bars that looked strong enough to hold a pissed-off rhino.

To my untrained eye, Samson didn't look too happy. But then, maybe he never did. Some people don't. I don't know about pigs.

"Does he bite?" I asked.

This time Frank's chuckle turned into a full-fledged laugh. "He doesn't only bite, Tom. He *eats.* He'll eat anything, and that would include *us* if we get too close. He's got a nasty temperament for a hog. Usually they're kinda sweet, but not Samson. Pop says Samson's overgrown hormones must have fucked up his sense of restraint, because he ain't got one. Sense of restraint, I mean."

"Like a tractor without a governor."

Frank chucked me on the arm. "Very good. You were paying attention. I'll make a farmer out of you yet."

Fat chance.

I shook my head. "It must cost a fortune to feed this monster. Why does your dad keep him around?"

"State Fair. Pop wanted to take him up to Indy and show him off. There's always somebody willing to pay good money for any kind of livestock that doesn't fit the mold. Freaks and all. Two-headed calves, that sort of thing. Samson would make a real good sideshow attraction, if you could manage to keep him from eating the audience. I don't guess Pop will get the chance to show him off now."

We shared a glance, both knowing it was true. Joe's days of showing anything off were pretty much over. Frank sighed, then turned his attention back to the pig from hell.

I guess Samson was one of those pigs who doesn't like being talked about. He gave a nasty roar and charged the fence like a freight train trying to plow through a depot. Mud and pig snot flew everywhere as he came barreling toward us, head down, tusks slashing left and right. Thank God the fence was made of iron. It stopped him cold, but just barely. I could hear the fence rattle and twang and hum for about ten seconds after Samson crashed his head into it like a battering ram.

Frank stepped cautiously back when Samson began his attack while I took a more definitive approach and leaped straight up into the air like Apollo 11. I figure if a thing is worth doing, it's worth doing right. When I leap in fear, I *soar*. Pride be damned.

Frank employed a bit of tact by not mentioning my leap of terror. Or the fact I had screamed like a little girl. After I came back down, he kissed me on the lips as if glad to see me safely back on Earth after my long flight. "Ready for breakfast?" he asked with a determined show of good cheer and desperately trying not to laugh.

I wiped the sweat off my forehead and gingerly patted the seat of my pants to clandestinely check whether or not I had soiled myself, what with the unintended inertia of my unscheduled blastoff and all. Reassured that I had not, I said, "Sure, Frank. Let's go eat."

It was with a great deal of satisfaction that I turned my back on Samson, who was still shaking his head and grumbling and flinging pig slobber everywhere. The fucker.

I hoped we were having bacon for breakfast. Lots and lots of bacon.

Chapter Ten

JOE was so weak we had to stuff pillows between him and the arms of the chair to keep him sitting upright at the breakfast table. With each of us taking an arm, it took both Frank and me to get him to the kitchen from his bed. We had exchanged worried and knowing glances behind Joe's head along the way. We would have to get a wheelchair, and soon. And probably a bunch of other stuff too. A walker, maybe. A bath chair. A bed tray. God knew what else.

"Guess maybe I've turned into more trouble than I'm worth," Joe said, obviously mortified by his helplessness. His face was the color of volcanic ash, and he was still listing a bit to the left, but no matter what we did we couldn't seem to straighten him up completely. His hands were trembling as they lay atop the kitchen table. Just the effort of getting to the kitchen had caused a sheen of sweat to glisten across his forehead.

Frank stopped piddling around with the pillows long enough to give his dad a kiss on the cheek. There was a lot of hurt going on behind Frank's eyes, but he didn't let it be heard in his voice.

"Don't be silly, Pop. You're having a bad day is all. You'll get your strength back real quick. Wait and see if you don't. First thing you have to do is eat."

"I'm not really hungry, son."

"That's okay," Frank said. "You'll eat anyway."

Joe cast a sheepish glance in my direction as I scraped eggs and sausage and fried potatoes onto plates and plopped them on the table. "One of my sons is mean and worthless, Tom. The other one is sweet and dumb. Frank's the sweet one."

I nodded, my mind elsewhere. Since everything was cooked in bacon grease and slathered with butter, I figured our cholesterol levels should be spiking around noon and our arteries completely clogged by sunset. That's probably when the strokes would hit. A lot of people seemed to die of stroke at sunset. Biorhythms and all that.

If I hadn't been so tied up worrying about the fat content in our breakfasts and the state of our arteries, I could have talked to Joe all day about his observation concerning his two sons. No one knew better than I how sweet the one was and what a prick the other had turned out to be. But at the moment I had more important matters to fret about.

"I'm sorry, Frank. Where did you say the milk was?" I had my head in the refrigerator all the way up to the fourteenth vertebrae. I was starting to get cold.

"In the crock. Just scoop it out with a ladle. The ladle's in the top drawer. You'll have to crawl back out of the fridge to get it." I got the impression Frank was trying not to laugh and cry at the same time, what with his dad being so sick and me being so stupid.

Ah. So that's what that white stuff in the big bowl under my chin was. It's hard being a cook in someone else's kitchen. And in a different century.

"So it's just milk then," I said, carefully dragging the huge, heavy crock out of the fridge and clunking it down on the counter, trying not to let it slosh all over the place. "Milk straight out of the cow. Unsterilized, unpasteurized, unhomogenized, unfortified with Vitamin D. Just plain old milk. Cow milk. Hot off the press, so to speak. Mmm. That should be healthy."

Or deadly. Hadn't these people ever heard of *E. coli*? Or tuberculosis? Or mad cow disease? Didn't brucellosis ring a bell? *Coxiella burnetii*? *Bacillus cereus*? Good Lord, I was going to have to either start drinking water or stop watching The Learning Channel.

To hell with it. I ladled the milk into glasses and served them up, wondering how long it takes *E. coli* to strike. Then I wondered if anyone had ever survived a stroke and an outbreak of mad cow disease at the same time. Would they cancel each other out, or would you die that much quicker? Was it painful? Why the hell wouldn't it be? I hoped someone would take care of Pedro when I was gone.

My concerns made Joe smile. I wondered how he could do it, as weak as he was. Smile, I mean. "Don't worry, son. People were drinking unsterilized milk for centuries before Pasteur came along. Now it's called organic health food and costs twice as much. We get it free on the farm. Drink up."

So I did. We all have to die sometime.

While Frank and I wolfed down our food (cholesterol be damned, I was starving), Joe moved his around with his fork every now and then but very little of it ever seemed to make it to his mouth.

"Tom, I've let things go the last couple of weeks. Just haven't felt like doing much, I guess. You and Frank here are going to have to get the work caught up. Think you can do that? Moody was kind enough to give us a hand this morning but from here on out we'll manage on our own. Okay?"

"No problem, sir," I said. "That's why I came along. To help out. I'm a little worried about those chickens though."

Frank cleared his throat to shut me up. I guess I couldn't blame him. "Don't worry, Dad. We came here to work and that's what we intend to do."

"I know you will, boys. And I'll make it worth your while, don't think I won't. 'Cause I appreciate it. I do. One day this farm will be yours, Frank." Joe turned a sheepish eye to me. "And I think maybe yours too, Tom."

I started. "What?"

Joe gave his head a little shake. "I didn't just fall off the turnip truck, Tom. I may be a simple farmer from Indiana but I know how the world works. And I know love when I see it. The way you look at my boy, and the way my boy looks at you, makes it pretty clear how things stand. And I've got no problem with it whatsoever. As long as you make each other happy, that's good enough for me. Frank deserves to be happy. He's a good boy. Just treat him right. That's all I ask. Think you can do that, Tom? Think you can treat my son right?"

I wasn't sure what to say, so I said nothing. I think maybe I couldn't have said anything anyway, since my heart seemed to be stuffed up into my throat like a rag in an air duct. It meant a lot having Joe welcome me into the family and to understand and accept the love I felt for his son.

I could see that it meant a lot to Frank too. He reached out and covered his dad's hand with his own. "Don't worry, Pop. He treats me right. But I think you already know that." If anything else needed to be said, Frank let the touch of his hand say it. Frank smiled at me across the table, and I could see the pride he felt for his father shine brightly in those heavenly green eyes.

I reached out and took Joe's other hand. "Thank you, sir. I will. It's all I want to do. Frank is the best thing that's ever happened to me. I intend to be the same to him."

"You already are," Frank said, reaching across the table to grasp my hand too.

A tear glistened in each of Joe's eyes as he looked from Frank, to me, then back to Frank. He smiled a weary smile as the three of us held hands in a circle. And it was then that the coughing commenced again.

This time it struck with such force that Frank and I both wondered if it would ever stop, and if Joe's weakened body would survive the onslaught. Even Joe seemed rattled by the intensity of it. I saw fear on his face this time. Real fear. And pain. The coughing was tearing him apart.

While Frank tried to help Joe through it, I cleared the table and wondered about Stanley. Wasn't he included in any business concerning the farm? Shouldn't he be helping out? The way Joe had talked, the whole shebang would be going to Frank when he was gone. Surely that couldn't be. Wouldn't Stanley contest the will? There would have to be one, or the farm would be split between the two sons no matter what Joe wished.

But after washing the breakfast dishes and getting Joe settled back in bed, Frank and I found too many other things to occupy our time. I almost forgot about Stanley in the shuffle that followed, and any questions I meant to ask were forgotten real fast when I heard the list of things Joe expected us to do before the sun went down. It was going to be a busy day.

I suddenly realized that Pedro was missing in action. I searched the house twice without any luck. Finally, I stepped out the back door, and there he was, asleep in the backyard snuggled up close to one of the farm hounds that outweighed him by fifty or sixty pounds.

While I watched, Pedro snapped at the monster beside him so as to carve a little more room for himself on the two-acre lawn, which should have been big enough for Pedro and a *thousand* farm dogs and a couple of elephants besides, but apparently Pedro was feeling a little cramped, or maybe he was just asserting his authority. The hound yipped in pain, looked at Pedro in surprise, as if he was expecting a rattlesnake or something instead of a squirrel, or whatever the hell this little creature was—surely it wasn't a dog—and then the big mutt reluctantly scooted over and made Pedro some room.

Pedro took it as his due and immediately went back to sleep, sprawled out flat on his back with all four legs pointing off in different directions, soaking up the morning sun like a fat tourist on the beach at Rio.

The huge mongrel looked down at him for a minute, then yawned and went back to sleep.

I felt hot breath on the back of my neck. It was Frank, chuckling.

"I see Pedro has carved a niche for himself."

"Yeah." I grinned. "He carved a niche in that big-ass dog too."

"Well, good," Frank said, sliding his lips across my ear. "Now they're friends."

"How's your dad?" I asked. "Did the coughing stop?"

"Yeah. Finally. He's sleeping now. At least, I hope he is. You ready to go to work?"

"Sure," I lied. "Let's do what we came here to do."

Frank gave me a sidelong glance, like he was wondering if I knew what I was getting myself into. Instead of saying anything, he simply took my hand and dragged me toward the barn.

Thus began our longest journey together.

Oh wait. Sorry. Wrong book. Even if, as you'll soon see, that line from *To Kill a Mockingbird does* fit this juncture of our story like a fucking glove.

WE FOUND Moody pouring the fresh, foaming milk from his milk bucket into a shiny waist-high container made of stainless steel. It was pristinely spotless, glistening with condensation, and obviously ice-cold. When he was finished pouring, he slapped a metal lid onto the container, banged it down with the heel of his hand, and hefted the container into an old refrigerator which had had the inside shelves removed. The refrigerator stood in the shadows among a stack of hay bales at the back of the barn. Moody nudged the refrigerator door closed with his boot when he was done.

"This one's about full," was all he said. I noticed that, except for the three of us, the barn was empty. The cows were gone. Probably out pooping somewhere. Maybe they had a quota to fill.

Frank explained about the fridge. "We sell whole milk to a health food store in town. They pick it up twice a week. Sell 'em butter too. And eggs. And sometimes meat when it's freshly slaughtered."

"Good," I said. "Slaughter Samson. That should make you rich. And me happy."

Moody laughed. "I thought I heard a cry of terror earlier out behind the barn. Sounded just like a little girl. At first I thought maybe it was Heidi, falling off the Alps, it was such a high-pitched scream. Then I figured it was just you, Tom, having an audience with his royal highness." He didn't say it with malice, but he did say it. Kidding, I supposed. I felt myself blush but I didn't take his comment too much to heart. After all, I still had Frank and Moody didn't. I figured that made me the winner in any sort of pissing contest he might decide to initiate.

Frank gave me a sidelong glance to see how I was taking the ribbing. He seemed relieved to see me give a good-natured shrug. "Samson would scare the pants off anybody," Frank kindly interjected into the conversation in an obvious attempt to bolster my ego. Then he playfully bumped me with his hip. "Mmm. There's a thought," he added with a wink, glancing down at my trousers like Mae West looking for that hard man she was always talking about.

"*Well,* then," Moody said, glancing at the two of us bumping hips, then he too glanced down at my pants as if reassuring himself they were still in place. "All sexual innuendos aside, on *that* happy note I think I'll head on up the road and start my *own* chores."

Frank thanked him, and there was an awkward moment when they were about to hug, then thought better of it since I was standing right there.

"S'okay, guys. You can hug. Just no tongues," I added.

And everybody laughed. Their hug was short and sincere and kissless. By God.

"Thanks, Jeff," Frank said, releasing him. "If you need any favors in return, just let me know."

"*Farm* favors," I clarified, and everybody laughed again. Except me. This time I was serious.

I stuck my hand out to give Moody a businesslike good-bye shake, but he scooped me into those muscle-bound arms of his and gave me a squeeze that almost made me gasp.

"It was good to meet you, Tom. I'm glad you're here."

He sounded like he meant it. *I* wouldn't have if *I'd* been him. "Nice to meet you too," I said, almost sincerely. Frank flashed his dimples, trying not to laugh at the wary look on my face. I rolled my eyes at him over Moody's shoulder, as if to say, "So sue me, I'm not used to sincere gay people."

Moody released me and grabbed Frank's hand one last time. "Keep me posted on your dad. Hope he gets better real fast." He didn't say it with much sense of hope, and by the sad look that dimmed Frank's eyes, I knew Frank didn't harbor much hope of that happening either.

It was a sad good-bye full of sad possibilities all around. Then Moody was gone and Frank and I were on our own.

"Ready to learn the ropes?" Frank asked, rubbing his hands together, apparently eager to get to work and take his mind off his dad's illness, even if it meant the herculean task of trying to turn me into what I clearly was not, and probably would never, never, *never* be—a farmer.

"Kiss me first," I said.

So he did, and it was a long one. My favorite kind. By the time our kiss ended, Moody was half a mile down the road, the sun was a wee bit higher in the sky, and I was ready to toss Frank into the hay and have my way with him. Tom Junior was ready to back me up. By the bulge in Frank's jeans, it looked like Frankie Junior wasn't exactly averse to the idea of a little one-on-one action in the hay either.

Unfortunately, *big* Frank had other ideas. He stepped away and readjusted his dick in a saintly manner (if saints ever actually do that), then he tried to readjust mine, which didn't seem saintly at all. Plus, it made matters worse, because he sort of lingered awhile doing it, poking, prodding, pulling this way, then that way, and all the time he tried to make my dick less conspicuous the damn thing kept growing. Finally, he gave up. "Hell, we'll just have to work with hard-ons. Won't be the first time. Come on. I want to introduce you to about nine hundred chickens. Give or take."

Suddenly sex was the last thing on my mind. Well, maybe next to last.

"Have I ever told you that I really hate chickens?" I asked, shooting for a conversational tone but failing miserably.

Frank stuck his tongue down my throat one last time. Probably to shut me up. Then he said, "I seem to recall you mentioning something to that effect. We'll just work around it, okay? Trust me, Tom. Chickens aren't nearly as vicious as everybody says they are."

I had a sneaky suspicion Frank was being sarcastic. Unusual for him. Usually he's so sweet.

I WAS wearing my old painting sneakers now for work shoes so I at least didn't have to worry too much about treading in poop, which was a good thing, because frankly, it was everywhere. Dog poop, cow poop, pig poop, chicken poop, cat poop, and in Samson's pen, several gigantic mounds that looked suspiciously like elephant poop, although they must have come from Samson himself, which made the rear end of that animal just as scary as the front end. Almost.

All the while we walked around the edge of Samson's pen, getting to where we were going, wherever the hell that was, Samson trailed along beside us on the other side of the fence, snorting and farting and grumbling out threats like a psychotic stalker.

"Ignore him," Frank said. "He can't get out."

I *tried* to ignore him. I swear I did. But with every step that humongous pig took, I kept imagining the world tilting a little more precariously on its axis. Samson's shadow followed him around like an eclipse as he stomped along, occasionally nudging the fence with his snout looking for weaknesses, rattling his tusks against the metal bars, grunting and snorting and shaking the earth beneath him. Man, he was fat. I can't say I was truly frightened, but I thought Frank might be, so I made it a point to hold his hand as we trudged along through the mud and the poop and the weeds.

The air was alive with the sound of honey bees. One flew past my nose and I jumped. Frank laughed. "You'll get used to them. Pop has four hives down by the pond. He harvests the honey every autumn. He's been thinking about putting in a few more hives. Maybe we can do that for him."

Great, I thought. Psychotic killer pigs and hordes of chickens aren't enough to deal with. Let's just add a few million stinging insects to the mix. That'll be fun. I thought it wise to keep my thoughts to myself, so for once in my life, I did. Maybe if I never mentioned the bees again, Frank would forget about setting up condos for a couple million more of the little bastards. I hate bees.

At the back of Samson's pen, the farm opened up, and it was really quite pretty. A copse of trees stood by a small pond, where I could see one lone calf standing straddled-legged, drinking from the water. Among the shadows of the trees, I saw the rest of the cattle grazing. There were maybe ten or twelve of them. They were all facing the same direction, just like Mark Twain said cows do. I was impressed. Who would have thought Mark Twain would know such a thing as that?

Surrounding the pond was pastureland. It was the peak of summer now, and the pasture was carpeted with either wildflowers or very pretty weeds, I didn't know which. They created a riot of color as the ground sloped down the hillside toward a long skinny building, maybe a city block long, that stood against another line of trees that followed a creek bed around the edge of the property.

"Chicken house," Frank explained, looking at me askance. I suppose he was wondering if I would just take off and run back up the hill to the car and drive off into the sunset rather than face nine hundred frigging chickens, but I fooled him by playing it cool.

"Nice," I said. "Looks functional." I casually plucked a daisy (or maybe it was poison oak, hell, I didn't know) and sniffed the blossom as we walked along. Trying to look nonchalant, I stuck the stem in my mouth like I've seen farmers do in a thousand movies, then spat it out and tried not to gag. Geez, it tasted like battery acid.

Frank laughed. "Ragweed. Tastes terrible, huh? Come on, let's get this over with. I can hear the blood surging through your veins from where I stand. Your blood pressure must be hitting four hundred over two hundred and fifty. You're a stroke waiting to happen. The sooner you see that chickens are harmless, the better your chances are of surviving the day long enough for me to ravage your body this evening."

I could hear the chickens now. It sounded like a cell block riot, except with clucking and flapping and cock-a-doodle-dooing. Personally, I would rather have faced the riot. Some of those prison inmates are hot. The only time a chicken is hot is when it's right out of the skillet.

"They know we're coming," Frank said. "Haven't been fed yet this morning."

"Oh good," I said. "Let's feed them and go then, shall we?"

Frank gave me a gentle pat on the ass as we trudged along through the weeds. "Don't worry. You'll be fine. We have to gather the eggs too. Won't take long. Maybe an hour."

An *hour*? I blinked three times, trying to avert the Aunt Pittypat swoon I felt coming on. Be butch, be butch, be butch. I kept repeating that mantra silently in my head as Frank pulled open the chicken house door and the sound of nine hundred screaming chickens intensified to about the same decibel level as a Boeing 747 hurling itself into the sky.

Boy, those chickens were loud. And friendly. They came running at us from every direction. Treading on our toes. Brushing up against our legs. Flapping their wings and bobbing their heads and squirting poop all over the place in their excitement. The air was dense with dust and feathers and probably parasitic chicken mites. I clapped my mouth shut, trying to keep them out of my lungs.

Frank laughed again. "You have to breathe some time. Just relax, Tom. Look how happy they are to see you."

And I had to admit, they were. Of course, they didn't fool me. Pedro has played that ruse for years. He always acts like he's happy to see me too. Until he gets his treat, that is. Then it's toodles, see you later, ta-ta. The only difference here was that these damn chickens wanted chicken feed while Pedro wanted a biscuit, or a belly rub, or half my sandwich. Same principle, different species. It was all a big scam. Of course, Pedro had a personality to back him up. Not much personality on a chicken. Not that I can see, anyway.

The chicken house was one long room, with roosts and tiers of nests built into the walls on both sides and skylights stuck in the ceiling for light. The skylights were propped open for fresh air, which the place was desperately in need of. I supposed they were closed during the winter months so the chickens wouldn't freeze to death. Not that I would care.

Halfway down the length of the long, skinny room, the building was separated by a wall of chicken wire. There was a chicken wire door stuck in the middle of it. On the other side of the wire, there were no nests, just poles arranged along the walls for roosts. And even more chickens than there were on this side.

"Are these chickens being punished?" I asked. "Is this side of the wire like the cooler in stalag movies? They've got no beds. No reading materials. No Coke machine."

Frank ruffled my hair. Thank God, he still seemed to find my stupidity charming. I wondered how long that would last.

"These chickens are sold for food. The chickens on the *other* side of the wire, the ones with the nests, we keep for their eggs. That's why they need the nests. To lay the eggs in. Every spring Pop gets in a truckload of baby chicks, eight or nine hundred, and we grow them right here. In the fall, we sell them. The next year we do it all over again. But the egg chickens, we keep."

I was beginning to understand the basics of chicken farming. It seemed a little light on the financial end, though.

"You mean your dad makes a living doing this?"

Frank sighed. "Well, no. You have to put everything together. He rents out a couple hundred acres of farmland for crops. He sells the eggs and chickens and milk and butter and hogs, and sometimes a calf now and then, and maybe some things out of the garden, and if you add it all together, and throw in a few farm subsidies from the government, he makes about enough to survive and pay the taxes. People like my dad don't farm for the money, Tom. They farm for the way of life it offers. And it's a good one. Just not moneywise. On the bright side, nobody eats better than we do. And everything is fresh. Plus, you're your own boss."

A feather wafted down from the ceiling and landed on top of Frank's head. I fondly plucked it away.

He rested his hand on the back of my neck and gave me an affectionate squeeze. "I wish you'd learn to like it here, Tom. It would mean a lot to me."

I smiled at him and took a deep breath. "Then I will, by God. So let's feed these bastards and gather the eggs. Show me what to do. Mold me. Make a farmer out of me."

Frank looked startled for a moment, then he laughed so hard he had to bend over and hold onto his knees to prop himself up. A little rope of snot even dribbled out of his nose. After what seemed like about three hours, he finally pulled himself together and looking a little shamefaced, wiped the tears from his eyes and proceeded to show me what to do, still chuckling now and then in a stunned sort of way. I guess he didn't see me as farmer material. Well, I'd show him. I'd work really hard. I would, by God.

Because it suddenly dawned on me—what a wonderful sort of life this might be for a couple of guys with terminal shyness and social anxiety disorder. No people. No bosses. No asshole brothers or exes lurking around to ruin your day and invite you to parties. If it wasn't for the goddamn animals and the poop and the mud and the bees and the poverty and all the back-breaking work, it might even be *fun*. Sort of. At least we would be together, Frank and I. And Lord, we wouldn't even have to pay any apartment rent.

Hmm. That last thought really grabbed me. No rent. I'd have to give this some serious thought.

But first, I had to extract this chicken's beak from my forearm. It seems they don't like having their eggs scooped out from under them by erstwhile bankers. Who knew? I danced around in pain and terror for a minute while the chicken and I screamed and flapped at each other, then I got hold of my senses and got that damned egg. Of course, it shattered twelve ways from Sunday before I could get it out from under the chicken's fat ass, but still the effort was noteworthy. Dripping egg yolk and shell fragments and a considerable amount of blood, mine, I turned to see what Frank thought of my noble effort. He was in the process of digging around for a handkerchief because he was laughing all bent over with snot hanging out of his nose again.

I wondered if he was getting a cold.

Altogether, we gathered sixty-four eggs. There would have been seventy-eight, but some of the chickens didn't like me. We held the eggs up to candles in a darkened back room to make sure they were sound (Frank seemed to know what to look for, I sure didn't), and once they were checked and wiped free of chicken poop we stashed them in gigantic egg crates that held about a bazillion eggs each.

I lost less than a pint of blood and I still had full use of my fingers, or most of them, so I guess the mission was a success. I was pretty pleased with myself until Frank told me we had to do the same thing twice a day, every single day until either us or the chickens were dead of old age, and it was about that time that I had an uncontrollable urge to sit down and blubber like a baby but I held it in. I figured if I was going to be a farmer I would have to learn to be stoic, and trust me, so far in my life, stoicism wasn't exactly one of my calling cards, if you know what I mean.

As Frank and I were leaving the chicken house, he gave me a kiss and told me I did just fine. I spit out a feather and said thank you.

I was exhausted already, and the day was just beginning.

Chapter Eleven

WE DUCKED into the house long enough to tiptoe into the back bedroom and check on Frank's dad. He was asleep, but it didn't look like a restful sleep. There was a sheen of perspiration on his face, and his hair was lank and damp and stuck to his forehead. His breathing was heavy and rasping, just short of a snore. Pedro was snoozing on his back between Joe's legs, all sprawled out like he had just fallen out of a tree. He lifted his head when we peeked in the door, but he didn't rise. Maybe I read more into it than there really was, but I got the distinct impression that Pedro didn't want to disturb Joe by moving. He also seemed to resent our intrusion. He gave a soft growl, and we took the hint and quietly closed the door on our way out.

In the kitchen, we each guzzled half a crock of ice-cold unpasteurized milk to wash down the chicken mites. I was still waiting for the *E. coli* to strike me down, or maybe bird flu would be the culprit now after our little interlude in the chicken house. Frank rummaged through a first aid kit to find alcohol and bandages for my injured forearm thanks to my altercation with the deranged chicken.

"Next time a chicken acts like that, I'll shoot it for you," Frank promised. "Chickens shouldn't be so cranky."

No wonder I was in love with the guy. While he wiped my arm down with alcohol and wrapped the bandage around my wound, I stuck my tongue in his ear and nudged his crotch with my knee. The bandage I finally ended up with looked more like a three-year-old's version of First Aid 101. It was so big you could have used it for a hammock.

Frank and I laughed until we almost peed our pants, but at least my wounds were sterilized and dressed. If flesh-eating bacteria didn't set in, I would probably survive.

Back outside, Frank led me to the summer garden. It covered perhaps half an acre at the north side of the house and was neatly laid out in perfectly straight rows with labels tied to sticks at the end of each row to show what was planted there. It looked to me like a *dozen* families could have survived on the amount of food Joe was growing in that garden. Rows of sweet corn stood tall at one end, their crisp long leaves rustling in the hot breeze. Next to the corn were russet potato plants in full flower, tomatoes fat on the vine, then sweet potatoes, carrots, peas, green beans, lettuce, broccoli, beets, cucumbers, hot peppers, thick clumps of rhubarb, plus, at one end of the garden, a carpet of vines with bright red strawberries peeping through. And it all looked neglected. Even a city boy like me could see that the weeds were taking over. That would have to be remedied.

Frank introduced me to a hoe, told me which end was the business end, as if I couldn't figure it out for myself, and told me to use it between the plants to chop out the weeds. I guess he didn't trust me with the monstrous rototiller he chose for himself. I daintily pecked away at a few weeds, scared to death I would mow down an innocent vegetable, while Frank cranked up the rototiller and in a cloud of exhaust fumes and enough racket to deafen a stone wall, dug his way between the rows, churning up dirt and weeds and obliterating everything in a horrendous cloud of dust. Trillions of bugs ran or flew or crawled for their lives.

It was during the mass exodus of those trillions of bugs that a big fat bumblebee, who must have been having a bad day to begin with, he was so short-tempered, took it into his head to have a go at my ear. He stung me before I knew what was happening, and when a bumblebee stings you, you know it. Pain? Oh, no, not much. I yelped and took off running and when I stopped running I was two fields away. I could see Frank way off in the distance behind me, standing in the middle of the garden behind his rototiller, looking in my direction and scratching his head, wondering what the hell I was up to.

Too mad and in way too much pain to be embarrassed, I traipsed back to Frank, then spent twenty minutes looking for the hoe. In my panic I had flung it into a tree.

By the time I was back in the swing of things and we were an hour into the work, Frank and I were both sweating bullets, so we shed our shirts. It was a hot day, and the sun blasted down on us like a forced-air furnace. While I chipped away at the weeds with my trusty hoe (which I already hated with every fiber of my being), my dirty arm bandage flapped around like a war-battered flag, and my poor ear wailed an off-key aria from *Aida*. Trying to take my mind off my woes and tribulations, I concentrated on watching Frank's back muscles slide around beneath his gorgeous sweat-soaked skin. With his blue jeans barely hanging onto the curve of his scrumptious pale ass, he manhandled that rototiller up and down the rows of vegetables like a cowboy steering a bucking bronco through the shoot. God, he was something. Even with all my miseries, after watching him for three minutes, my dick was as hard as the hoe handle. I finally had to tear my eyes away from Frank before I chopped my foot off.

By the time we finished slaughtering weeds and the garden was looking halfway respectable, the sun was almost straight up in the sky, and my ear felt like someone had spliced an electric wire to it and turned on the juice.

"You hungry?" Frank asked, looking at me with considerable sympathy. I must have been a sight.

"No," I grouched, wiping the sweat from my eyes. "I'm too tired to be hungry. And too much in pain. Horny, though."

Frank grinned. "I'll fix that little problem later, babe. But first let's pick some of these vegetables before the birds get them."

Let's don't, I thought. But we did. We shucked sweet corn, gathered up enough lettuce to stuff a mattress, picked all the tomatoes that were ripe, which was about a ton and a half, not counting the ones we gobbled up while we worked. They were the best-tasting tomatoes I had ever eaten, even if they were covered with dirt and bug poop and possibly fertilizer made from some sort of fecal matter, as fertilizer so often is. Now I had hepatitis and dysentery and maybe dengue fever to add to my list of things to worry about, but I was too hot and tired and grumpy and horny to care. We pulled a few hundred carrots, plucked a thousand or so cucumbers off the vines, and filled two buckets with strawberries. By the time we were finished, my back muscles were screaming in outrage, and I never wanted to eat another fucking vegetable as long as I lived.

But oddly enough, I was still horny.

We stashed the vegetables on the back porch, drank another crockful of poisonous milk, and headed for the barn.

"Let's check on Grace," Frank said.

I was too tired to ask who Grace was. Couldn't have cared less. All I wanted to do was burrow into Frank's crotch, root around for a while, then sleep for a week. But it wasn't meant to be.

On the opposite side of the barn from Samson were more pig pens. Unlike Samson, these pigs were cute and not intent on killing us, which was a nice change. They stood about a foot tall and were running around, snorting, and humping each other and frolicking like a schoolyard full of kids. There must have been forty of them. When they saw us approaching their pen, they all came running, galloping along like a tiny herd of buffalo. They stuck their snouts through the fence to say hello. They were white and fat and cute as hell. Little pink ears. Little curly tails. Little distended bellies.

Frank saw my infatuated expression and gave out a sigh. "Tom, I hate to tell you this, but these guys will be slaughtered in about five months so don't get too attached."

"What, *all* of them?"

"'Fraid so."

I was slowly coming to the conclusion that the chuckles in being a farmer came few and far between. "So which one is Grace?" I asked, resigned.

Frank pointed to a row of ramshackle huts at the back of the pen. "Grace is back there. She's having trouble farrowing. It's one of the first things Pop told me when we arrived. We'll see how she's doing, but I have to warn you, we may have to intervene." And for some reason, he looked appraisingly at my hands.

I had no idea what "farrowing" meant, but I sure didn't like the sound of that "intervening" part. Or the way he was sizing up my hands. What the hell was that all about?

"Let's have sex instead," I suggested without much hope. At least I *knew* what sex was all about, or I liked to think I did.

"Later," Frank promised with a naughty little smile, chucking me gently on the chin and taking another swift glance at my hands. The next thing I knew we were wading through a mob of tiny pigs, shin-deep, heading toward the back of the pen. "We'll take care of Grace then we'll feed these little guys."

Frank peeked into three hog houses before he found the right one. We didn't bother knocking, I guess one simply doesn't. We ducked our heads and scooted inside all doubled over because the roof was only about four feet off the ground. The hut was dark and sweltering and smelled like a hog house, natch. If you've never smelled one, consider yourself lucky. I won't ruin your run of good luck by explaining it to you. Let's just say a whole truckload of those little Christmas tree deodorizers you hang on the rearview mirror of your car wouldn't have made a dent in that god-awful stench. Not a dent.

Grace was a full-grown version of the little fat guys outside. Not quite as cute, but still a large improvement over Samson. At least she didn't have any tusks and she didn't look like she wanted to eat us. In fact, unless my imagination was playing tricks on me, she seemed inordinately glad to see us. She was lying on her side in the corner, and her belly was bouncing up and down as she fought for breath. Her eyes were big and round and panicky. There was a bloody mass of some really disgusting matter dangling out of her rear end. After seeing that, I figured I would never eat again.

I hated to say it, but Grace looked considerably worse than I did, believe it or not.

"Oh man," Frank sighed. "This is going to be a problem. Stay with her. I'll be right back."

"Say what—" But Frank was already gone. Not knowing what else to do, I squatted down by Grace's head and tentatively patted her forehead. She closed her eyes as if she liked being touched so I tickled her ear. "How are you feeling?" I asked, trying to be sociable. "Seen any good movies lately?" She grunted and gave a snort.

Encouraged by Grace's receptive manner, I was just about to give her stubbly chin an affectionate tweak, when she let out a feeble groan and another glob of bloody tissue oozed out of her rear end. It looked sort of like a magician pulling a long red scarf out of his sleeve. Except for the squishing sound. And the smell.

I almost fainted.

Grace started panting again, and thank God Frank chose that moment to crawl back through the hog house door. He had a bunch of rags in one hand and a huge dirty jar of petroleum jelly in the other.

"That's a big-ass jar of lubricant you've got there, Frank. We gonna fuck?" I asked it without much hope. I didn't figure my luck was running in that direction, and I was right.

"I've never done this without Pop around to help," Frank said, "but I think I know what to do. Take your shirt off, Tom. Your hands are smaller than mine."

I didn't like the sound of that. "Uhh—"

"Slather up your arm with jelly, and then I'll tell you what to do."

"Uhh—"

"Don't worry if they bite you. They don't have any teeth."

That got my attention. "Who? Who don't have any teeth?"

"The baby pigs."

I looked around the hut. "*What* baby pigs?"

"The ones trying to get out."

I looked down at Grace. "You mean trying to get out of *her?*" Suddenly I knew what "farrowing" meant.

"They probably just don't want to face the world. They're all comfy and cozy in there. Or maybe one is turned sideways and blocking all the rest. We won't know until you're in there."

"Until I'm in *where*?"

He pointed to Grace's hind end and the horrendous glop of crap dangling out of it. "In there."

And suddenly I understood. Everything. I grabbed Frank's shoulders and made him look me in the eye. "Frank, I can't go in there. What if I hurt her? What if my hand gets stuck and I have to walk around with Grace on the end of my arm for the rest of my life? I can't even reach in and pull that little packet of turkey guts out of a Thanksgiving turkey without barfing. Last year I had to get Miss Wiggins to retrieve it. Please, Frank, don't make me do this."

Frank gave me a shake. "If we *don't* do it, Grace could die. And all the little pigs too. Come on, Tom. Help me out here. Your hands are the right size. Mine aren't. They're too big. You *have* to be the one to do it."

Then he kissed me.

I narrowed my eyes and kissed him back, but it was a pretty perfunctory kiss. I wasn't happy.

Grumbling, I peeled off my shirt and Frank scooped up a handful of petroleum jelly and proceeded to grease my arm from fingertips to elbow.

"Feels funky," I groused, and Frank smiled.

"Lie down behind her," Frank said.

"What, in the mud?"

"Yes."

So I did, grumbling even louder.

"Now, just go to it," Frank said. "Stick your hand in there. Think of it as fist-fucking. Make sure you go in the right hole."

"Huh?" Then I saw what he meant. "Oh yeah."

So I did that too. Or tried to. I picked my hole very, very carefully, don't think I didn't, but still the "fist-fucking" analogy wasn't working for me, so I imagined myself sticking my arm through a big fat white gooshy coat sleeve. It worked. I was up to my wrist in no time. In the proper hole too, thank God. I didn't much care for it, but Grace didn't seem to mind. Go figure.

I burrowed my arm into the moist heat of Grace's twat a little farther and then I felt it. Something hard. Something moving. Then I lost it. I pressed my cheek into Grace's butt and dug my arm in deeper, groping around with my fingers, seeking, seeking. And there it was again. It felt like—a chin. A tiny chin. I prodded it with my finger and it bit me.

"Yeeouch!"

Frank grinned. "Found 'em, huh?"

I nodded. Frank was right. Whatever was nibbling on my finger didn't have any teeth. Had some pretty good jaw pressure though. Desperate to get my hand out of there as soon as possible, I wrapped my fingers around that tiny chin and without any further ado, gave it a yank, praying to God the head wouldn't come off in my hand. Out came the cutest, tiniest little pig you ever saw in your life. All of it. In one piece. And alive. I don't know which of us looked more surprised. Me or the pig. I just lay there in the mud and laughed, he was so cute. Then, to my astonishment, out slid another. And another. And still another. Apparently pig number one had been blocking the road for everybody else. Before Grace was finished, I was lying in the mud with nine little piggies flopping around my head, trying to walk, trying to nibble my nose, giving out weak little squeals, rooting through my hair looking for a nipple, jostling for position.

I was elated and disgusted at the same time. It was an odd feeling. Elated by the lives I had saved and disgusted by the mud and the Vaseline and the pig poop and the afterbirth which was still sliding out of poor Grace's rear end, and disgusted too, by the fact that that same said rear end was still only inches away from my nose.

I looked up into Frank's beaming face and grinned. "Wow."

"Wow indeed," Frank laughed. "Just look at 'em go."

All the little pigs got their GPSs up and running in no time. They unerringly scrambled over Grace's back legs and wended their way toward her double row of teats, all swollen tight with milk, having given me up as a lost cause, I guess, since I didn't have any chow to offer.

I was as tired as I had ever been in my life, but happy too. And proud. Even *with* all my injuries. I lay there in the mud and gazed one last time at all the little lives (and the one big one) I had saved, and it was then that Grace decided to stretch her aching muscles after everything she'd gone through. She gave a kick with her back leg and caught me smack in the eye with her hoof. It was like being whapped in the head with a hammer. I saw stars. Lots and lots of stars. Big fat ones.

I was still cussing when Frank hauled me out of the hog house, tsking and apologizing as if he was the one who had kicked me in the head. I was dripping afterbirth and pig poop and three or four pounds of mud and stunned senseless by the pain, not to mention wondering if I had an indelible cloven hoofprint embedded forever in my face and worrying if I would ever be able to see again out of both eyeballs at the same time.

While Frank watched in horror, the eye swelled shut and turned black in twelve seconds flat. Twelve seconds. He timed it.

I WAS sitting in the middle of the pig pen with the first herd of little pigs, all bumping into each other and squealing for their dinner. Somehow they weren't quite as cute as they had been earlier. Now they were just annoying. I guess the pain of being kicked in the head was making me grumpy.

I tried to put on a brave face and be butch about the whole "kicked in the head" thing, but it was an uphill battle. I'm not built for butch. I'm built for snits and tirades and pouty little sympathy ploys, none of which are to be found on the standard farmer's playlist of top ten character traits. At least I didn't cry. And God knows I wanted to. I couldn't play the social anxiety card either. That doesn't work with hogs.

"Think I should go to the hospital, Frank?"

"I don't know. Are you thinking straight?"

"As straight as I ever did."

Frank looked like he was trying not to smile at that. "Then I think you're fine. Maybe we should put some ice on your injury though."

Poor Frank. He looked closer to crying than I was. At least I think he looked that way. I could only see through one eye, and that one had mud in it.

I wasn't sure what part of me hurt the most. My arm, my ear, my eye, or my ego.

"Which injury?" I observed drily. "We can't put ice on everything. Let's just finish the day's work, then if I'm still alive we can try to put me back together. Okay? Besides, ice just keeps things from swelling and turning black. My eye already did that, didn't it?"

"It sure did," Frank declared with enough conviction to make me wonder what the hell I looked like. If Joe had used a little common sense and put a mirror in the pig pen like he should have when he built the place, I could have seen for myself what sort of condition I was in, but of course he didn't. There is never a mirror around when you need one. Never. I guess pigs don't primp. Or farmers.

"Then let's get back to work," I said again. "I'll be fine. I'll be just fine." Geez, I sounded like the brave little toaster. Just before it blew up.

"Are you sure?" Frank asked.

"Yes. I'm sure. At least I'm not horny anymore. Grace and her magic hoof fixed that problem."

Frank nuzzled my neck, nibbled on my good ear, and laid his hand on my crotch in a friendly manner. The only uninjured part of my anatomy jerked awake, lifted its little head, and tried to peel open my zipper from the inside.

"Well, maybe she didn't *completely* fix that problem," I rasped, and Frank smiled.

"Thank God," he said, sounding like he meant it. He was obviously enjoying the feel of the bulge growing in the crotch of my pants. He gave the bulge a final pat. Sort of a fond farewell for the time being.

"All that's left is to feed these little guys," he said, looking down fondly at the sea of squirming, oinking pigs jostling and squealing around us. "Why don't you perch yourself on the edge of the fence there, Tom, and watch. Won't take long."

Frank gave me another tiny chuck on the chin, although he didn't really make physical contact. He was probably afraid my damaged head would fall off. "Good man," he said, by way of encouragement.

"Thanks." I rolled my good eye around inside my aching head and clattered to my feet like a bucket of bolts. "Let's get it over with then. I don't think I've got much time left."

Frank laughed and helped me climb the fence. "I love you," he said as I settled myself on the top board like a true cowpoke. "And don't fall off the fence."

"Shut up, Frank," I said, and he very wisely did.

EVENING shadows were crawling across the grass as I limped my way toward the farmhouse with Frank at my side. Pedro met us at the back gate, took one look at me, and ran back into the house. So much for loyalty.

Frank steered me into the shed by the back door.

"What's this?" I asked, too weary to really care.

"Washhouse," Frank explained. "This is where we clean up when we're too dirty to traipse through the house to the bathroom."

I looked down at myself and understood completely. I wouldn't have let me into the house either. I was a mess. And Frank wasn't much better.

The washhouse was nicely laid out, with straw mats on the floor, two showerheads on the wall, and a cabinet packed with towels and soaps and shampoos standing in the corner out of the way. In another corner stood a big electric heater for cooler months than this. Next to the electric heater were a washer and dryer. All three appliances stood on concrete blocks to keep them away from the water.

"Nice," I said, and meant it.

Frank seemed relieved. "It's really an old smokehouse, but we converted it to a big shower stall and wash room a few years back since nobody really smokes meat anymore. Don't worry, Tom. It's clean."

"I'm not worried," I said truthfully. "Not about that anyway."

"Then what is it? Something's wrong. I can tell."

I was already peeling my clothes off and trying not to grunt and groan while I did it. "It's my foot. Something's inside my shoe, I think. Something's moving around."

"You're kidding." Frank already had his own clothes off. Naked, he dropped to his knees in front of me and solicitously untied my shoelaces one at a time. He slipped my sneakers off, threw them in a corner, then peeled off my stinking socks.

"Oh crap," he said, examining my foot while I unbuckled my pants and slid them down my legs. Frank released my foot long enough to let me kick *those* into a corner, along with my BVDs, then he lifted my foot from the floor and eyed it more closely. "Gee, Tom, I haven't seen one of these in years."

"One of what?"

"Leech. It's on the side of your foot. You must have got it in the garden when we were churning up the dirt."

I looked down at Frank cradling my naked foot. "I'm sorry. Did you say 'leech'?"

"Yeah. Leech. A really big one."

I could feel a scream crawling up my throat like a shot of magma surging up through the middle of a volcano. "Did you say *leech*?"

Frank patted my bare knee. "Don't worry. I'll fix it right up." Still naked, he flew through the washhouse door and disappeared.

I looked down and almost keeled over in terror. The leech was fat and black and pulsating. I guess it was pulsating because it was busy sucking away at my circulatory system like a kid with a straw and a bottle of Yoo-Hoo. Oh God. Oh Jesus. I couldn't really feel the leech now that my shoe was off, but seeing it was more than enough to give me the heebie-jeebies.

"Come on, Frank. Come on, Frank. Come on, Frank."

And there he was. He had one of those long skinny fireplace lighters in his hand and the first aid kit we had rummaged through earlier after the homicidal chicken mangled my arm.

He dropped to his knees in front of me again, took a firm grip on my foot, and flicked the fire stick to life. Very carefully, he touched the flame to the leech, and it immediately curled up and fell off, leaving behind a smear of blood and a tiny hole in the side of my filthy foot.

Since I wasn't screaming, or passing out, or losing bowel control, I figured I was handling this latest outrage with considerable aplomb. Frank flung the leech through the doorway. It landed out in the yard, and one of the farm dogs immediately gobbled it up. Guess they weren't too particular about what they ate.

Frank poured alcohol over my foot, then settled back on his haunches and looked up into my face. "You're just having one hell of a day, aren't you?" he asked.

I gave him a feeble shrug. I seemed to be at a loss for words. If one of my eyes hadn't been swelled shut, I would have been bug-eyed with shock.

"Let's clean you up," Frank said.

He turned on both showerheads, aimed them into one powerful stream, and adjusted the water temperature. Side by side we stood there for a couple of minutes letting the water wash away the day. I closed my eyes and soaked up the water like a sponge. Frank lathered up a washcloth and proceeded to lather himself up. Then he did the same for me, gently soaping me down from the top of my head to the soles of my feet. He lingered in a few areas a little more than was truly necessary, but since those were some of our favorite areas, neither of us complained.

When we were both sparkly clean and pink from the hot water and smelling of Ivory soap, we ducked under the spray and rinsed off. Then Frank once again dropped to his knees in front of me on the pretense of examining my foot, which he did, but only for a second. As the water ran down my body, Frank forgot about the foot and slid his hands across my stomach, caressing me here, stroking me there. He massaged my thighs, and while he was doing that, he pressed his face into my groin, nuzzling my dripping pubic hair, sliding his tongue along my lengthening cock. When my dick was standing straight out from my body and begging for attention in no uncertain terms, Frank gently peeled back the foreskin and encircled the engorged tip with his soft lips. Slowly, he drew me in as deep as he could.

I clutched his head and closed my eyes. God, his mouth felt wonderful. Everything else hurt, but my dick was in heaven. Slowly, I slid myself in and out of Frank's hot mouth. In and out. In and out. Frank continued to stroke my stomach as the water poured over us. He looked up at my face as he worked away at me, obviously relishing every moment. Every taste. He smiled around me when I groaned in pleasure. He grinned when I said ouch, but didn't bother asking what hurt. He knew it wasn't my dick. That part of my body was doing just fine and dandy, thank you very much, and Frank knew it perfectly well.

He let me slide from his mouth, and when I did, he pressed his lips to my balls. I could see him inhaling the clean soapy scent of me as he slowly slid his lathered hand along the length of my rigid cock. It was so filled with blood by now it was damn near blue. I shuddered at the sensation of Frank's hand around me, and once again Frank peered up across the expanse of my heaving chest to see the look of pleasure on my face. He smiled and continued to pump my cock with his soapy fist, occasionally stopping long enough to take his lips from my balls and press them to the underside of my dick, just to let it know it hadn't been forgotten, drawing the foreskin back when he did, tasting me, enjoying the heat of my cock against his face.

Frank and I both cried out when the semen came surging out of me, filling his hand. He continued to stroke me until the last drop was extracted and my knees started to buckle. He grinned, watching me tremble.

"Ouch," I said, and he laughed.

Pulling himself to his feet, he pressed his lips to mine and once again aimed the showerheads in our direction. Never once taking his mouth off mine, he soaped us down once again.

When I moved to bend down and press my lips to his throat, he gently pushed me away.

"You're not up to it," he said. "You just stand here and let me do it myself."

Frank was right. If I got down on my knees I would probably never get back up. And I was man enough to admit it. So I did what he said. Happily.

Once again, Frank pressed his lips to mine, and while we kissed, he stroked his cock. Slowly, at first. Then more rapidly. He pulled his hand away and laid his cock against my soapy stomach. On tiptoe, he pressed himself to me, creating friction in the soap suds, his strong, hairy legs hard against my own, his hands caressing my back. His tongue found mine and with a tiny shudder, I felt his hot come shoot across my stomach. We stood like that for perhaps a minute, while Frank continued to drag his cock back and forth across my belly, squeezing out every last trace of semen.

When he pulled his lips from mine, his eyes were still closed and his cheeks were flushed. After a moment, those fabulous green eyes opened wide and he smiled at me.

"You okay?" he asked. "Didn't hurt you, did I?"

I couldn't speak. I was too drained. In every respect. I merely shook my head and Frank grinned. "I love you so much," he said, pulling me into his arms as the water continued to sluice over us, washing away his come, gradually becoming cooler as it sprayed against our bodies. We seemed to have drained the water heater.

I held him close. I still couldn't speak. Too weary. Too many emotions thundering through me. All I could do was nod, but that seemed to be enough. Frank understood.

"Hungry?" he gently asked. "It's time for supper, you know."

And I nodded yet again.

Arm in arm, we dripped our way into the house, toweled each other off, and dressed in shorts and T-shirts. Frank's dad was just waking up.

FOR dinner I tossed a gigantic salad with the veggies we had picked from the garden. Then I boiled sweet corn on the cob and fried up some pork chops for the main course. While I worked in the kitchen and tried not to whimper, I was so damned tired and sore, Frank spent time with his dad, helping him bathe and getting him dressed in a clean pair of pajamas. I could hear Joe grumbling now and then about all the attention and the pampering, but I heard them laughing too, so I knew things were okay. When Joe was cleaned up to Frank's satisfaction, Frank led his dad into the kitchen and together we got Joe situated at the table. He seemed a little stronger than he had that morning. This time we didn't need to prop him up with pillows to keep him sitting upright. But still, there was a weariness in Joe's eyes that was troubling. He looked to me like a man who was giving up. I guess pain can do that to anyone. Not the fleeting kind of pain I was dealing with at the moment, but the kind of pain there is no hope of getting away from. The kind of pain that gets into the bones and just won't leave. The terminal kind of pain.

But even with everything going against him, Joe managed to wear his sense of humor like a suit of armor: against the pain; against his embarrassment at being so helpless; against the fate he must have known was waiting for him. Joe was no fool. He had to realize there would be no escape from the illness that was wearing him down. He knew he couldn't laugh his way out of this one. I imagined that Joe's sense of humor had shielded him from a lot of miseries over the years, but it would not be able to shield him this time around. Not from the treachery of his own failing body. That is a misery that cannot be remedied. And Joe knew it. I could see the acceptance of the fact in his pain-wearied eyes.

Those eyes did manage to light up considerably, however, when they settled themselves on me as I stood at the stove, barefoot, limping and grunting, trailing bandages like a mummy in one of those old fifties horror flicks. Of course, for sheer ugliness, I had the mummy beat by a long shot, what with my black eye and swollen ear and sundry scrapes and contusions. For some reason, Joe seemed to find my injuries a matter of considerable glee.

"My God, Tom. You're a sight to behold, you truly are. I gotta tell you, I spent three years in Vietnam when I was a young man about your age, and I saw guys stumble out of the jungle after three months that looked better than you do right now. And you've only been here one day. Hell, son, you look worse than I do and I'm about as wrung out and beat to death as a man can get."

"Thanks," I grumped, trying to drag up a smile, just to be polite.

Frank laughed. "He's had quite a day, Pop. So don't rag on him too much. He did an honest day's work, though. He surely did."

"So I see, son. So I see. Looks like it just about killed him too." Joe held his hand out to me and I took it. He gave it a vigorous shake. "We thank you, Tom. Your help is truly appreciated. I dare say we'll make a farmer out of you yet."

I wished he would let go of my hand. The blisters I had acquired from wielding that damned hoe were just about killing me. "Maybe if I live," I said, only half joking.

Joe seemed to find that pretty amusing. He pointed to my eye. It was still swollen shut and black as the ace of spades. "What happened there?"

"Kicked by a pig."

Joe nodded as if he understood. "Uh-huh. Uh-huh. I know what that's like. And there?" He pointed to my ear, which was still roughly the size of a catcher's mitt and burning like a forest fire.

"Bumblebee," I replied. "Mean one."

"Uh-huh. Nasty things, bumblebees. Had one sting me on my tallywacker once when I was peeing in the bushes. Don't think *that* didn't hurt." He looked down at my bare foot. It was bright red since Frank had decided to slather it with Mercurochrome to ward off infection from the fucking leech. "And that?"

"Fucking leech."

Joe nodded. "I see. They have to fuck some time or other, I suppose." Which wasn't exactly what I meant.

Lastly he pointed to the yards of fresh bandage Frank had rewrapped around my forearm after our little interlude in the shower had washed away the other one. "And what the hell happened *there*, Tom? Did somebody shoot you?"

My face turned bright red. I know it did. I could feel it. "Chicken," I mumbled softly.

Joe leaned in closer. "I'm sorry, did you say 'chicken'?"

I straightened my back and cleared my throat, trying not to look at Frank. If he was bent over laughing with snot dangling out of his nose, I didn't want to know it. "Yes, sir. Chicken."

Joe's eyes glittered. He was having a wonderful time. "Must have been a real nasty one."

"It was. Mangled me pretty good."

"Big was it? I mean, for a chicken?"

"Big as an ostrich."

"And you say it was just one? Just one chicken? Not a whole flock? Just one?"

"Yes sir," I said, getting redder by the minute. "Just one. But she was upset. Didn't like me trying to rob her nest. I think it pissed her off. Either that or she had some psychological problems to deal with and took them out on me."

"Well," Joe commiserated, "insane people sometimes acquire supernatural strength. Maybe it's the same with insane chickens."

"Maybe it is."

"Did you get the egg?" Joe asked, nodding, looking sympathetic. His shoulders were starting to quiver.

"Got it all over me," I answered truthfully. "Fucking thing exploded when I yanked it out from under the chicken's ass."

And at that, Joe started laughing. He laughed so hard he took a fit of coughing that almost carried him off to the promised land right then and there. After about fifteen minutes, we finally managed to get Joe's coughing spell under control. Then the three of us settled in for a pleasant dinner, although once again, Joe didn't eat enough to keep a bird alive. He seemed to be more in a mood to talk. So we let him.

"Speaking of 'Nam," he said, looking meditative, thinking back forty years or more. "I probably never told you, Frank, but there were two guys in my platoon that were as tight as you and Tom here. Both gay, I guess, though nobody ever talked about it. They were good soldiers, that's all we cared about."

"That war must have been awful," I said.

Joe nodded. "It was, son. It was. And we were all just kids. That was the saddest part. None of us knew what we were doing. We just wanted to go home."

"Did they make it home?" Frank asked. "The two gay guys? Did they survive the war?"

Joe nudged his pork chop with his fork. He hadn't tasted it yet, and I could tell he had no intention of doing so. "One did. The other one didn't make it. The one that survived had a hard time getting over losing his friend, or I should say his lover, I guess, but he finally came out okay. I still see him now and then. It was really sad what happened. He was a good man, the one that died. Hell, they both were. The one still is. Being gay didn't make them otherwise than what they had it in them to be. I'm telling you this 'cause I don't want any misimpressions here between the three of us. I want you to know that I'm glad you're here. And that means both of you. And I'm glad you've got each other. You look happy. I hope you can stay that way. I have no issues whatsoever with you being the way you are. Just be good to each other.

That's all I ask. And be happy. Everything else will work itself out on its own."

Tears glimmered in Frank's eyes as he studied his father's face. He cleared his throat. "We are happy, Pop. You know we are. So don't worry about us. All we want you to do is concentrate on getting better. We'll take care of the farm. You just take care of yourself. Together we'll get through this. You'll see."

Joe gave Frank a sad smile. "You're smarter than that. I know you are, Frank. This is about the end of me, I reckon. I reckon you know it too, so let's not pretend otherwise. I'm not afraid of dying. Pretty pissed off about it, but not afraid. I don't want you to be afraid either. If I've learned one thing being a farmer all my life, it's that dying is just as much a part of life as living. Death comes to all of us in one way or another. The only thing we have to figure out is how we want to meet it. I've decided to meet it head-on. If you love me, you'll let me do it. I intend to go out on my own terms, Frank. No doctors. No hospitals. No weeping. And that's not something that's open for discussion."

Frank nodded. "Okay, Pop. Okay. We'll do it your way. There's no reason we can't try to make you comfortable though, is there? A little comfort wouldn't break the rules, would it?"

Joe shrugged. "Do what you think you have to do. There's some stuff up in the attic that we bought when your mom got sick. Go through it if you like. Maybe you'll find something I can use. I'll leave it up to you boys. Just no doctors. Are we clear on that point? I don't want to be drugged or stuck in a room with a bunch of sick people and poked and prodded and charged up the ying-yang by every quack with a license until there's nothing left for you to inherit and then end up dying anyway. Got it? I just want to stay right here in my own house on my own farm until the Lord comes to get me. Is that a deal?"

"It's a deal," Frank said.

"Deal," I said.

Joe was getting tired. I could see it in the lines of his face and the way his hands were shaking more and more as the minutes passed, but still he must have felt a need to get certain things off his chest while he was able to do it. Again, he took Frank's hand. "Son, I'm leaving the farm to you. Everything. You stayed with me for six years after you graduated from high school. You didn't have to do that, but I appreciate the fact that you did. Stanley left two minutes after he graduated, and I've never seen him or heard from him since. He doesn't deserve the farm. You do. Do whatever you want with it. Sell it. Work it. Whatever you and Tom want. And don't let Stanley make you feel guilty about it. There's a will so he can't fight you. The will is valid. Notarized and everything. And I explained my reasoning for leaving the farm solely to you in the will too. If Stanley gets litigious, he'll be sorry, 'cause I've spelled it all out in simple enough language even the dumbest judge in the world can figure it out and do what's right. You know, if you boys want to stay here and make a life for yourselves, I'd be proud to see it happen. You could be happy here. But maybe you'd rather go back to the city. I don't know. And that's up to you. I won't try to sway you either way."

Suddenly Joe's voice just about gave out. He pushed his plate away. "I'm sorry, Tom, you went to all that trouble cooking, I know, and it looks great, but I just—I just can't—"

Frank reached out and laid a hand to the side of his father's face. "Please try to eat just a little. Please, Pop."

But it was useless. "Just help me back to bed, will you, son? I'm too worn out to eat."

So while I cleared the table, Frank led his father back to the bedroom and tucked him into bed. I went in a few minutes later and stood in the doorway while Frank bent down and kissed his father's forehead. "Sleep tight, Pop. Tomorrow we'll make you better."

"I know, son. I know." And he closed his eyes.

Frank switched off the light and we left the room, leaving the door ajar in case Pedro wanted to join Joe in the middle of the night.

In the morning we would find the little guy curled up once again between Joe's legs. Pedro seemed to know exactly where he was needed most, and I was proud of him for the knowing.

He was a good little dog with a good heart.

It was just his pooper that had no common sense.

Chapter Twelve

FRANK was determined to stay with his dad until the end. And I was determined to stay with Frank until Frank was ready to leave Indiana for good. I had enough money not to worry about having to find a job for a while. We still had a few weeks of rent paid on our apartment back in San Diego, and the other bills that came in from back there were forwarded to me by Miss Wiggins, God bless her. I usually just paid the bills and never mentioned them to Frank. Without his job at the nursery, he once again had no money coming in, and he was so busy caring for his father and trying to keep the farm running that I decided not to bother him with anything else. Plus, I knew Frank. If he found out I was paying all the San Diego bills behind his back, he would feel guilty about it, and that I could not let happen. He had enough misery on his plate already. He didn't need to top it off with a big glob of guilt.

So I settled into farm life with as much will as I could muster. And I was so nuts about Frank that, while my talents were minimal, my will was considerable. I had no intention of letting Frank slip through my fingers over a lousy work ethic on my part. I knew I would never be the farmer he was, but by God, I could try my best not to humiliate myself every five minutes. After that first horrific day, I knew all subsequent days would have to be an improvement, and they were. Marginally. After I learned a few basic rules, the injuries to my person became fewer and farther between, and those rules were fairly simple. Never wield a hoe, or any other handheld implement, for more than three minutes without first donning a pair of gloves. Never put your face, or any other body part you are particularly fond of, within six inches of a hoof. And stay the hell away from Samson. That was it. Oh, and never underestimate a live chicken. I had been right all along in hating the little bastards. They can be mean, snarky, temperamental, and just plain untrustworthy. And I had the scars to prove it.

While my life on the farm improved daily, Joe's life most certainly did not. Poor Joe. It must be hard for a man used to taking care of himself and dealing with life on his own terms to suddenly find he isn't up to the task. He rarely left his bedroom now. He could barely walk on his own. He seldom ate. He had lost so much weight that his skin was like parchment, his bones threatening to tear their way through it every time he moved. He was a small man when I met him. Now he was even smaller.

But still, out of that sallow, angular face, Joe's green eyes, eyes just like Frank's, would sometimes glitter like emeralds. Those eyes were too big for his face now, and packed full of hurt, but Lord, they could draw you in. Many evenings, while Frank slept exhausted on the sofa in the living room after working like a dog all day long—usually having done half of my work as well as his own since I was so inept—I would sit with Joe beside his bed and read aloud to him. It seemed to take Joe's mind away from the pain that was forever tearing through him. Occasionally he would open his eyes and immediately begin telling a story. It was as if that story had been lurking there, just beneath the surface, waiting for the perfect moment to burst out into the light, like a fish leaping up through the surface of a lake to glitter and shine and sparkle for one brief moment in the light of the sun. They were stories of Frank's childhood usually, or of Joe's life here on the farm. And at those times, as Joe shared his memories with me, as he shared his life, even from the well of misery he was drowning in, Joe could dredge up the strength for a smile now and then. I wondered if I would have had the courage to do that.

I had never known my own father. He took off before I was born, the irresponsible shit. But I very quickly found a father in Joe. And I hope he found another son in me. He seemed to. He honestly seemed to like me. And that made me happy.

Another fact that astonished me concerning my deepening relationship with Frank's father was that not once had I ever felt shy around him. I had never felt judged. Even on that first day when we first laid eyes on each other, he seemed to accept me immediately, and I him. I never quite understood the easy way that our friendship fell into place. And I never took it for granted. Joe was a friend from day one. I never intended to let him become anything less.

Joe held true to his word concerning no doctors. He wouldn't have let one on the place, and coercing him into going to see one would have been impossible. Joe got mad if the subject was even broached. So Frank and I did as Joe suggested. We rummaged through the attic and found all manner of sickroom supplies to help in our struggle to keep him alive in a reasonably comfortable manner. A walker. A bed tray. Handrails which we screwed into the walls so he could make it to the bathroom on his own at night. Otherwise he would have lain in bed all night needing to go, but refusing to wake us up to help him.

I think it was a confusing time for Frank, being torn in two different directions as he was. He was happy with our relationship. I know he was. And so was I. On the farm, Frank and I became closer than we ever had in the city. Yet it tore him apart to see his father's health decline so rapidly. I began to seriously doubt Joe would still be with us when autumn rolled around.

I never mentioned my fear to Frank. I figured he had enough fears of his own concerning his father's health.

It was during this period that Frank came to me one evening with tears in his eyes. He was clutching a sheaf of medical papers he had found in Joe's desk. Without saying a word, Frank handed them to me, then went to the window to look out at the darkness while I perused them. I quickly realized I was looking at Joe's test results from his first (and last) visit to a doctor in Terre Haute. X-ray images. MRI findings. Amid pages and pages of confusing medical jargon which I could make neither heads nor tails of, I found a few coherent sentences. Those sentences read in part, "…the cancer has fully spread to both lungs and it appears the lymph glands are now affected. From there the cancer will spread quickly to other organs. Unfortunately, surgery is not an option at this point. Perhaps if the patient had sought medical treatment earlier, this would not be the case. Dr. Graham suggests an aggressive regimen of chemotherapy combined with radiation, although the result of such a regimen will not be enough to stem the disease. It may, however, extend Mr. Wells's life by a few weeks or months. Since the patient refuses to consider such an aggressive form of treatment, there is really nothing more to be done. I have suggested to Mr. Wells that he put his affairs in order, and he has indicated to me that he understands and accepts my diagnosis."

"So that explains it," I said, moving to Frank and pressing my face to the back of his neck. He turned and let me fold him into my arms. His shoulders were trembling. He was quietly crying.

"He's always so goddamn stubborn," Frank said, wiping a tear from his cheek. "Maybe the chemo and radiation would save his life."

Gently, I said, "That's not what the doctor thinks, Frank. And if it's in his lymph glands—"

Frank laid his head on my chest. "I know, Tom. I know. I was just hoping, I guess. All the chemo and stuff would probably just make him sicker. Maybe Pop is right."

"I'm sure he is," I said. "I don't think I would do it either."

Frank nodded. "I know. Neither would I. Poor Pop."

Poor Pop indeed. We stumbled into bed that night, exhausted as usual, but heartsore on top of it. I held Frank long into the night. It was our first night together when we did not think of sex. When I finally fell asleep with Frank still in my arms, it was long past midnight. Frank was awake until morning. Not once did he leave my embrace.

The next day, for some obscure reason, and God knows he should have known better, Frank took it into his head to teach me how to milk. Until now, he had insisted he do it alone. Maybe he was bored with the job. Or maybe he thought it was something I might truly need to know. Or maybe after that long night of worrying about his dad, Frank just decided he needed a good hearty laugh. Who knows? Suffice it to say, I tackled the task with my usual ineptitude, which must have pleased him. I, in fact, used milking class as a backdrop for grilling Frank about Jeff Moody. In my mind, that subject still hung over our heads like a dangling saber.

Instead of being honest and straightforward and simply asking my questions outright, I thought I might reap better rewards by being devious and sneaking in the back door concerning Frank and his past relationship with Moody. I should have known better.

"Sure was nice of that Moody fellow to help your dad out that day we arrived, coming over here at dawn and everything to milk the cows for Joe."

"Sure was," Frank said with a chuckle. He knew what I was doing. Frank didn't just fall off the turnip truck, as Joe was fond of saying. Whatever the hell that meant.

I repositioned my ass on the milking stool. I had repositioned it six times already, and still it didn't feel right. Frank was next to me on another stool milking Betty Ann, a nice brindle cow with big soulful eyes. Frank's bucket was half full already. My bucket was clean as a whistle. Not a drop of milk in it. That's because I had Mary Lou. I didn't like Mary Lou. For one thing, she had horns. Betty Ann just had ears. I didn't like Mary Lou's horns, and I didn't trust her with them. She had a habit of flinging them around the barn like a drunken pirate with two swords. There was poop on the end of her tail too, so I was watching that tail pretty closely, don't think I wasn't. Didn't want to get slapped in the face with that thing.

As far as the milking went, I was still trying to get the fingering right. It was funny. I could milk a dick until the cows came home, so to speak, but milking an udder was a totally different procedure, and I couldn't get the knack of it. "Her nipples don't want to squirt," I griped. "She's holding back. Maybe something's plugged up."

Frank giggled. He had his cheek resting against Betty Ann's flank, and I could hear the milk squirting into his bucket. Squoosh. Squoosh. Squoosh. Squoosh. "Try it again," Frank said. "Do it like I showed you."

I tried again, but nothing was squooshing. "Yeah, that Jeff Moody is a really nice guy," I said, once again clumsily pawing away at Mary Lou's undercarriage. "Good looking too. Don't you think so, Frank?"

"Naw," Frank said. "He's got a little bitty dick."

"Really?" I chirped happily, and Frank laughed like a hyena. He was lying. At least I hoped he was lying.

Apparently Mary Lou didn't like the sound of Frank's laughter. Or maybe it was the way I was pulling at her tits. Her hoof came down on my foot like a sledgehammer. While my stool went rolling across the barn and I was screaming and cussing and trying to drag my foot out from under her hoof and the six hundred pounds on *top* of her hoof, I forgot to watch Mary Lou's tail, and that's when she nailed me with it. Right in the mouth.

Mary Lou could be a real bitch when she wanted to be.

Still, as much as I hated to admit it, I was actually becoming acclimated to poop. When you are around it as much as I was, you sort of have to. It hardly bothered me anymore. So I just spat the cow poop out of my mouth, finally managed to extricate my mangled foot, and kept on talking. "A little bitty dick, huh? Well that must have been disappointing. Especially because you seem like a guy who appreciates the more ample ones. You know, the *bigger* ones. Like say, *mine*, for example."

Frank was still filling his bucket. (Squoosh. Squoosh. Squoosh.) And I still wasn't. (Crickets.) It was disheartening. Plus now the toes on my right foot were numb. And I thought I may have lost a toenail on the big one, thanks to Mary Lou. The cow.

"You do have a nice pecker, Tom. I've never denied it," Frank said. "So tell me, do *you* think Jeff is cute?"

"Naw," I said. "Too blond. Too muscle-bound. And his jeans are too tight."

This time Frank really laughed. "Yeah, right."

"Plus, he isn't you."

I could hear the smile in Frank's voice even though a cow was blocking my view. "Now there's an answer I like," he said.

He set his milk bucket out of reach of Betty Ann's hind legs and came and stood behind me where I was once again sitting on my little stool, trying to part Mary Lou from her milk. "Don't worry about Jeff,

Tom. I never loved him and as far as I know, he never loved me. We were just friends who used each other a few times to satisfy some urges that we couldn't satisfy anywhere else. Okay? It's you I love, not Jeff Moody. Remember that."

Before I could answer, Frank leaned over my shoulder and covered my hands with his as I manipulated Mary Lou's nipples, and suddenly they worked. Her nipples, I mean. Milk was shooting into the bucket like nobody's business. Squoosh. Squoosh. Squoosh. Squoosh. Not that I cared. I was too busy enjoying the feel of Frank's crotch pressing against the back of my head. The only thing I could think of that might feel better than Frank's crotch pressing against the back of my head was Frank's crotch pressing against the *front* of my head.

And now that I wasn't worried about Jeff Moody any longer, I thought I might just spin around and put that crotch exactly where I wanted it, when an eerily familiar voice gave a sarcastic "tut tut" from the vicinity of the barn door.

"Well, isn't this cozy."

Frank and I both turned to see who it was, and trust me, it didn't exactly make our day to see Stanley standing there, leaning on the doorjamb. Yep. Stanley. In the flesh. Remember him?

He looked like he had just stepped out of Abercrombie and Fitch. Khaki trousers, brown muscle tee, black canvas deck shoes with bright orange shoelaces. The bastard looked great, just like he always did. Handsome, buff, tanned. But that was just the outside. Inside, he was most assuredly still a dick. I wouldn't have to book an ultrasound to figure that out. It was a given.

Frank was about as thrilled to see Stanley as I was. "What the hell are *you* doing here?" he asked, straightening up, leaving his hand resting possessively on my shoulder. "Come to take another stab at breaking Pop's heart?"

Stanley looked around the barn, as if the memories he had of the place were just about as depressing as actually seeing it again. "Thought you might need a little help with the family crisis. Can't leave it all up to my little brother now, can I?"

"Admirable," Frank said. His fingers tightened on my shoulders. "You gonna say hi to Tom or are you just going to ignore him?"

Stanley smiled, never taking his eyes off Frank's face. "I thought I'd ignore him," he said, and turned and walked toward the house.

We watched him go.

"Still a sweetheart," I said.

"I don't like this," Frank said, gathering up his milk bucket and kicking the stool out of the way so Betty Ann wouldn't break a leg on it. "Pop has enough to contend with. This isn't going to make his last few weeks any easier. You finish the milking, Tom. I want to be there when those two confront each other for the first time. I'll be back."

I looked down the row of cows, each one patiently chewing a mouthful of hay and waiting her turn to be milked. Jeez. If I couldn't get milk out of Mary Lou, how was I supposed to get milk out of the rest of them? Now I remembered why I hated Stanley so much. Every time he did *anything*, he tossed a monkey wrench into the works for everybody else. And he got a kick out of tossing in those monkey wrenches too. That was the most annoying part.

I scooted my own bucket and stool out of the way. "Sorry, girls, you'll just have to hang loose for a while. Don't be gossiping while I'm gone and try not to fret. I shan't be long." Yes, I was talking to cows now. Life on a farm does that to you eventually. And cows are actually very sweet. Nicer than chickens, anyway. You just have to remember to stay out from under their feet. And away from their horns. And poopy tails.

Brushing myself off, I followed along behind Frank and Stanley. Frank and I punched Stanley's lights out once. It was one of my fondest memories. Frank's too, I think. With any luck, the day could take a turn for the better, and we might get a chance to do it again.

AS HE almost always was these days, Joe was lying in his big four-poster bed when I walked into the room. He had three or four pillows stuffed under his head and an open book lying across his chest. It was a book about animal husbandry. There were a cow and a sheep and a horse on the cover. Frank was standing by the window nervously fiddling with the hem of the curtain. Stanley was at the foot of the bed looking down at his father. Pedro was curled up in the crook of Joe's arm and growling at Stanley like a miniature Hound of the Baskervilles. Come to think of it, Joe and Frank were pretty much growling at Stanley too. They all ignored me like I was just another daisy in the wallpaper.

There were tears in Joe's eyes, but I didn't think they were *emotional* tears. I think he had just survived another fit of coughing in the moments before I walked through the door.

Stanley whirled on Frank. "Why the hell isn't he in a hospital?"

I could tell by his stance that Frank was trying to stay calm. Probably for the sake of his dad. "He doesn't want to go to a hospital. He wants to stay here."

"Does the doctor come all the way out here? I thought house calls were a thing of the past."

"They are," Frank said. "There hasn't been a doctor on the place."

"What about hospice?" Stanley asked, and that word "hospice" hung in the air like a bad smell. Frank and I made it a point never to utter the word "hospice" within earshot of Joe. To Joe, hospice meant not only death. It meant far worse things. It meant strangers in the house and feeding tubes and loss of privacy. Everything, in fact, that Joe had told us he did not want.

Frank's eye narrowed and his fists clenched. "Shut up, Stanley. Just shut up. If you have to talk about this, we'll do it somewhere else. Not here." He flicked his eyes at his dad, just long enough to make Stanley understand. Unfortunately, Joe understood that flickering glance too.

"I'll not have you boys discussing my fate behind my back. In fact, I'd just as soon you didn't discuss it *at all*, seeing as how it's not really up to either one of you to be making any decisions here. I'll make the decisions. It's my life, and I'll damn well see it end any way I see fit. It's also my house, and I'll decide who comes inside my door. Frank knows how I want things to be, Stanley. You just stay out of it, you hear? If you intend on staying for a while, don't be making any waves while you're here. Just let things be. Let 'em be. Please. I don't have the energy to fight."

Joe's pale head fell back on the pillow. He closed his eyes, obviously exhausted. One trembling hand still clutched the book on his chest, while the other idly stroked Pedro's ear. Stanley stood his ground at the foot of the bed, glowering down at Joe for all the world like a man looking down upon a total stranger. He gripped the high foot posts of Joe's four-poster bed so tightly his knuckles were white. It was Frank who went to his dad's side and wiped the sweat from his father's brow with a corner of the sheet. It was Frank who then patted his dad's hand and kissed him on the forehead, giving Pedro an idle pat in passing as well. And it was Frank who said, "Don't worry, Pop. We'll do it your way. I promise."

At that, Stanley stormed out of the room. He shot me a look of pure hatred as he stomped past.

I glanced at Frank. We shared a look. And it was pretty obvious we were sharing the same thought as well.

What a dick, we silently communicated to each other.

Joe had other thoughts on the matter, anatomically speaking.

"That boy sure turned out to be an asshole," he muttered to no one in particular, eyes still closed and clucking his tongue like a disappointed schoolmarm. "And who in the hell ever heard of anybody wearing orange shoelaces?"

Then he opened his eyes up wide and the three of us grinned at each other while Pedro wagged his tail in agreement.

STANLEY had a shiny new rental car squeezed in between my crippled Toyota and Joe's old battered F-10 pickup out on the driveway in front of the house. We assumed he'd picked the rental up at the Indianapolis airport after flying in. Frank and I had left Joe to rest and we were in the kitchen making ourselves a sandwich before going back out to finish milking the cows. Pedro had tagged along in case there was any droppage of sandwich makings. Pedro was a big fan of droppage. We could hear Stanley tossing things around as he settled into his old childhood bedroom across the hall from the room where Frank and I slept.

All of a sudden Frank was looking almost as worn out as Joe did. "What the heck did Stanley have to come here for? He's just going to make it hard on everybody, sulking around, starting arguments. Plus he's another mouth to feed. It's not like he's going to chip in with the work or donate any grocery money or anything. He's too selfish and too damn contrary and way too lazy to think of doing anything like that."

I stroked the back of Frank's neck and leaned in to give him a hug. Then, with our sandwiches made, I helped him put the sandwich makings back in the fridge. "I think you've got a bigger problem than groceries, babe."

"Like what?" Frank asked, turning to me. I could see the weariness in those fabulous green eyes. He looked exhausted. What with his dad's illness, and all the hard work which never seemed to get caught up, and now Stanley's arrival, it's a wonder Frank was still on his feet.

"Like the will," I said, lowering my voice. "Stanley isn't going to be too thrilled when he finds out the farm is going to you alone. I think maybe if I were you, I would find out where that will is and make sure it's safe. Put it in a safe deposit box where Stanley can't get at it."

"I don't have a safe deposit box."

"Then get one. I'll even spring for it. My treat."

Leaning up against the sink, Frank took a huge bite out of his ham and rye. "I'm sure Pop's got that all taken care of. He knows what Stanley's like. And maybe Stanley won't stay that long. I guess we'll just have to try to make the best of things until he leaves. I wonder how he found out Pop was sick. I sure didn't tell him. And we know Pop didn't."

I tried not to shuffle my feet or look guilty. "I think I might have had a hand in that. I told Jerry I was coming here. And I told him why. He must have told Stanley. I'm sorry."

Before Frank could comment, Stanley strode into the kitchen like he owned the place, peeked in the fridge, and pulled out all the sandwich makings we had just put back in. "Starving," he said to the ham. I guess he was talking to the ham. He certainly didn't seem to be talking to us. He laid it all out on the kitchen table, grabbed a plate and utensils from the cupboard, swung his long legs into a chair, and commenced building the biggest sandwich I had ever seen in my life.

Satisfied with his construction, he finally tore off a mouthful, and while he was chewing he aimed a few words in my direction. "Sorry about what, Tom?"

"Huh?" I asked.

"You were just telling my brother you were sorry. Sorry about what?" He was striving to appear casual, but he looked a little intense about it all the same. I got the feeling Stanley *really* wanted to know what Frank and I had been talking about. Assholes always think people are plotting against them. Of course, in this case—

Frank came to my rescue. "Tom was just saying how sorry he was that we didn't get you a 'welcome home' cake."

"Yeah," I said. "Something with hemlock in it. And maybe a sprinkling of gunpowder for kick."

Frank elucidated. "He means poison with an explosive chaser. Yummy."

Stanley just kept on chewing, nodding a little, looking first at me, then at Frank, then back to me. "Couple of wise guys," he sneered.

Stanley turned to Frank. "I guess Pop's about done for. Cancer, huh?"

Frank turned to the sink and rinsed off his plate. Then he dried it and tucked it back into the cupboard. His shoulders were stooped with either weariness or sadness or both. Like his dad, Frank looked like he didn't have the energy to fight any more. "He's got a few weeks left, at the most. The cancer is in both lungs and spreading. Surgery won't help, so don't be talking to him about it. He'll just get upset."

Frank dragged a chair out from under the dining room table and parked himself in it across from his brother, elbows on the table, his hands splayed out flat in front of him. I moved to his side and rested my hand across the back of Frank's neck, just so he would know I was there.

"Stan," Frank said, reaching back to hold my hand, "this ordeal we've got coming up is not going to be pleasant. Please don't do anything to make it worse. Don't hassle Pop about doctors. Please. He's too weak to argue with you, but he'll fight you tooth and nail if he thinks he has to."

Stanley polished off his sandwich and pushed the plate away. "I'm not here to cause trouble, bro. I'm here to help. Honest. You can't close out the farm on your own." He cast a supercilious glance in my direction. "And I don't imagine Tom here is much help."

Frank's shoulders tensed, and his grip tightened on my hand. "Tom does just fine, and what the hell do you mean by 'closing out the farm'?"

Stanley waved a hand around, encompassing his surroundings. "It's pretty obvious, isn't it? Frank, when Pop is gone there is going to be a lot of work to do to get this place ready to sell. Public auctions will have to be arranged for the equipment and the livestock. A real estate agent will have to be found to handle the paperwork and help us advertise the property. We're sitting on two hundred acres of prime Indiana farmland. With a perfectly good house and farm buildings on top of it. It won't come cheap to whoever buys it. We may not be set for life, dear brother, but the proceeds will keep us in clover for a while. We have to do it right."

I waited for the bomb to fall, but I guess Frank wasn't quite ready to disclose that little oops moment quite yet. Oops, as in, "Oops, I forgot to mention that you aren't even *in* the will, dipshit."

Gee, and I was so looking forward to seeing the look on Stanley's face when Frank told him.

But all Frank said was, "I guess you're right." And that was it.

Later, I decided Frank had taken the right approach. Joe would have to be the one to tell Stanley that being an insufferable peckerhead for the major part of his life had pretty much precluded him from being named cobeneficiary of this handsome parcel of prime Indiana farmland (as Stanley put it), and more's the pity. If he had just been a little nicer and not such a snot for the past decade or so, things might have turned out differently, but alas, they had not.

"I'm always right," Stanley flatly stated. He unfolded himself from the dining room chair and sauntered off to the living room where he plopped himself down in Joe's recliner with a groan and hit the on button on the TV remote. He looked like he planned on parking himself there for a while. The incredibly annoying voice of Judge Judy suddenly echoed through the house.

Frank glowered at Stanley's dirty plate and silverware still scattered across the kitchen table where the schmuck had left them and sadly shook his head. He finally heaved himself to his feet, gave me a peck on the cheek, and together we cleaned up Stanley's mess and mine and tucked all the food back in the fridge for the second time. Then we headed off to finish the milking.

I didn't know about Frank, but I was really looking forward to the moment when his brother learned the truth about his nonexistent inheritance. I hoped I would be present when that glorious moment unfolded in all its pyrotechnic splendor.

It might even be *better* than clocking the guy in the puss. Sometimes wallet smacks hurt even worse than head smacks.

Just thinking about Stanley's upcoming comeuppance made the scowl on my face do a happy somersault and transform itself into a scoundrelly grin. I love it when scowls do that.

"You're gloating," Frank said, without even looking at me. But he smiled when he said it. I'm pretty sure he was looking forward to those pyrotechnics too.

Chapter
Thirteen

STANLEY turned out to be just as useless as Frank predicted he would be. He spent his days glued to the TV. He gobbled up food like the ass-end of a garbage truck, all the while lounging around on Joe's recliner like a fat, lazy lizard on a rock. He also made an inordinate number of phone calls for someone without any friends, although if either Frank or I walked into a room while he was in the middle of one of these mysteriously whispered conversations, Stanley would execute a hasty good-bye, slam down the phone, kick the footrest up on the recliner, and go back to watching *Jeopardy*. Or *Days of Our Lives*. Or *Cops*. Or head off to the kitchen to forage for more food.

Stanley rarely went in to visit with Joe, and when he did, they would inevitably end up arguing.

Poor Joe. As if he didn't have enough to contend with. Now he had Stanley too. Frank and I weren't too thrilled about dealing with Stanley either, but we tried to manage it with a minimum of fuss. We didn't have much choice. Frank kept hoping Stanley would leave, just go back to San Diego and the life he had there, the life he had carved out of meanness and spite and being a slut and a home-wrecker and a first-class dick. But I knew better. Stanley was entrenched. He wasn't going anywhere. For all intents and purposes, he was here for the duration. I knew it for a fact, even if Frank wouldn't admit it.

Stanley was protecting his interests, you see, or he thought he was. He figured his interests included half of the farm and everything on it. All he had to do was wait for Joe to die to get his hands on what was coming to him. Then he would sell out fast, gather up as much money as he could in the transaction, and skedaddle. And in a perfect world, this might have been true. Unfortunately, Stanley still did not know he had been excluded from the will for being a poophead. Frank and I saw no reason to break the news to him while Joe was still alive. It would only create more drama. And drama was one thing Joe could do without. Hanging onto life by your fingernails, day after day after day, was drama enough for anyone to cope with, thank you very much.

I turned out to be almost as useless as Stanley, at least as far as the milking was concerned. I simply could not get the hang of it. So now, when morning and evening chores rolled around, morning and evening chores being cow milking and egg gathering, Frank and I had a whole new system in place. Frank went off on his own to do the milking, and I went off on my own to gather the eggs. He had the cows and I had the chickens. The goddamn chickens. Twice a day. Every single frigging day of the week. Chickens, chickens, chickens, and more chickens.

A normal person would have gotten used to the little fuckers after a while. I said a *normal* person. Apparently, I'm not among their ranks. Consequently, me and those nine hundred chickens drew a line in the sand—scratch that—drew a line in the chicken poop and chopped up corncobs, and squared off twice a day in a grudge match of epic proportions. They didn't like me and I didn't like them, and neither of us was averse to demonstrating the fact.

In the barn, I had found a massive pair of leather gloves that looked like something Hagrid might have worn while handling dragons. These I commandeered as my egg-gathering gloves, and no chicken could have drawn my blood through them with anything short of a nine millimeter Glock. I found an old lace curtain in the attic with jonquils appliquéd around the hem that I laboriously sewed onto the brim of a beat-up straw hat I discovered under a bed. This I wore as a sort of veil to keep the feathers out of my mouth and the chicken mites out of my lungs. Combine this with Velcro ankle straps to tie my pant legs down, hip boots to wade through the chicken shit with, and a long-sleeved leather jacket I snatched from Joe's closet when he wasn't looking, just on the off-chance that I would fall down and a gang of pissed-off pullets would jump me in retaliation for stealing their children, and you have a fair idea of the egg-gathering garb I donned twice a day to get the job done.

Actually, it took longer to get dressed for the job than it did to *do* the job. But that is neither here nor there. The point is the job got done. Without bloodshed. And when I say bloodshed, I mean mine.

While I groped around under their butts and snatched their offspring, all decked out in my bizarre ensemble of leather and lace and rubber and straw, I rattled off an endless litany of possible consequences for the chickens to ponder which I thought might keep the little blighters on their best behavior and quell any ideas of future rebellion.

"Chicken and dumplings, chicken à la king, chicken salad, chicken fricassee, chicken tacos, Kentucky Fried Chicken, chicken burritos, chicken marinara. Sound good? How about this, you little peckerheads. Chicken and rice, chicken almondine, chicken croquettes, spicy chicken wings, sweet and sour chicken, chicken fried rice, chicken florentine. Yummy, huh? That could be you, you know. Oh yeah. Mess with me, you clucky fuckers, and you'll be chopped up in little pieces and wearing a garnish of parsley and parmesan and crusted up to your eyeballs. Your kids'll be omelets. You know why the chicken crossed the road? *To get away from me!*" And on and on I'd ramble and rant as I gathered up the eggs, nest after nest after nest, leaving tiers of childless, squawking mothers behind. Did it bother me? Hell, no. Like I might have mentioned before, I *hated* the little bastards.

My death threats and my long string of recipes certainly seemed to keep the chickens civil. Whether it was because they were appalled by my culinary bloodthirstiness or simply enthralled by the melodious timbre of my homicidal ravings, who knows? When I ran this by Frank, he told me he thought the calming effect I was having on the chickens had more to do with the fact they were either stunned I was talking to them at all, or trying to be polite and not cackle uproariously at the getup I was wearing.

I found it sad that Frank could grow up on a farm, spend all his formative years there, and still end up knowing so little about chickens.

After gathering the eggs and wiping them clean of any lingering traces of chicken poop, I shut myself up in the candling room and checked their viability. Yes, I actually knew what candling an egg meant now. Holding the eggs one by one before a candle's flame, I looked for imperfections such as specks of blood inside the egg, hairline cracks in the shell, or double yolks. The first time I showed my prowess at candling to Frank, he gave me a big hug and said I'd make a farmer yet, assuming I didn't get my chintz veil with the jonquils appliquéd around the hem too close to the candle and set myself on fire, or simply die of a heat stroke underneath all that leather I was wearing.

It was a good thing Frank was great at sex because his comedic instincts sucked.

After candling the eggs and carefully crating them up, I thought I would visit Grace and her young ones. Since I was the one who brought Grace's litter *into* the world, I felt it was up to me to stop by and say hello every now and then.

I avoided the east side of the barn like the plague. That's where Samson resided. Grace's townhouse was on the west side, behind the pen where all the young shoats were kept. Those shoats had grown considerably since my arrival on the farm. They were knee-high now and growing like weeds. They were marginally less cute than they were before, but they were still friendly and still enthusiastic when anyone came within hailing distance of their enclosure. Wading through them now was a bit tricky, but I managed it. I was still trying to think of a way to make Frank rethink his plan to have them stuffed into sausages when their time came, but so far I had been unsuccessful in posing a reasonable argument. Poor little guys.

Grace poked her head out of her hog house door when she heard me coming, and galloping out behind her like a little avalanche of pink flesh came her nine tiny offspring. They all seemed just as happy to see me as Grace did. I climbed the fence, gave Grace a pat on the snout, and sat down on the driest patch of ground I could find. The little piglets swarmed all over me while Grace stood back and watched with motherly pride.

I carefully pulled two eggs with cracked shells from my shirt pocket and held them out to Grace, who deftly scooped them out of my palm and chomped them up like popcorn, squeezing her eyes shut in bliss. Technically speaking, those two cracked eggs should have found their way to our breakfast table, but I thought Grace might like them more. And she clearly did.

Spending a few minutes giving each of the nine piggies a good chin scratch, I finally heaved myself up, gave Grace a pleasant "Good day," and headed off to the barn to see how Frank was doing.

Before I took two steps I spotted Stanley. He was perched on the top rail of the shoats' pen, watching me like a hawk. He gave me a friendly wave, obviously insincere, and I was reminded of one of those fish in the ocean that has a replica of a worm dangling off its forehead to attract innocent passersby and then sucks them down its gullet when they come to investigate. A friendly wave from Stanley was a warning sign if there ever was one.

"What do *you* want?" I sighed, trying to stay on my feet while I waded through those forty or so pigs, each and every one of them as happy as a kid on Christmas morning. They were far happier than I was, in fact. I had *been* happy, of course, before Stanley came along to spoil the mood. I had no idea what he wanted but I knew it couldn't be good.

Stanley laughed. If I didn't know him so well, that laugh would have charmed the pants off me. Possibly quite literally. Just as I'm sure it once charmed the pants off Jerry. The slut.

"Well now, Tom, you're looking like a regular farmer these days. Talking to the piggies and all."

Thank God I wasn't still wearing my egg-gathering ensemble or he might have formed a different opinion.

"Like I said before, Stanley. What do *you* want?"

Stanley pulled a hard candy from his shirt pocket, tore off its little paper wrapper, and tossed the candy in his mouth. He let the wrapper drift from between his fingertips and waft to the ground where it was snatched up by one of the pigs. They'll eat anything.

"You know you're breaking Jerry's heart, don't you, Tom? He's never gotten over you. I have to admit I don't quite see the attraction, but love is blind, as they say. Maybe it's your big dick, huh? God knows Jerry talked about it often enough. And now you're poking my brother with it, I guess. Makes me wonder if maybe I might be missing something."

I climbed out of the pen, all the while attempting not to eyeball Stanley who was now tugging at his crotch, looking sexy as hell, trying to turn me on. If I hadn't known him so well, his little act might have worked. "You can keep right on wondering, Stanley. You and my dick are never going to get up close and personal, if you catch my drift. I'd rather poke one of those pigs with it than offer it up to a creep like you. I have standards, you see. Not many, but a few. And you don't quite make the cut."

He laughed. He was still rubbing his crotch, and his cock was inching its way down his trouser leg even as I watched. Or tried *not* to watch. With his other hand he was now tweaking his own nipple through his unbuttoned shirt, watching me every second, smiling that nasty sexy smile. Unlike Frank's elegant smooth chest, Stanley's chest was hairy and bulging and muscled up to the max. He looked like he worked out. A lot.

Of course, he was still an asshole. Plus, like Joe said, who the hell wears orange shoelaces? They made the guy look ridiculous sitting there on the fence playing with himself with those damn stupid orange shoelaces flashing in the sun. Stanley was thirty, not thirteen. Orange shoelaces? Puh-lease.

"You're wasting your time," I said, and took off for the barn. The growing lump in my own trousers might have had something to do with my hasty retreat. I wasn't about to give Stanley the satisfaction of knowing I might have found his little exhibition arousing, in a disgusting sort of way. But even so, I would still rather have had a love affair with Samson than give Stanley the sexual time of day. I wouldn't have fucked him with someone *else's* dick, as the quaint old saying goes.

I had no idea what he was playing at, but it seemed clear that he wouldn't mind sticking a wedge between me and Frank, just like he had between me and Jerry. Maybe he couldn't help himself, maybe he just enjoyed causing trouble. Or maybe he was beginning to worry about his inheritance. Frank and I obviously didn't consider him a threat. Even Joe was pretty cavalier in his attitude toward Stanley. It must be really annoying for someone like Stanley who enjoys making waves to find the water around him as persistently smooth as glass. Must be disconcerting. I suspected Stanley would ask questions about the proposed distribution of his father's estate pretty soon. He would want to see the will. He would try a little harder to make some waves and turn Joe's misery into a sizable lump of cold, hard cash for himself.

Yep, I decided. That was it. Stanley was getting worried. Greedy people always do. Might as well egg him on a bit.

I did an about-face and climbed up beside Stanley on the fence. He still had a fairly attractive boner laid out beneath the fabric of his pant leg, but happily he wasn't playing with it anymore. He looked at me with considerable suspicion when I plopped my ass down beside him on the top rail in a companionable sort of way. I looked out over the forty or so prepubescent piggies milling around at our feet like they were my own personal property, a look that wasn't lost on Stanley one little bit.

"Looking a little proprietary there, Tom," he noted with a smirk. "Hope you're not getting any homey feelings about the old farmstead. It's as good as sold already, you know. You probably won't be here much longer."

"Found a buyer for the farm, did you, Stanley?" I asked, nonchalant as hell.

"Maybe I did, maybe I didn't."

"Guess that's what all those whispered phone calls were about, huh?"

He was still smirking. "Could be."

I twiddled my pinky around in my ear like I was trying to dig up something to say. It was a ruse. I already knew what to say. "The last I heard, *Stanley*, you have to own something before you can sell it. This farm still belongs to Joe. And I think maybe Frank might have a sizable share in it too."

Stanley gazed past the pigpen to the pond and the chicken house off in the distance. "I'm afraid Pop isn't up to caring for the place properly. He's too sick to make business decisions. Some days he can't even pour milk into his cornflakes without getting more in his lap than he does in the bowl. I don't want to sound hard-hearted or anything, but it's time Pop was put some place where he can get proper care. And once he no longer resides on this farm, well, he'll no longer need to concern himself with what happens to it. It'll pass on to his sons. Me and Frank. Just like he always intended it to. So don't be gazing around like you own the place, Tom. It sure as hell isn't going to you."

God, if he only knew the truth. But it wasn't up to me to tell him. It was up to Joe.

"I never thought it was going to me," I said. Trying to diffuse his suspicion, I added, "I'm not a farmer, I'm a banker. Sort of. I just hate to see Joe lose it is all. He loves this farm. So does Frank."

"And you think I don't, I suppose," he snarled. "Jesus, you're a suspicious little fucker. What the hell did Jerry ever see in you?"

That got a laugh out of me. "Geez, how many times did I ask that question about you and Jerry? What the hell did he ever see in *you*? Why the hell did he leave me for *you*? And once he did, why the hell did I care anymore? Well, now I don't. Now I've got Frank. And Frank would never cheat on me with a lowlife like you. With Frank I have trust. And trust is something you will never have, because to have trust, you have to be trust*worthy*. And *that*, shit for brains, you most definitely are *not*."

I hoisted my ass up off the fence and stalked off toward the barn.

If Stanley wasn't an enemy before, he certainly was now. I'd have to watch my back. And I'd have to watch Frank's and Joe's backs too. Stanley was up to something. And whatever he was up to, I was pretty sure it would benefit no one but Stanley.

And way off in the back of my mind was a tiny niggle of guilt. It was pecking away at my brain stem like an itsy bitsy woodpecker with a really sharp beak.

Had I really broken Jerry's heart?

BEFORE I could round the corner of the barn on my way to find Frank, I heard a racket coming from the direction of Samson's pen. Christ, what a noise! It sounded sort of like a T. rex going head-to-head with a bigass pterodactyl in the middle of a flock of ostriches.

I took off running and by the time I reached Samson's pen, Frank and a handful of free-range chickens were already there. They were standing like statues, Frank and the chickens, mute with horror. Two seconds later, Stanley arrived. The bunch of us drew close together, as creatures often do in times of catastrophe, shoulder to shoulder and wing to wing, to peer through Samson's cast-iron fence at the winding down of what would have undoubtedly been a horrific sight, had we arrived in time to watch it all unfold. As it was, we barely caught the final act.

There were always a few free-range chickens roaming around the place pooping and pecking and popping up when you least expected them, but what could have possessed one of them to take a stroll through Samson's pen was beyond me. It had been a serious lapse in judgment even for a chicken. Still, he wouldn't be making the same mistake again, and a lesson learned is a lesson remembered, or so they say. Of course, the lesson is pretty much wasted when you get yourself killed learning it, and this chicken was about as dead as you can get.

His bloodied feathers were plastered all over Samson's face, and one scaly chicken foot still poked out of the side of Samson's mouth like an exploded cheroot. The foot was still twitching. Samson was chomping away like a starving man with a Big Mac. His eyes were rolling around in gluttonous satisfaction while his tusks slashed left and right, flinging ropes of slobber and chicken blood through the air. Samson's ugly stubby tail trembled with euphoric glee behind him.

"Stupid chicken," Stanley said, turning on his heel and heading for the house.

Frank and I ignored him. We leaned over the fence and watched the poor dead chicken slide down Samson's gullet. Samson gave a manly burp and a feather floated out. Then he squinted his evil piggy eyes in our direction, lowered his head like a charging bull, and came right at us.

Boy, this guy never learns, I thought. Frank and I stood our ground this time, trusting in the fence to save us, and happily, it did. Samson plowed into it with such force he almost knocked himself out. Feathers flew everywhere. His eyes crossed while the metal fence twanged and hummed and vibrated, and Frank just shook his head and clucked his tongue.

"This animal has got to go," Frank said. "He's a menace. I'd hate to think what would happen if he ever got out."

"Maybe we could feed him Stanley first."

Frank turned to me. "Why? What happened?"

"Big brother tried to seduce me."

Frank grinned. "I figured he would."

"You did?"

"Yeah. Stanley's the kind of person who always wants what he can't have. I figured he'd go after you sooner or later. What'd you say to him?"

"You're not jealous?"

He scooped me into his arms and nuzzled my neck. "I trust you, Tom. You trust me. I trust you. That's how it works. What'd you say to him?"

"I told him I'd rather fuck a pig." And while Frank was laughing, I looked over the fence at Samson who was still reeling from his collision with the fence. Even now, still cross-eyed from the impact, he appeared to be contemplating taking *another* shot at us. Don Quixote with hooves. "Well, maybe not *this* pig," I clarified. "This pig is pretty much unfuckable, I think."

"That would be my assessment," Frank said, glancing at Samson, then gazing back at me. "Eggs gathered?"

I nodded. "Cows milked?"

"Yep."

We nodded good-bye to the chickens that were still milling about. They seemed to be talking quietly among themselves, as grieving friends do, no doubt praising their late acquaintance, whatever his name was, and wondering what had possessed him to play chicken (if you'll pardon the expression) with a demented fourteen hundred-pound hog.

In a companionable sort of way, Frank took my hand and led me toward the barn. I wondered what was up. Then, glancing down at Frank's crotch, I saw what was up.

Holding my hand, he dragged me past the cows that were just finishing up the hay in their mangers, which they had been plucking at while Frank relieved them of their milk. Then, one by one, as they finished their evening snack, they would wander back out into the barn lot. From there they would take their customary evening constitutional down to the pond and soak their feet, or feed on wildflowers in the pasture, or simply stand around in the copse of trees by the chicken house and watch the sun go down as they talked quietly among themselves of world events.

Deep inside the barn was a rickety wooden ladder that climbed up the back wall and disappeared into a hole in the ceiling. I could hear faint music wafting down from somewhere above. Frank climbed up the ladder first, with me hot on his heels. By the time I reached the top rung and followed him through the hole, he was already standing among the hay bales, tugging himself out of his clothes. I saw that this was no spur of the moment decision on Frank's part. He had planned this little tryst, right down to a milk bucket with ice in it and a six-pack of beer cans cooling inside, a blanket strewn in a corner with a mattress of loose hay tucked underneath, and a beat-up old portable radio playing soft music, hanging on a nail from the rafters.

The door that opened from the second-floor hayloft at the back of the barn was flung wide, and in the distance we could see the pond and the trees and the sun setting slowly behind the tree line on the horizon. The passing clouds made the pasture piebald with gliding splotches of sunlight and shadow. A gentle evening breeze cooled my skin as I followed Frank's example and stripped down to absolutely nothing. When we were both naked, he popped two beer cans, handed me one, stretched himself out on the blanket in the corner, and patted the floor beside him. I dropped down at his side and pressed my body alongside his. We lay there sipping our beers and watching the sun set through the hayloft door. Frank's dick lay hot against my leg. My dick lay hot against my stomach, or it did until Frank casually scooped it into his paw and gently held it there throbbing, while he clutched his beer with his other hand.

In the cool of evening, in the silent shadowy barn, as we lay watching the sun ducking behind the treetops in the distance, I could hear my heart beating out the rhythm of my love for Frank. And when I rested my head against Frank's warm chest, I could hear his heart beating out the same sweet song for me.

"Very nice," I sighed, enjoying the beer and the quiet sunset and the wee movements of Frank's fingers twiddling with my dick in a casual, yet not so casual way. I felt moisture on my leg where Frank had pressed himself against me. Hot moisture. Looking down, I saw that Frank was already starting to drip. So was I, as a matter of fact. Frank gently smeared the precome oozing out of my cock across my slit with his thumb. Once in a while, he would put his thumb to his mouth and kiss it away. My dick throbbed in hopeful anticipation every time he did. I began to tremble. Frank felt it, and pulled me closer with a satisfied sigh.

"Can I have another beer?" I asked, trying to sound casual, but my voice was little more than an excited croak, and Frank smiled at it.

"Sure," he said, reaching for the milk bucket. His voice was pretty croaky too, and he smiled even wider when he heard himself speak. With our sex hormones in hyperdrive, we sounded like a couple of tree frogs.

I wrapped my fingers around his cock just like he was doing for me, and together we lay there, sipping our beers, casually stroking each other until we were as hard as fence posts, and occasionally brushing our lips together just to let each other know that we had more than sex on our minds. There was love there too, we seemed to be saying, as if we both didn't know it already.

"Stanley's sniffing around," Frank whispered, and I realized immediately that we were not up in this secluded hayloft just for a romantic interlude. There were things besides romance that Frank wanted to talk about.

"He's doing more than sniffing around," I whispered back. "He's actively seeking a buyer for the farm, or that's what he was intimating while he sat on the fence playing with himself for my benefit."

"All those phone calls." Frank grinned.

"Yep."

"He can't sell it, you know. It's not his to sell."

"That's what I told him."

"You didn't tell him about the will, did you?"

"Nope. Not a word."

Silence fell as we sipped our beers. We watched the evening sky darken through the hayloft door as we thought things over. My leg was starting to thump like Pedro's does when he's getting his ass scratched. Lord, Frank's fingers felt good on my dick.

Finally, Frank spoke. "We're going to have to talk to Dad. Find out exactly where the will is, maybe see exactly what it says and make sure it's as ironclad as Pop implied it is. I can't imagine Pop going to a lawyer to have the will drawn up. He probably did it himself. I suppose it's legal doing it that way, but that doesn't mean it's Stanley-proof."

"We also have to make sure there are duplicate copies," I said. "If there's only one, and Stanley doesn't like what it says, all he has to do is destroy the thing and there will be no proof there was ever a will at all. Then half of everything will go to him no matter what your dad's wishes are."

I looked up into Frank's face and saw a lot of hurt going on behind his eyes. "I wouldn't mind giving Stanley half of everything anyway. He's Pop's son too, after all. But, God, the guy just keeps doing mean things. He really is a rotten human being, not helping me out in San Diego, treating you like pond scum, breaking up your relationship with Jerry, and now trying to seduce you and come between us. These are not nice things to do. What is it you always call Stanley?"

"A dick?"

"That's it."

Silence reigned again. I looked down at Frank's fingers manipulating my cock, then over at my fingers manipulating Frank's cock. Both cocks were so engorged with blood they were standing up like parking meters. They even had little slits in the top to stick your coins in, if one wanted to be fanciful about the whole "parking meter" analogy.

After thirty minutes of stroking I was ready to pop.

"Frank," I said, breathless. "If you keep doing that, I'm going to come. In fact, I think I'm going to come whether you keep doing it or not."

"Oh dear," Frank said with a gentle smile. "Mustn't let *that* go to waste."

He set his beer aside and slid down on the blanket until his lips were at the same level as my dick, which was throbbing and bobbing around in his fist like a snake about to strike. Looking up at me with his heavenly green eyes, Frank slid my foreskin down and pressed his lips to the underside of my cock, just below the head. He gently nipped me there with his snow-white teeth.

Oddly enough, that's all it took. When my come shot out and splattered his face, his hair, and part of the barn wall behind him, Frank cried out louder than I did.

He took me into his mouth to finish the job, and damned if I didn't come again. I clutched a fistful of his hair, and his eyes opened wide as my sperm hit the back of his throat. He laughed and a little stream of come dribbled out the corner of his mouth. He licked it back in with his tongue. I released my grip on his scalp before I snatched him bald-headed, then fell back on the blanket and tried not to die of happiness as his mouth continued to suck me dry.

"Wow," he breathed, when he was sure I was finished. "That was something." Then he said, "My turn."

He gently laid me back on the blanket and squatted over me, his hot fuzzy ass splayed out on my chest, his balls on my chin. I scooted down a tad and scooped those gorgeous plump balls into my mouth, one after the other, while Frank took matters into his own hands. Eyes closed, he pumped his cock directly over my face, occasionally stopping to rub the length of it along my cheek or bop me in the forehead with it just for fun. I stroked his strong hairy legs, his perfect back, his beautiful smooth chest, all the while looking up into his handsome face as he looked down at me and pounded away at his beautiful hard cock directly above my nose.

Soon he was breathing in frantic little puffs, and his thighs were tensed tight around my chest. He scooted his ass back a smidgeon to position the head of his dick in the place it most wanted to go, and I opened my mouth wide and happily invited it in. Frank slid his luscious cock between my lips and clamped his eyes shut as I closed my mouth around it and drew it in. Every fabulous inch. And just as my lips traveled so far down his cock that his pubic hair was tickling my nose and it was all I could do not to sneeze and giggle and praise God Almighty for making me gay and giving me Frank, both in the same lifetime, Frank clutched my head in his hands and launched his seed into me with a happy series of grunts and groans and gasps and shudders. Hugging his ass, I lapped his juices up like well water, every drop, until finally Frank collapsed on top of me, just as contented and spent as I was.

This time it was my turn to say wow.

So as soon as I could talk, I did say it.

Twice.

Chapter
Fourteen

IT WAS a Saturday morning in early August. I had been with Frank on his dad's farm for the better part of two months. The work was hard and never ending, but my love for Frank, and his love for me, and those wonderful moments we found to sneak off and be alone, carried me happily through it. As time passed, I grew even closer to Frank's dad, and I know Frank was pleased by that. Once in a while he would simply sit back and watch Joe and me interact with each other. During those times there was always a gratified sparkle in Frank's green eyes and a gentle smile twisting his lips. He was thrilled that Joe and I got along so well, and somehow, I think, in Frank's eyes, it confirmed his own good sense in falling in love with me. At least I hoped that's what was making him smile, and not the memory of how I looked in my egg-gathering outfit.

I was still a bumbling fool when it came to helping out around the place, but my heart was in the work, and God knows I tried, and that seemed to be enough for Frank. It was with more than a little astonishment that I finally faced the fact that I was actually beginning to enjoy life on the farm. I hadn't had to breathe into a paper bag for weeks and weeks. Social anxiety disorder? Since I was rarely off the farm, and with no social life to speak of, it wasn't a problem. Shyness? I was surrounded by animals. Who the hell is shy around animals? Well, except for Samson. You'd have to be nuts not to be shy around that crazy fucker. But still, even Samson wasn't enough to make me stick my head in a paper bag. Only Stanley could make me do that.

Even then, it wasn't from shyness. It was just so I wouldn't have to look at him.

I had just sent a check to Miss Wiggins to cover our apartment rent back in San Diego for another month, but I didn't mention it to Frank. He had enough to worry about without fretting over money.

Joe was fading fast. The constant pain and incessant coughing was wearing him down. As bad as he looked when I first met him, he looked infinitely worse now. Always a little guy, now he couldn't have weighed more than a hundred pounds. Obviously, the cancer was eating him up, and there was absolutely nothing we could do about it.

Stanley wasn't helping either. He was always poking around the place, digging through Joe's papers when Joe wasn't watching, making strange phone calls, sending off letters which he never let anyone see. We knew what he was doing, of course. It was the same thing he had been doing since he first arrived. He was sending out feelers, seeking a buyer for the farm, and digging around trying to find out if there was a will. But even Stanley wasn't dumb enough to come right out and ask Joe about a will point-blank. He had no idea Frank and I both knew more about the matter than he did, and if he ever did learn that little fact, I figured we would be in for some rip-roaring battles. All of us. Joe included.

This morning, Stanley had driven off in his rental car to visit friends, or so he said, although Frank couldn't imagine who his brother was referring to when he talked about friends. Stanley had not been in Indiana for years, and even when he had lived here, through high school and all, the guy was already well on his way to being a first-class jerk. Consequently, he didn't have many friends even then. According to Frank, if Stanley had said he was off to visit *enemies*, he would have had a broad range to choose from. If Stanley were to visit *all* of his enemies, Frank figured he would be gone through Christmas. If he was truly visiting friends, he would probably be back in about five minutes.

With Stanley out of the picture for a while, Frank and I thought it would be a good opportunity to try yet again to talk some sense into Joe. It was pointless for him to suffer. There was pain medication readily available. All we had to do was ask for it. With our chores caught up, we trooped into Joe's bedroom on the pretense of stopping by for a simple chat, but by the leery look in Joe's eyes, I figured he knew we were up to something, and he was pretty sure he knew what it was.

Joe's pajamas hung all over him now. He looked like a sick little kid wearing his dad's pj's. Frank perched himself on the edge of Joe's bed and set about nervously smoothing the sheet over Joe's stick-thin legs, trying to build up the courage to start the argument over pain medication one more time. We had already been through it twice with Joe, and both times Joe got upset with us for interfering with what he called "my own personal business and nobody else's." The last thing Frank wanted to do was upset his dad again, but something had to be done. The constant pain was simply killing the man. It had to be reined in. Joe was so tiny now, so wasted away, that even his bed looked too big for him when he lay in it. And these days, Joe could rarely be found anywhere else.

I stood at the window gazing out at the lawn, where Pedro was humping away at the back leg of one of the farm dogs. He looked like he was having a real good time. His tongue was hanging out, his little Chihuahua pecker was all over the place, and his eyes were bugged out in carnal bliss. He looked like a tiny lumberjack hugging a tree, only most lumberjacks don't get that excited about it. Pedro's humper was going a mile a minute. The farm dog was two feet taller than Pedro, and unless his chosen paramour had a vagina on her ankle, I figured good old Pedro wouldn't be having any paternity papers served on him anytime in the near future. He could hump away to his heart's content, as long as the big-ass hound he was humping didn't get annoyed enough to spin around and bite his head off. So far she merely looked bored. I read in *Cosmo* that a lot of women aren't turned on by short guys. Too bad for Pedro. Maybe he should go find a squirrel to hump.

I turned from the window, and my grin faded quickly enough when I saw Frank reach out and gently brush the hair away from Joe's eyes. The man's hair was always wet these days. Weakness will do that. I had pneumonia once, and my hair was wet for a month. Couldn't keep it dry.

Frank gave his dad a little smile. "You need a haircut, Pop. You're starting to look like a Yeti."

Joe tried to smile back, but the effort was obviously too much. A flash of pain dimmed his eyes even while he fondly aimed them at Frank. "I need more than a haircut, son. I need a new me."

Frank nodded. "I know, Pop. I wish I had one to give you."

Joe looked over at me with his wide concentration camp eyes. So much misery in there. Misery and courage. He was facing his own death just like he said he would—head-on, apologies to no one. He cleared his throat, dredging up the energy to speak. "How's Grace, Tom? Been to see her lately?"

My face lit up. I could feel it. I loved talking about Grace. I had never saved a life before. Or brought new ones into the world. I figured it was a major turning point in my career as a farmer. At least it was one of the few things I had somehow managed to do right. "She's great. She and the baby pigs were lying out in the sun soaking up the rays the last time I looked. Pigs are getting big. I think they know me. Grace said to tell you hello," I added with a grin.

Joe grinned back. It was feeble but it was definitely a grin. "I'm sure she did," he said. "Hogs are always sociable that way. Very polite."

"Except for Samson," Frank said.

Joe nodded. "Except for Samson. He'd rather eat you than say hello."

"He's tried more than once," I said, shuddering at the memory.

"I'm sure he has," Joe started to say, but a coughing spell stopped him cold. It took a couple of minutes for him to quiet down, and by the time he did, he was truly exhausted. Tears streamed from his eyes, and his skinny chest heaved under the sheet as he tried to draw in enough oxygen to stay alive just a little bit longer. Another day, another week, another month. Whatever God would give him.

I could see he wanted us to leave, his illness always embarrassed him so, but Frank was determined to do what he had come to do.

"You need medicine, Pop. We can make you a lot more comfortable than you are. Why are you being so damned stubborn about it? Give in on something just this once. What's the point of suffering? Come on, Pop. I'm begging you. I can't stand to see you like this anymore."

Joe reached out a trembling hand and ran a gentle finger along Frank's jawline. "I know it's not easy for you, Frank, but it's not easy for me either. And I know what will happen if you bring a doctor around to prescribe me medicine. He'll insist on getting hospice involved, and they'll start running the show. The next thing you know they'll start doing exactly what they want without listening to anybody's wishes, and I'll be laying here with a dozen tubes sticking out of me and doctor bills piling up like snow in January. I won't have it, Frank. I won't. I watched your mother die that way. They said they were easing her passing. My ass. They didn't ease nothing. They just added to her misery. And that's what it was too. Pure, unblemished misery. If she had been here in this bed where she belonged, she wouldn't have died alone in the middle of the night like she did in that cold hospital without a familiar face anywhere near. I would have been right beside her. Holding her hand. Stroking her hair. Don't do it to me, Frank. I'm begging you. I've lived my whole life the way I wanted. Let me die the same way. Not all doped up and dumb as an ox. I want to know what's happening. I want to see it come."

The long speech all but knocked him out. He was so tired by the time he finished, he was almost sobbing. The coughing started up again, and Frank and I bustled around trying to ease Joe through it, offering water, sitting him up and patting his back, pushing the hair out of his eyes and wiping his sweaty brow, apologizing for getting him upset. In the end, the coughing stopped, but not because of anything we did. It just stopped because Joe was too weak to let it go on.

As soon as he quieted down we heard a whimper in the doorway, and turning, we saw Pedro standing there looking up at Joe as he lay in the bed trying to breathe. When Joe looked over at him, Pedro's tail started doing its happy thing, whipping back and forth like a metronome. He gave a yip and flew across the room and into Joe's bed like he had been shot out of a catapult.

As weak as he was, Joe found a smile to greet his little friend with. Pedro gave Joe's face a good washing, then curled up in the crook of his arm where he always lay when he was spending time with Joe. He looked at me as if daring me to argue. Pedro knew where he belonged. Damned if he was going to let me or anyone else tell him otherwise.

Joe watched Pedro twist around in a circle two or three times before settling down, then he turned to Frank and said, "This is all the medicine I need, son. I've got you and Tom and Tom's dog, who's a fine little rascal, there's no two ways around that, and I honest to God don't need anything else. You might light a firecracker under Stanley's ass to get him moving and maybe help you boys out with the chores, but that's about all that's needed. Things'll work out just fine on their own. You'll see. So don't be pestering me anymore about doctors and medicine. Okay? Do we have a deal?"

Frank gave a big sigh and said, "Okay, Pop. If that's the way you want it."

I could tell Frank didn't like it, but what could he do? In the end, I supposed it really should be Joe's decision. Nobody else had earned the privilege of telling him how to die, least of all us.

Frank looked over at me, and by the time we both looked back at Joe, Joe was asleep. Or pretending to be.

We quietly left the room.

Pedro watched us go, and while we were closing the bedroom door behind us, he burrowed his nose under Joe's hand and calmly closed his eyes.

FRANK was off working in the garden and I was dropping hay bales through the hayloft door for the milk cows' evening meal when my cell phone rang. It startled me so, I almost fell out of the barn. It hadn't rung for weeks. In fact, I was seriously considering tossing it into the pond and ridding myself of the monthly bill.

I checked the readout, and the number was vaguely familiar, but I couldn't quite place it. At least it wasn't Jerry.

"Yes?"

"Tom? Is that you?"

"Yes. Who's this?"

The caller went through a slightly pompous throat-clearing routine which was also vaguely familiar, but still I couldn't place who it was.

Finally, the mystery was solved. "Mr. Moonhouse here, Tom. From the bank. How have you been, son?"

That was a bit much for me to wrap my head around on this fine Indiana afternoon. "Son? You're calling me, 'son'? It seems like only yesterday that you were firing my ass and telling me to empty out my desk. Son? Fuck you, Moony."

"Ha. Ha. You always were a kidder. No, seriously, Tom, I'm calling to offer you your job back. I, hmm, uhh, may have been a tiny bit precipitous in making my decision to let you go. Perhaps you could drop by the bank, and we could talk over the particulars of your coming back to work with us. I might even be able to resurrect that idea you had about a wee raise for your services. How would you like that, Tom?"

"Moony, I'm in Indiana."

"You are? What in the world are you doing there?"

"Living."

"What about the lawsuit?"

"What lawsuit?"

Moony's voice tightened. "I just got a call from your lawyer, let me see now, where's that card, oh, well, your lawyer Mr. Jerry Somebody, and he informed me that a lawsuit was about to be filed against me personally and against the bank in general for unlawful termination on the basis of discrimination against a member of the

LTBG community, or BLGB or GLGT or BLT or whatever the hell it is. I assume it means queers. I mean gays. I mean you."

I bit back a giggle. Jerry was up to his old tricks again. First he got me fired, now he had managed to get me reinstated. Or he was trying to. I guess he was getting worried that I wouldn't come back to San Diego, and if I didn't come back to San Diego he wouldn't have anybody to harangue for the rest of his natural life. Lord, that guy could be a pain in the ass. I couldn't deny the fact, however, that he certainly still seemed to be in love with me, for all the good it would do him.

Apparently, Mr. Moonhouse was getting worried by the continued silence on the other end of the line. I had visions of him imagining himself at the unemployment office being interviewed by a fifty-year-old queen, currently out of drag for his day job. The queen would be sitting there with an eyebrow pencil poking out of his pocket protector and just a teeny smear of blush coloring his five o'clock shadow. The queen would check Moony's paperwork, then eye him coldly after seeing the reason Moony was fired from his *last* job. Queens are so sensitive about discrimination. Especially ugly queens. And they'll take it out on anybody in spitting distance. Maybe Moony was imagining the old queen pulling out a rubber stamp as big as a dinner plate and, being careful not to break a nail, slamming it down on his request form for benefits. *Bam!* DENIED. *Bam!* DENIED.

Moony hemmed and hawed and cleared his throat again. Sounded like he had a seat cushion stuck in there. "Son, I don't know where you got the idea that I'm prejudiced, I truly don't. The head office frowns on this sort of hullabaloo, Tom. Gives the public a bad impression of the bank. A lot of queers keep their money with us. I mean gays. I mean people like you. We can't have them thinking we don't like them, now can we? I want you to drop this lawsuit business before the legal department gets wind of it. Let's let bygones be bygones, what do you say? No hard feelings?"

I hated to let the guy off the hook so easily, but aside from sheer petulance, there was really no reason to make him dangle.

"Moony, relax. There will be no lawsuit. On one condition."

He sounded wary. "What might that be?"

This should be good. "Tell me the truth, Moony. Were you really looking for rolls of quarters all those time you scoped out my crotch at work?"

"*What—why I never—*"

I clucked. "Moooonyyy—"

He gave a sigh that sounded like it came all the way up from his shoes. "Well, I suppose I might have been a *wee* bit curious about that bulge in your—"

That was all I needed to hear to confirm my suspicions. Being the nice guy that I am, I clicked off my cell phone and stuck it back in my pocket, leaving Moony with at least a smattering of his former dignity.

Smiling, I went back to work.

Later, after tearing the hay bales apart and stuffing them into the mangers for the cows to feed from, my cell phone rang again. Wow. Twice in one day.

I flipped it open without checking the readout. It had to be Jerry. "Hello?"

It wasn't Jerry. It was Miss Wiggins, my apartment manager back in San Diego.

"Tommy! Is that you? It's so nice to hear your voice! I just want you to know that all your houseplants are back in the apartment and they're in considerably better condition now than they were when you left them with me, dear. Not much of a gardener, are you? Oh, and I had a girl come in to give your place a good cleaning since it's been empty so long. Jerry's got his stuff moved in, and there certainly is a lot of furniture in there now. You couldn't fall down if you wanted to, but if that's the way you boys want it, it's no skin off my nose. I'm sorry things didn't work out with Frank, he was such a nice boy, but life goes on, and at least now you're back with Jerry. I'm so glad you're coming home, Tom, things have been far too quiet around here. That nice couple in 2B are getting divorced, did I tell you? I'm not surprised, really. Did you see that kid they spawned? Ugliest child I ever saw in my life. That would be enough to wreck *any* marriage. Turn you off sex completely, that would. Such a shame, though. But by golly I told them the same thing I told you. Life goes on. Of course, if it goes on long enough you get to be an old lady like me, ha ha, but that's grist for *another* mill, if you take my meaning. What's the matter, boy, cat got your tongue? Say something!"

All I could manage to stutter was, "Did you say Jerry is back in my apartment?"

"That's right, dear. He moved in this morning."

"With all his stuff?"

"That's right, dear. Furniture and everything. He has a cat now, but I'm sure you already knew that. Cute little thing. I hope Pedro doesn't eat it. That dog isn't quite normal, is he?"

"And you let him?"

"Who, dear?"

"*Jerry! You let him move back in?*"

"Yes, dear. Him and the cat. He still had his key, so I knew it was all right. Now don't you worry about a thing. Everything is under control, and we'll all be waiting with bated breath for your happy return. Jerry looked so pleased to have you back. I'm sure you've made the right decision, the two of you, although I do feel sorry for that nice Frank. I hope he'll be all right. He seemed to love you so. But then we never know what goes on behind closed doors, do we, dear? Oh, my, Oprah's just coming on. It's a rerun. She's talking about poop today. Human poop. With a doctor. Nothing is sacred anymore, is it? Well, I'll see you when I see you. And watch out driving back from Indiana, dear, there are still serial killers lurking behind practically every tree, I saw it on *Jerry Springer*. Well, gotta run. Bye, dear!"

And with that, the phone went dead in my hand.

For three seconds.

Then it rang again. By this time I was so stunned, all I could do was flip it open and mutter a maniacal, "Who the hell is *this*?"

"Me." This time it *was* Jerry, and he sounded a little nervous. Well, maybe more than a little. Actually he sounded like a demolitions expert who suddenly wakes up to find himself in a roomful of nitroglycerine. *Old, sweating* nitroglycerine. With a pile of lit dynamite sputtering in the corner. And a box of C4 strapped to his chest. Hooked up to an alarm clock about to go off. In a burning house. On the edge of a crumbling cliff. On a Monday. You know. *Nervous.*

"Hello, *Roomy!*" I spat. "Get moved in okay?"

"I had to," he muttered. "I want you back."

"*You don't need me!*" I screamed. "*You've got a cat!*"

"Miss Wiggins missed me. She said so."

"*Well, I didn't!*"

"I got you your job back at the bank."

"*You got me fired from that job to begin with!*"

"We were lovers once."

"*'Til you cheated on me and broke my heart!*"

"I didn't mean to."

"*How can you 'not mean' to cheat? Did your dick just go off and cheat on its own?*"

"I'm sorry."

"*And now you've stolen my apartment—*"

"My name is still on the lease."

"*—and got a cat!*"

"It's a loaner."

"*Fuck you, Jerry!*"

"Wow. You're grumpy. How's Frank?"

"You leave Frank out of this! And where did you get a key to my apartment?"

"I kept one when we broke up. Thought it might come in handy. And voilà! It did."

I clutched my chest. Great. Now I was probably having a heart attack. Boy, some days you just shouldn't get out of bed. I took a series of deep breaths which I learned watching yoga on TV because I was too shy to go to a *real* yoga class and learn how to do it firsthand. I began to think maybe it was working, maybe I was really calming down a little bit, but then I thought, nope, maybe not. And why the hell *should* I calm down? My blood pressure shot back up like Old Faithful, just the way I wanted it to.

"*What the fuck do you want, Jerry? Why are you calling me and what the fuck do you want?*"

"Well, babe—"

"*Don't call me babe!*" I took one more deep breath. A long, shaky one. This time it seemed to work. Maybe I wouldn't die of a stroke brought on by aggravation at the tender age of twenty-seven after all. "Okay, Jerry, forget I asked that question. I don't care what you want. You can even stay in the apartment until Frank and I decide to come home. The minute we do, I'll let you know and you'll have three days to get out. You and all your shit. Got it? Now then, if you can't think of anything else to piss me off, I'm going to hang up the phone. If your loaner cat gets fleas in my carpet, I'll hunt you down and murder you like a dog. Fleas are probably the only thing in the world that I hate more than I hate you." (Chickens, too, but I was in no mood to go into the whole chicken thing with Jerry.)

And with that "hate you!" parting shot, feeble as it was, I finally snapped the phone shut and stuffed it in my pocket. If it rang again I was going to feed it to Samson.

I threw my gloves up through the hole in the hayloft floor so they would be there when I needed them the next time I was chucking hay and took off for the garden. I needed to talk to Frank. I needed to tell him about Jerry being in the apartment and I needed to hear him tell me how much he loved me. Somehow that seemed real important right now.

I wished I hadn't told Jerry I hated him. I didn't hate him. I just didn't love him anymore. Plus, once someone has cheated on you, how do you go back to trusting them again?

The short answer? You don't. Ever.

Maybe one day Jerry would understand that.

FRANK wasn't in the garden, although it did look freshly tilled.

I circled the house, thinking Frank might be somewhere in the yard, but he wasn't. I went through the front door of the farmhouse and checked out every room inside. I found Joe lying in bed giving Pedro a belly rub with one hand and holding a book up to his face with the other. No Frank. Joe said he didn't know where Frank was. Just keep looking, he said, he's bound to turn up sooner or later. He said it like a farmer says everything—as if his words were packed with wisdom. Oddly enough, usually they were. I nodded, backing out, and Joe went back to his book, squinting like he could barely see. His eyes had been failing him lately. Just one more tribulation for the man to go through. Pedro never looked up once while I was inside the room. Give him a belly rub and he was lost to the world.

Back outside, I looked toward the fields, gazed off toward the barn, and checked the driveway for Joe's truck, which was still there, parked alongside my Toyota. Then I did a double take. Stanley's rental car was gone, and in its place, tucked in among the other vehicles like it belonged there, was Jeff Moody's old yellow pickup. That was strange. What the hell was he doing here?

I was about to head off toward the pasture and the chicken house and the pigpen behind the barn, figuring Frank had to be in one of those three places, maybe with Moody, since they didn't seem to be anywhere else around, when I heard the sound of running water coming from the washhouse by the back door.

I grinned. That had to be Frank, all heated up and cooling off with a quick shower after toiling away in the garden under a burning summer sun. I stepped over a couple of sleeping dogs, who barely stirred when I straddled them, and approached the washhouse door, thinking maybe I would give Frank a little scare.

Then I thought, wait a minute. If Frank is taking a shower, then where the hell is Moody?

Then I heard the moans.

They weren't the kind of moans you make when you're hurting. They were the kind of moans you make when you're *not* hurting. When you're not hurting *at all*.

I reached out a hand to push open the washhouse door, then stopped. Suddenly I didn't want to know what was going on behind that door. Suddenly I didn't want to know why my heart was thudding away inside my chest, or why an ache had started up behind my rib cage that seemed to be squeezing the air right out of me. I didn't want to know why I had this sudden urge to plop myself down in the dusty backyard beside the mangy farm dogs and the big-ass tractor tire painted white and filled with petunias, and sob like a baby.

Already blinking back tears, I shut my mind to the pain and quietly pushed open the rickety old door with a trembling hand just enough to peek inside. Suddenly the moans were a whole lot louder. I could hear the water splashing and the slap of flesh against flesh, and as my eyes adjusted to the dim light, I saw, standing beneath one of the showerheads, in a deluge of water, a pale naked ass, handsome and strong, pumping away at another naked ass, this one slimmer and deeply tanned. That second ass had the kind of tan that comes from the genes, not from the sun. Their four long legs were intertwined, the water sluicing down them in buckets, sharpening the outlines of their calves and thighs. The arms holding the ass in position in front were rock-hard and packed with biceps that rolled around like croquet balls when they moved. Blond hair was plastered wet to the top of the man's head, and one brown arm from the body of the man in front was reaching around to clutch the pale ass and pull the pale body closer to his own.

It was Moody doing the fucking, of course. Moody with his pale ass and beautiful strong arms. Moody and—

The man in front said something I couldn't understand, and Moody pressed his lips to the back of the man's neck while his ass started pumping even faster. The man in front gave a loud groan. I could see him shudder. His brown legs, strong and hairy, quivered as Moody held his hips in place and drove his cock into that eager ass like a pile driver.

They were both groaning now. Things were coming to a head.

"No—" I whispered. "No—" And I quietly closed the washhouse door and leaned against it. I couldn't look anymore, but I had to listen. I had to hear.

Frank. Oh God.

And then the tears came, hot and furious. And no sooner did they come than a hand came out of nowhere and laid itself atop my shoulder.

"Tom, what's wrong?"

I spun around so fast I almost passed out. The day dimmed around me and stars blinked in front of my eyes.

Then my vision cleared and I saw Frank standing there. Bone-dry, except for the sweat pouring down his face. He was dirty as hell, his shirt soaked with grime, his hands still tucked into big filthy work gloves. The knees of his jeans were stained green. His shoes were two big mud clods, so coated with crap you couldn't even see the laces. Sweet Jesus. I had never seen anything so beautiful in all my life.

I threw myself into his arms, and that's when the tears really came. I cried like a baby, and I'm not ashamed to admit it. Frank didn't seem ashamed to see me cry either, although he did look powerfully confused. He clutched me close, patted my back, cooed sweet things in my ear that I didn't really hear except for the loving tone in which he said them.

"Baby, what's wrong?" Then he tensed up. "Is it Pop? Did he—"

I managed to shake my head and find my voice. "No, Frank. No. Your dad's okay. I was just with him."

Frank heard the shower going through the washhouse door. "Who's taking a shower?" he asked. "Stanley?"

And that's when I realized, yes, by God, that tanned ass and those strong hairy legs *had* belonged to Stanley. Who else could they have belonged to?

Then Frank heard the groaning coming from behind the closed door, and as if the groaning wasn't enough, someone inside the washhouse, either the fucker or the fuckee, either Moody or Stanley, let out a wail that would have startled a dead man. It was a happy wail. An

"Oh, sweet Jesus, here I come!" wail. I had made that wail myself a few times with Frank. I knew it well.

Frank removed a work glove with his teeth and squeegeed off one of my tears with his thumb. I hiccupped and said thank you.

Frank nodded toward the door. "Who's in there?"

"Well—"

A grin started to spread across Frank's face. His dimple deepened. A knowing light came into his green, shimmering eyes. "You thought it was me, didn't you?"

I blinked back more tears. This time they were guilty tears. That's what comes from having one slut for a lover. Makes you think they all are. "I'm sorry, Frank. I should have known better."

Frank's smile faltered when he said, "Yeah, Tom, you should have." But then he saw the hurt look on my face, and his smile popped back in all its glory. He chucked me under the chin, for all the world like a coach sending his worst player out onto the field in the middle of the biggest game of the year. "I forgive you. It'll take more than one isolated moment of stupidity to get me to throw you to the wolves. If the way you gather eggs hasn't done it, this won't. We're still an item. I'll prove it to you later. Just have a little more faith next time, okay? Have a little trust. And yes, I still love you, Tom. So stop looking so worried."

I hiccupped again and said thank you very politely, like he had just passed me the potatoes or something instead of giving me my life back. My life with him. The best life I had ever known. Even if I was working my ass off.

Frank brushed his lips against mine, knowing that was what I wanted him to do. We were still standing by the washhouse door, and there was still a whole lot of groaning happening on the other side of it. Frank listened to the groaning for a moment longer, then gave out a quiet chuckle. "I know that groan," he said. "Jeff's truck is out front, isn't it?"

"Yep."

"It's Jeff and Stanley in the washhouse, isn't it?"

"Yep."

"Wasting water."

"Yep."

"And fucking."

"Yep. Fucking up a storm."

Frank shook his head in wonder, then scooped me back into his arms. "Jesus, what a slut."

"Which one?" I asked, burying my face in his collar.

Chapter Fifteen

THE four of us were sitting around the kitchen table a few days later. Summer was at its peak, and the days were so hot that at noon you could griddle pancakes on the hood of Joe's pickup truck. Nights were even hotter. On this particular Sunday evening, the kitchen was sweltering, even with all the doors and windows flung open. Joe's old fan was propped up on the kitchen counter, screaming out a one-note tune and blowing the heat around, cooling nothing.

Pedro was lying on his side on a dishtowel in the middle of the kitchen table like a holiday centerpiece. His fat little tummy was pumping up and down as he panted his way through the heat and humidity. He rarely left Joe's side these days. I couldn't help wondering sometimes if maybe Pedro knew something about Joe that we didn't. Like how much time Joe had left. Or how much time Joe *didn't* have left. Does Old Man Death have a quantifiable smell? Could Pedro sense that ancient creature in black robes hovering at Joe's side, biding his time maybe, enjoying the wait, savoring Joe's suffering, taking it as his due, before finally stepping out of the shadows to snatch Joe off to oblivion?

Or maybe Pedro's motives were a whole lot simpler than that. Maybe Pedro simply *liked* Joe. I couldn't discount that possibility either.

Joe had called a family meeting. It was the first time we had seen him out of his bedroom in a week, and I could tell it was taking every ounce of what strength he had left to remain upright on the kitchen chair, even *with* a bunch of pillows poked in around him to hold him up. The man was so shriveled up now, and the never-ending pain was so indelibly etched on his corneas, that I wondered just what it was that kept him going. Was it maybe love that kept the wheels of his life turning? Love for his sons. Love for his farm. What exactly was it that kept Joe's poor heart beating? I knew, deep in my own heart, that I was not as strong as this simple Indiana farmer. If I had to suffer like Joe had suffered, I would have laid down the weary, miserable load long before this and considered myself lucky to be rid of it.

Frank and I had said nothing to Stanley about that day in the washhouse, but Stanley knew we knew. You could see in his eyes that he was hoping one of us would mention it so he could jump down our throats and tell us to mind our own business, but we refused to give him the satisfaction. I also think Stanley entertained a certain perverse satisfaction in knowing he had seduced what had once belonged to Frank alone. Perhaps it was just another example of Stanley's greed. He couldn't bear to think Frank might have had something that he himself had never tasted. Which was probably why he had tried to seduce me. Greed. He would have bedded me even if he didn't want me, just to show he could.

We hadn't seen Jeff Moody since that day. He was probably hiding out on his own farm, mortified, and hopefully running into town now and then to have some blood work done. Medically speaking, I wouldn't trust Stanley's ass any farther than I could throw it. I certainly wouldn't feel comfortable sticking any of my own body parts into it that weren't first properly sheathed in eight or nine layers of polyurethane, then thoroughly sprayed with disinfectant and dipped in Raid and possibly roasted over an open flame afterward.

Needless to say, Stanley was still being a pain. Lazy, sneaky, and no help whatsoever. Frank and I bore the brunt of the farm work, and if we complained, it was only to each other. Complaining to Stanley would have pleased him no end, so we weren't about to do that. Besides, not *expecting* any help goes a long way in keeping you happy when you don't *get* any help. You can't miss what you know you'll never have, and Stanley was a master at never offering anybody anything but grief. He seemed to thrive on it.

True to his character, Joe got right to the point. He looked around the table at each of us in turn. Pedro was snoring softly, lying there sound asleep on the dish towel between us, his gentle noises barely audible above the cacophonous thrumming of the old electric fan. Joe seemed to be keeping his voice down so he wouldn't wake Pedro. Even with Death tapping him on the shoulder, Joe could find consideration for a napping Chihuahua. The immensity of kindness in that act staggered me.

Already, Joe was fighting back a cough, gently touching his tender throat with a trembling hand, massaging it, coaxing it to silence. "My time is running out, boys. We need to clear a few things up. I don't want any surprises or disappointments after I'm gone."

"Pop—" Frank said.

Joe gently cut him off. "Let me say what I have to say first. Then you can do all the talking you want."

Frank's hand reached out to me under the table. I took it, twining my fingers through his, and together we waited. Silent and respectful.

Stanley was tilted back on the two hind legs of his kitchen chair, chewing a kitchen match. He was eyeing his father coldly, at least when Joe wasn't watching. It was as if Stanley was bored and resentful of the fact that Joe had pulled him away from the *real* drama of *Days of Our Lives* for this horseshit. Not for the first time, I wondered how a guy as handsome as Stanley could turn out to be so damn mean. Was he missing a chromosome or something? Was there a kink in his DNA chain that made him act the way he did? Did nature stick a rusty link in there? Once again I found myself wondering what it was that had made Jerry fall in love with this creep. Not that I much cared anymore now that I had Frank. And if you looked at it obliquely, if Jerry hadn't dumped me for this Neanderthal, Frank and I would have never come together. Funny how things work out. One day you have a broken heart, and the next day you're so damned happy you can't see straight. Life's a trip and that's a fact. New surprises at every turn.

With a start, I realized that Joe's eyes were not centered on his sons anymore. They were aimed directly at me. It seemed like a good time to stop thinking about myself and start paying attention, so I did.

"Tom," Joe said, "you're a third party in all this, so I'm going to say what I have to say to you. That way I won't feel guilty when certain people that I love find out things they may not want to hear. Is that all right with you?"

"Yes, sir," I said, gripping Frank's hand a little tighter, pleased when he gave me a reassuring squeeze back. "I guess so."

I saw Stanley tense up when Joe spoke those words. Maybe Stanley knew what was coming, or maybe he just suspected. Either way, he didn't look happy.

Joe trained his eyes on me. Those eyes were teary and red and weary beyond all imagining. They were deep-set in a face so strained with the suffering the man had endured the last few months that it made your heart ache to look at them. But those eyes still had a flame of purpose burning bright somewhere deep down in their troubled green depths. And they still looked out at the world with determination. It was pretty obvious that Joe had no intention of letting a little thing like his own suffering derail his intentions as far as the execution of his estate was concerned.

"I've done a lot of soul-searching about my two boys, Tom. And being a farmer, I've had to rely on the conventional wisdom about what you get out of life. The conventional wisdom is 'you reap what you sow'. Pretty profound, huh?"

"No, sir," I said.

Joe smiled. "You're right, Tom. It ain't profound at all. It's a simple truth. You reap what you sow. Any farmer in the world will tell you the same. If you plant corn, you get corn. If you plant wheat, you get wheat. If you don't plant anything, you get weeds. Or nothing."

Joe took a moment to wipe his lips with a broad red handkerchief he plucked from his pocket. I thought he was going to start coughing, but he didn't. I think he thought so too. He looked immensely grateful when he didn't.

"Well, now, Tom, I know my boys are sitting here chomping at the bit to find out what my will says. I'm afraid they're going to have to wait a little longer. I didn't gather everybody here to tell them what they're getting. I gathered them here to tell them what I *want*."

"This is nuts," Stanley stated. "So there's a will, huh? So what's the big mystery? Just tell us what it says, or better yet just show it to us and end the suspense. We're adults. We can take it."

"No," Joe said. "I won't watch you boys fight while I'm laying in that bed in there dying a slow, miserable death. You can fight all you want after I'm dead and gone, and I don't doubt you will. But it'll all be a waste of time if you do. The will is airtight. Even if I did draw it up myself."

Stanley's voice was the only cold thing in that sweltering kitchen. His words sliced through the air like knives made of ice. "I guess you left me out of it then, is that what you're trying to say, Pop? This farm is worth a fortune, you know. You could sell it right now for a pretty penny."

"I didn't leave anybody out," Joe said. "The will includes both of you. Maybe not equally, but it includes both of you."

Frank shot a glance at me, then looked back at his father. I knew what Frank was thinking as well as Frank did. Joe told us the farm was going to him. Now he was telling us something different. I couldn't imagine why. It wasn't like Joe to sneak around and play one side against the other like this. Had his pain addled his mind? Was he confused? Did he even know what the hell he was talking about?

Stanley certainly seemed to think so. "I won't be left out of my share, Pop. Half this farm is mine. I'll drag Frank through every court in the country before I let him walk off with everything. He's always been your favorite. You've always loved him more." He rolled his eyes. "Christ, I sound like Tommy Smothers."

"If I love him more," Joe said, ignoring the jest, "then I would have left you nothing. You're taken care of. I'm not so sure you deserve it, but you are taken care of. Does that satisfy you?"

"Taken care of *how*?" Stanley insisted. One would have thought he was arguing with a car salesman over the price of a new car, not dealing with a dying father about the dispensation of his estate. Stanley really was a cold son of a bitch. One look into his pitiless eyes as he sat there coolly appraising Joe was enough to prove it. Even his father's misery meant nothing to him. Stanley cared only about himself.

"Where is this will?" Stanley asked. "We'll need to know where it is anyway, so you might as well tell us now."

"You mean you'll need to know where it is when I'm dead."

"Yes," Stanley flatly stated. "When you're dead."

Joe took a click of time to contemplate the heartless way Stanley had spoken those words. Then he seemed to let it go. Maybe he expected nothing more from his eldest son than what he was getting. If it hurt him, he didn't let it show. "It's well-guarded, believe me. You'd be hard-pressed to find a better guard than the one watching over that will," Joe said with a mysterious smile. "That's all you need to know. And if you know what's good for you, you won't go looking for it. You'll find out what it says when the time is right, and not a minute before."

Even Frank looked faintly confused by that statement. "Pop, when the time is right, you'll already be gone. You won't be able to lead us to it."

"That's what you think," Joe said. "I've got ways. Even beyond the grave, I've got ways."

Stanley gave a derisive snort. "Well, I hope there's more than one copy of the damn thing floating around just in case."

"Nope," Joe said. "There's just one copy. One copy's all I needed to make my intentions known."

"Oh really," Stanley said, glancing first at Frank, then quickly at me. "One copy, huh?" It didn't take a genius to figure out what he was thinking. If he wasn't happy with the will he would destroy it and then half of everything would go to him, no matter what the damn thing said. It would be his word against ours.

"Oh really," he said again. This time he said it to himself, not to us. I wondered if he knew he had actually spoken the words out loud.

Joe's eyes had started to water up, but he wasn't crying. He was trying not to cough. He held the red handkerchief to his lips, just in case, but he never looked away from Stanley's face.

Silence reigned around the kitchen table while I wondered what the hell Joe had meant when he said the will was being guarded. Guarded by whom?

Frank tried to intercede in the growing animosity between Stanley and his father. "Pop, if you didn't call us together to tell us about the will, then what was it you *did* want to tell us?"

But suddenly Joe was no longer listening. Or, at least, he was no longer listening to *us*. He had the look of a man who has suddenly heard a voice inside his head, heard a voice speaking of things that he knew all along were true, but had never really allowed himself to believe before this moment.

He seemed to have learned, beyond all doubt, what it was he had come to this table to find out. One or both of his sons had made it clear to him at last.

As we sat there in a circle in that god-awful hot kitchen on that god-awful hot summer afternoon, I saw Joe gather his strength and push the voice in his head away. He had learned what he came here to learn, and now he would do what he had to do.

"I want to see the farm," he announced, turning his eyes to me. "Tom, I want to see the farm. Right now." And to Frank, he said, "You can roll me down to the pond in that old wheelchair of your mother's. I want to look the place over. I want to remember it the way it is."

Frank gave his dad a patient smile. "Pop, there's plenty of time for you to—"

"Now," Joe said. "I want to see the farm now. If you and Stanley don't want to come, then Tom won't mind taking me, will you Tom? You wouldn't deny an old man his final wish, would you?"

Stanley laughed at that. "Final wish, my ass. You'll probably outlive us all. Besides, I have to go into town. You boys can roll around the farm as much as you want. I've got things to do."

"Take the phone book with you," Joe said. "If you're scoping out lawyers, it'll make things a lot simpler to have all their addresses at hand. Save on the running around."

I could see by the startled look on Stanley's face that maybe Joe's statement wasn't too far off the mark. Maybe Stanley really was going to see what a couple of lawyers could make of all this.

But all he said was "Don't be silly."

And Joe said, "Okay, then, I won't."

I turned to Frank. "Where's the wheelchair?"

"Still in the attic, I think," he said.

"Well, then—"

We pushed ourselves away from the table while Stanley sat and watched us like we were all a bunch of whack jobs recently set loose from the local nuthouse. He made no move to join us, or to lend a hand, or to impede our leaving. He just sat there. I wondered if he was going to rifle Joe's bedroom while we were gone, searching for the will yet again.

At the squeak of chair legs on the kitchen linoleum, Pedro scrambled to his feet and gave himself a shake, causing the dining room table to rattle. By the time he was finished shaking, he was wide awake. He might not know where we were going, or what we intended to do when we got there, but it was obvious that he was more than ready to tag along for the ride. One destination to Pedro was pretty much the same as another. It was all about the journey for him. He didn't give two poops and a pop for where he ended up. (Listen to that. Two poops and a pop. I'm even starting to *talk* like an Indiana farmer.)

Joe patted his lap and Pedro leaped into it.

"Packed and ready to go," Joe said. "But first let me just do something in my bedroom. I'm sorry, boys, but I don't think I can walk."

So Frank and I dragged the dining room chair through the house with Joe and Pedro on it. It was the easiest way we could think of to get the job done. After Joe borrowed a pencil and paper from us, we left him by the window where the light was good and headed off to the attic to dig up Frank's mother's wheelchair.

IF JOE had weighed any more than the husk of the man he once was, it might have been a heck of a chore pushing that wheelchair around the farm. But as it was, he weighed about as much as a minute, so Frank and I, taking turns, managed the task fairly easily. We tried not to jar Joe's guts out, and he did groan a couple of times as we bounced him through mudholes and over rocks and across petrified wheel ruts and around assorted bumps and dips and piles of livestock poop, but usually he did all his groaning in a pretty good-natured way. Pedro, on the other hand, decided to walk after we collided with a fence post on our first trip through the backyard gate, sending him flying and very nearly unseating Joe as well. We were a little more careful after that, but as far as Pedro was concerned, our being careful was a matter of too little and too late. He'd take his chances on his feet, thank you very much, and if Joe wanted to risk his life sitting in that deathtrap of a vehicle, that was up to Joe, but Pedro was having no part of it. His mama didn't raise no fool. Chihuahua mamas rarely do.

Even I knew Joe was dying. And he was doing it before our very eyes. And I mean *soon*. The man was doing all he could just to sit upright as we bumped and banged our way across the barn lot in that squeaky old wheelchair. He gripped the armrests like they were the only things holding him to the planet. His knuckles were white, the veins on the backs of his gristly hands bulging like tree roots. He was using every ounce of strength he still wielded just to hang on.

But still, even as sick as he was, Joe looked about with a fine pride lighting his eyes as we trundled him around the place. He had lived his whole adult life on this spread of farmland. He had married here, raised two boys here, buried a wife here, and pretty much hung on to this farm by the skin of his teeth through all the slim times and the droughts and the market crashes when a bushel of wheat might not bring you enough to buy the loaf of bread that was made from it.

Frank kept giving me worried glances as we went along. His father's weakness was really scaring him now. Just since this morning, Joe seemed to have failed. When he coughed now, and that occurred more often than it ever had before, the cough was weak and barely audible. Joe kept the handkerchief to his mouth all the time. There was fear in his eyes but he tried not to let us see it.

As we moved along, Frank rested a hand on Joe's shoulder and in a gentle voice, pointed out different things he and I had accomplished in the weeks we had been here. A new stretch of fencing along the south side of the pasture. A new door on the hayloft because the other one had just about fallen off. A new framework of poles for the string beans in the garden. Sheets of tin we nailed into place at the side of the corncrib to prevent any more grain from leaking out. A dozen things. Most minor, but some that had taken a considerable amount of work. And those we were proudest of.

Joe praised it all. Every job. Big and small.

While Frank and I wrestled the wheelchair around the farm, sweating and grunting and burning up in the heat, Joe's skin felt cool to the touch. I wasn't sure how to explain that medically, but I didn't think it was good. Was his body shutting down? How could anyone *not* sweat in that heat and humidity?

"Joe, you feeling okay?" I asked.

He shrugged. "As good as a dying man *can* feel, I guess."

Frank started to protest but Joe didn't let him. He was tired of hearing people tell him he wasn't dying. I think I would have been a little tired of it myself. "You boys have done everything I asked you to do, and more. You managed to do some things I've been putting off for years. That hayloft door for instance. Tell me, and be honest. Did Stanley help at all?"

Frank looked embarrassed. "Well, you know Stanley—"

"Yeah, I do," Joe grinned. "That's why I'm asking. I want you boys to know that I played a pretty mean prank on Stanley just now, but dammit, he needed to be brought down a peg or two. He's just too all-fired cocky."

Frank laughed. "What'd you do?"

Joe shook his head. I'm not sure if he meant to answer, or he *didn't* mean to answer. And anyway, it doesn't matter. A coughing spell took him first, and this one was the worst we had seen. In the midst of it, a gout of blood issued from Joe's mouth and splattered down his shirtfront like magma overflowing the lip of a volcano. Joe's eyes popped open wide at the sight of all that blood, and I think he thought that was it. The end had come. I know I did.

"Oh Lord," Frank said, peeling off his T-shirt and using it to wipe the blood from Joe's face. Frank's hands were shaking. He looked at me with terrified eyes as he sopped up the mess. After that one spray of blood, the bleeding seemed to stop. Soon, Joe got his breath back. By this time, I had my shirt off too, and between the two of us, we got Joe pretty well cleaned up.

"Embarrassing," Joe managed to say.

Frank knelt down beside the wheelchair and took Joe's hands in his. "No, Pop. I'm just sorry you're going through it. Feeling better now? Want to go back to the house?" Frank touched his father's forehead. "You're too cool, Pop. I don't like it. It's hotter than hell out here and you feel like a popsicle."

"The pond," Joe said. "I want to see the pond. And feel the wind on my face. There's always a cool breeze down there. It'll be nice in the shade of the trees. You boys can sit for a spell. Maybe paddle your feet in the water."

Frank didn't seem to think it was such a good idea, but he wasn't about to argue. "Okay, Pop. If that's what you want."

We were still in the barn lot in sight of the house, so I took the chair handles and we set off for the pond, just like Joe wanted us to. I took it nice and slow so we wouldn't jar Joe any more than we had to. Pedro pranced alongside the wheelchair, now and then looking up at me, then looking at Joe, and occasionally looking at Frank. I don't think he knew what was going on, but he certainly knew something wasn't right. He had been around me long enough to sense a disaster building a mile off.

We rounded the barn, and as if we didn't have enough to worry about, we came face to face with Samson. He was inside his pen, rooting around in the mud by the carcass of that rusty old pickup truck. He looked up when he heard us coming.

He snorted like a locomotive, just like he usually did, and much to my surprise, Joe gathered up what little strength he had left and let out with a falsetto, "Soo, pig! Soo, pig!" And I'll be damned if Samson didn't come running like a mammoth cocker spaniel right up to the fence. The last time I saw Samson that close to the fence he was trying to plow his way through it so he could rip me and Frank to pieces. Now he just stuck his snout through the metal bars like Trigger saying howdy to his old pal Roy. Joe pulled an apple out of his trouser pocket, wiped a little blood from it on his pajama leg, and stuck his hand through the fence.

I figured that was the last we would see of Joe's hand, and probably a goodly portion of his arm too, but Samson spread wide those nasty jaws of his with the six-inch tusks going off in every direction like spearpoints, and as daintily as the Queen of England plucking a crumpet from her breakfast plate, Samson snagged that apple out of Joe's hand as slick as you please. A Vanderbilt couldn't have done it with more delicacy.

"Soo, pig," Joe said, softer this time, while Samson snorted and snuffled and chowed down on that apple like he hadn't eaten in a week, which was bullshit. I had fed him that morning. And as usual, I had fed him, then took off running like a rabbit. It seemed like a prudent thing to do when dealing with a fourteen hundred-pound insane hog with tusks.

Joe had a smile on his face as we sat there watching Samson make applesauce. I think Frank and I were too stunned to smile. We just watched that damned hog like we had never seen him before in our lives.

Joe's voice was hoarse, but still there was happiness in it. He had a pensive look on his face, like maybe he was being bombarded with a million memories at once. Not a bad thing for a dying man to experience, I suppose. "I had fun watching you boys grow up," he said, still watching Samson chomp away at the apple. "I wish your mom could've been around longer. She would be pleased by how you both turned out so handsome and strong."

Joe reached out from the wheelchair and took my hand with his one hand and Frank's hand with his other. "She loved you boys so much. She was a fine woman, your mom."

When I gathered enough courage to look in Frank's direction, I saw exactly what I expected to see. Tears. Coursing down his cheeks.

Joe looked up at me and gave a little jump. "Good lord, Tom. I'm sorry. I was thinking you were someone else for a minute. Daydreaming, I guess."

"It's okay, sir. I don't mind at all."

He squeezed my hand, then released me. He held onto Frank's while he said, "Let's go on down to the pond now, if it ain't too much trouble."

"No trouble at all, Pop," Frank said, his voice weak with emotion.

I nodded in agreement. "Just point the way."

We rounded Samson's pen and took off across the pasture through knee-high wildflowers and clover. Being only about nine inches tall, Pedro found the going a little rough, so he decided to ride the rest of the way in Joe's lap. Joe seemed glad to have him on board.

"Frank," Joe said. "I got a call from Jeff Moody's dad. He's interested in buying the farm when I'm gone."

Frank glanced at me and I knew what he was thinking. Maybe that's what was going on in the washhouse that day. Maybe Stanley was greasing the wheels of commerce, so to speak.

"I told him to talk to you, Frank. That means the word is out. I'm leaving the farm in your name. You'll have trouble with Stanley when he finds out."

Frank sighed. "I can handle Stanley."

"Good. Try to do it without a lawyer. A lawyer will end up owning the farm before he's done. Nobody pads a bill like a lawyer."

Frank laughed, but Joe looked up at him with one eyebrow cocked, as if to say, "You think I'm kidding?"

Frank finally had to ask. "You told us in the kitchen that we were both in the will. So if I'm getting the farm, what is Stanley getting, Pop?"

"Money. Your mother left a $20,000 savings account for you boys. It was an inheritance from her father who died when you were just a baby. We held onto it all these years without getting into it, and that wasn't easy, let me tell you. But we managed it somehow. I'm going to give Stanley that money, since he has no interest in the farm."

"He won't be satisfied with that," Frank said. "He's going to want half of everything."

"He'll get what he can get, and what he can get is the $20,000. He doesn't deserve anything else. He'll be satisfied. He doesn't have a choice."

I could see the cows off in the distance. They were escaping the heat of the day by lingering in the shade beneath the willows, occasionally dipping their noses into the pond for a cooling drink. Off to the right, I could hear nine hundred chickens bitching about something, probably me, but I chose to ignore them. As soon as we stepped into the shady patch under the trees and I felt the coolness of the air brush my face and dry the sweat on my back, I was in too much bliss to let myself be angered by a bunch of damned chickens. I'd argue with them later.

I found a nice level spot in the shade to park the wheelchair where Joe could look out over the pond and the pasture and the tree line that bordered his property off in the distance. The sun was yellow-white and as hot as fire in the afternoon sky, but under the trees, all that sizzling sunshine was little more than a memory. No wonder the cows spent their days down here. It was a lovely spot.

"You boys go sit by the water and relax," Joe said. "I'd like to be alone for a few minutes."

I was surprised when Frank took my hand and led me down to the water. Until that moment, we had rarely displayed our affection for each other in his father's presence. The fact that Frank chose this particular moment to do so, and the easy way he went about it, made me love the man even more than I already did.

We sat on the pond bank with our backs to Joe, to give him his privacy, and we did as he suggested. We kicked off our shoes and socks and rolled up our pant legs to dangle our feet in the cold water. We felt no need to speak, Frank and I. We felt no need to demonstrate our love any more than we already had. Frank and I knew the love was there. Joe knew it too. Smiling, I lay back in the grass and closed my eyes. I wiggled my toes in the cool mud at the bottom of the pond and hoped there weren't any snakes in the water.

"You're worried about snakes," Frank said.

"Maybe," I smiled.

"You'd be smarter to worry about snapping turtles," Frank said, and when I jerked my legs up out of the water, he laughed like a lunatic.

Frank pulled me back down beside him and coaxed my feet back into the water. Again we held hands. The buzz of insects and the song of sparrows in the treetops lulled us into silence. Amid the occasional huff and clomp of a cow stomping away a fly, and the soothing rustling of the willow branches overhead, gently swaying and billowing in the lazy summer breeze, I found myself dozing. I dreamed of lying beside a cool mountain stream. Frank and I were naked, making love on a mossy hillside. There were Alps in the background, and the mountain stream was quaintly babbling. Orchestra music was tuning up on the other side of the hill, and Julie Andrews's helicopter was just swooping in over the treetops to pan in for a close-up.

When I woke up I was grinning.

Until I heard Frank sob.

FRANK was kneeling in the grass beside Joe's wheelchair. We were both shirtless because we had used our shirts to clean the blood from

Joe earlier. Our pant legs were rolled up because we had been napping with our feet dangling in the cool pond. Joe sat just as we had left him, his arms on the armrests of the wheelchair, his feet properly placed on the footrests, his chin now down upon his chest as if he had fallen asleep.

But he wasn't asleep.

When I stirred, Frank turned to me. Tears streamed down his face and splashed onto his bare chest. He held his father's hand in one of his, and with his other hand, he stroked his father's hair. Dappled shadows fluttered over them where the sun peeked through the wind-tossed willows above their heads. The sun on the horizon was sliding toward evening, but I knew that away from the trees, the day would be just as hot as it was before. Maybe hotter. As usual, even nighttime would not bring relief from the heat.

Joe's eyes were closed, his face at peace for the first time since I had met him.

His pain was finally gone.

I didn't know how long Frank had been crying. Minutes maybe. Not longer.

"He was like this when I woke up," Frank said, reaching out to me. He bit back a sob and tried to pull himself together. "Just—gone. He slipped away while we were dozing."

Frank was only a couple of feet away, so I crawled toward him on my knees and drew him into my arms. He pressed his face into the crook of my neck and I stroked his smooth back, even then feeling urges I should have been ashamed of under the circumstances. The heat of his body. The texture of his flesh. The strength of his arms around me. The smell of the man. His gentleness. All the things that made Frank who he was. I ignored my urges as best I could, turning to Joe instead.

I stretched out my hand and patted Joe's knee to say good-bye. It seemed so thin and still beneath my hand. Like a child's knee.

Even now, with death at my elbow, earthly matters interceded. I looked around. "Where's Pedro?"

Frank pointed fifty yards into the pasture, where Pedro was chasing a young calf around in circles. They both seemed to be having a good time, the calf kicking up her hind legs now and then with the exuberance of youth while Pedro sped through the wildflowers, yipping happily, his ears erect, his tail slapping back and forth like a tiny windshield wiper. The calf's mother blandly watched their shenanigans, calmly chewing her cud while she peed on a bush with the force of a fire hose. I don't think she had ever seen a Chihuahua before. She looked mildly confused.

A sad smile played across Frank's face as he watched Pedro frolic with the calf. "Now that Pop is gone, maybe Pedro figures his work is done. Time for fun and games again."

"He stayed with Joe just about every minute these last few days," I said. "I guess the little guy has earned some time off."

"That he has," Frank said. "That he has."

I turned back to Frank. "What do we do?" I asked. "About your dad, I mean. I've never—"

Frank drew in a deep, shuddering breath. "Let's get him back to the house. We can call whoever needs to be called from there."

I put my hand to either side of Frank's face and kissed his forehead. "I'm so sorry, babe. He was a great guy, your dad. I'm going to miss him."

Frank nodded. "Me too. He liked you, you know."

"I know," I said. "I liked him too."

We let fond memories flood our minds for a minute as we knelt there in the weeds holding each other, with Frank still clutching his father's lifeless hand. Finally, we blinked ourselves back to reality. We fished around through the weeds until we found our shoes and socks. Once they were on, we set out for the farmhouse, pushing the silent wheelchair before us.

It seemed strange that Joe was no longer in it, yet the weight of him was still there.

We took our time, with Pedro following along in our trail of trampled weeds and wildflowers. He made no move to hitch a ride. I guess he knew his friend was no longer there to welcome him aboard. By the time we reached the farmhouse, the sun was sliding toward evening.

Stanley was nowhere around to greet us. He would not return until Joe had left his cherished farm forever, hauled away in a black vinyl body bag in the back of a 2003 Cadillac hearse with _Simmons Funeral Home_ etched on the side windows, and plates that said LOVED1.

Standing on the front porch, watching the hearse drive away with Joe, I almost lifted my hand to wave good-bye. I wonder if Joe would have seen me if I had.

Chapter
Sixteen

STANLEY came home at midnight. He was so drunk he could barely put one foot in front of the other. Frank and I were stretched out on the sofa in the living room in each other's arms, snuggling. I was comforting Frank the best way I knew how—by holding him, petting him, being there for him. Frank had been talking softly about what a wonderful father his dad had been. Pedro lay at our feet, sometimes watching us, sometimes snoring. His tummy was soft against my foot. Once in a while he would lick my ankle. That was Pedro's way of being there for me.

"He only spanked me once," Frank said, remembering. "And that was because I was threatening to kill Stanley with a butcher knife." He laughed a sad little laugh. "That boy and I just never did get along."

The farmhouse seemed oddly incomplete with Joe gone. We both sensed it. It was like someone had snipped out the heart of it. Without Joe, the shadows seemed a little drearier, the wallpaper a little more faded, the empty rooms a little lonelier. I looked around at the dimly lit walls, the family photos hanging on nails containing a million memories that didn't include me, the piano in the corner that no one ever played. Lace curtains, limp with age, moved in the wind from the ever-present fan sitting and thrumming on a side table. It was the same fan that had been in the kitchen earlier and it sounded like a Sherman tank grinding up a hill. I figured it would be giving up the ghost one of these days, and we'd have to buy a new one, thank God. I couldn't wait. I was tired of listening to it. The windows were pushed open as far as they would go to let in a little night air, but it didn't help much. Frank and I were both sweating, lying there in each other's arms.

"I don't remember my mom much," Frank said, his lips pressed against my cheek, his fingers idly moving through my hair. Our groins were pressed together, but not in a sexual way. It was more just a connection. A joining. I had never felt so close to anyone in my life. To my way of thinking, Frank and I were damn near one entity. It was an astonishing feeling, and one I had never experienced before with anyone, even Jerry. Sometimes I wondered if I had ever really known love at all before Frank came along.

"Mom was real pretty when she was young. I'll show you a picture later. Dad was pretty much a hottie too. They were a good-looking couple. She died when I was little, so there might be a memory of her stuck in my head somewhere, but it's pretty indistinct. I can't put my finger on it. I can't really see her."

That was when Stanley came stumbling through the front door, causing us both to jump.

He giggled when he saw us on the couch. "Uh-oh, little brother's having a sexual interlude."

We didn't bother denying it. He could see we had our clothes on. As clothed as the temperature would allow at least. Shorts and T-shirts, which was actually about two items too many, considering the weather.

Stanley stomped off toward the kitchen, probably to build one of his two-foot tall sandwiches. Drinking is hungry work. He was almost there when he sensed something was wrong and stopped dead in his tracks.

Before he could turn to face us, Frank said, "Pop is gone, Stanley. He passed away this afternoon. Down by the pond. Mr. Simmons came and got him about five o'clock. He's down at the funeral home. They're—getting him ready. First viewing'll be tomorrow, I guess. I would have called you but I didn't know where you were."

Stanley didn't seem to know what to say. First he turned to look at us. Then he blinked himself sober and ran a hand through his hair. Finally, he plopped himself down in Joe's old chair and kicked off his black tennis shoes with the orange laces. I couldn't believe he was still wearing those stupid things.

"I don't suppose Pop had the foresight to tell you where the will was stashed before he passed on, did he?"

Frank's eyes narrowed, his voice took on a slight edge. "No, he didn't."

Stanley grunted. "Figures."

I could see Frank forcing himself to be cordial. He didn't want to fight. He was so wrung out with grief he didn't have any fight left in him. "We'll have to go into town in the morning and make all the arrangements. Flowers. The service. What music we want them to play. Simmons said he'd find us a preacher, so we don't have to worry about that. And the funeral is paid for. Pop paid for his and Mom's at the same time when she died. I didn't know that until Simmons told me. At least it's one less thing we have to worry—"

"And he didn't say one goddamn word about where the will was." It wasn't a question, it was a statement. Stanley was getting mad.

Frank sighed. "No. I'm sorry. He didn't."

"Do you *know* what it says?"

"Not really," Frank lied.

I knew what he was thinking. He wasn't ready to open up that kettle of fish tonight. Not with Joe still warm, splayed out on a slab down at Simmons Funeral Home, and Stanley drunk, and himself exhausted to the bone. No one needed a knockdown drag-out battle before the funeral, even if Stanley was spoiling for one. Joe had told them everything concerning his wishes would come to light at the proper time. Frank was going to rely on that.

In other words, why make waves where there was a tsunami coming in anyway?

I watched Stanley during this exchange for any sign of mourning at his father's passing. I saw none. Zip. Nada. He did not shed a tear. He did not even have the good grace to pretend to look sad. The only emotion that registered on Stanley's face was anger that Joe had departed the planet without clearing everything up before he left. Everything concerning the will, that is. That was all Stanley cared about.

"We'll have to go into town early to make the arrangements," Frank said. "Apparently Pop already picked out a coffin way back when, but still there's a dozen other—"

"You handle it," Stanley said.

Frank was still in my arms, but he was so tense now it was like holding a stack of lumber.

"All right," Frank said, as if he had expected it all along. "I can do that."

Stanley stood and moved on his stockinged feet across the living room floor and down the hall to Joe's bedroom door. It was already open, so he reached in and flicked on the overhead light. He stood there a moment peering in.

"This is the one room I haven't really searched," he said, more to himself than to us.

I jumped when Frank yelled, *"Don't you care that Pop died? Don't you give a shit? What the hell is wrong with you?"*

When Stanley looked back at Frank, his eyes were cold. Emotionless. "I just want what's mine, little brother. And I intend to get it." With that, he turned and stepped into Joe's bedroom.

He softly closed the bedroom door behind him. We heard the lock click.

Apparently Stanley wished to conduct his search for the will without any interruptions from us.

If I was as big a dick as he was, I'd probably feel the same way.

Frank seemed to give up then. He rolled back into my arms, limp with sadness, and eventually we fell asleep.

Morning rolled around long before we were ready for it.

FRANK and I were showered and dressed and ready to go into town by nine. We had raced through the morning chores as quickly as possible and were now just sitting down for a bite of breakfast before we took off. I didn't tell Frank, but I had my checkbook and a couple of credit cards stashed in my back pocket just in case there were expenses to be paid that Joe had not arranged for, and I was sure there would be. Flowers for the service, the printing of announcements, a blurb in the local obits, death certificates. These things all cost money, and Frank was too upset to think about them, plus he didn't have any money on hand that I knew of. I was more than happy to help him out. I only hoped he wouldn't give me too much of an argument over it.

Stanley was still locked inside his father's bedroom. It sounded like he was rearranging the furniture.

"Hope he doesn't knock any walls out, the dumb shit," Frank said as he hurried through his cereal.

He hadn't cried yet this morning, but I knew the upcoming ordeal would be hard for Frank. He had loved his dad very much. And the business end of dying is truly an ordeal, an ordeal that comes right when a person is at their most vulnerable. Working in a bank, I had seen a lot of the turmoil firsthand. I had even caused a bit of it, refusing access to accounts to loved ones, freezing monies until a death certificate was provided, confiscating ATM cards. It was all perfectly legal, and sometimes a necessity, but it was still pretty cold-blooded. It was one of the things I had hated most about the job.

My Toyota was still acting goofy since our marathon ride across country, so we decided to take Joe's pickup into town. We were just headed out the door when Stanley finally emerged from Joe's bedroom.

He looked like he had been up all night—unshaven, still wearing the clothes he'd had on the night before, his hair sticking straight up off the top of his head like he had spent the last few hours experimenting with nuclear fusion. His eyes were red and bleary. I knew why when he reached into the fridge without so much as a how-do-you-do and snatched another beer off the rack. He had been drinking all night.

Not only did he look like crap, he also looked pretty darned pleased with himself. Even more than he usually did, and that was saying something, the prick.

"Found it," he announced, just one notch below gloating.

"The will?" I asked.

But Stanley ignored me. His eyes were trained on Frank. "Pop must have been cracking up those last few days. He actually drew a treasure map to the will. Anyway, I found the map. By the time you get back from town, I'll have it figured out and I'll have the will in my hot little hands, and I'll tell you something, Frank. If it says what I think it's going to say, you'd better find yourself a good lawyer. I'm not going to let him leave this spread to you alone. It's half mine. Just because you pulled a few more years' worth of weeds on it than I did is no reason for him to leave me out in the cold. I'll have my share, by God, or I'll burn the place to the ground. That's a promise."

By the time Stanley finished talking, Frank was so mad he was shaking. "Do what you have to do, *brother*." He spoke the words with a dangerous calm, then turned and walked away.

I meekly followed. I had never seen Frank that mad before. Wow. I was getting a hard-on. Of course, a happy Frank gave me a hard-on too, so I couldn't really read too much into it.

"Bye, girls," Stanley cooed as we walked out the door.

"Bye, shit-for-brains," I muttered, following Frank outside.

I heard Stanley spitting out a nasty laugh as I pulled the door shut behind us.

SIMMONS FUNERAL HOME was on the outskirts of town in a renovated gothic monstrosity that must have once housed the Hoosier version of the Addams family. Or the Munsters. I wasn't sure which. I fully expected Lurch or Thing to greet us at the door but they must have been out to lunch. Nothing met us at the door except the reek of a million forgotten mums and carnations and the faint, but lingering, stench of formaldehyde and heartache.

Simon Simmons was a little wiry guy who looked like he had been marinating in his own embalming fluid too long. There wasn't an ounce of fat on him. And not much meat either. We found him behind a desk in a back room filled with brochures of caskets and funeral plots and a full array of Amway products. I guess he offered a little something for everybody, dead or alive.

When he was at rest, Simmons wore a dour expression on his pinched little face, just as you would expect a mortician to do. But when he smiled, he positively glowed. Every square inch of his face came alive like the flowering of a neutron bomb. He was obviously a happy man deep down inside, in spite of his chosen line of work, and damned if he was going to let anyone prove otherwise.

Frank and I presented ourselves, and he flew to his feet all aflutter like a frightened starling. His black suit and wispy black hair and the fact he was so damned scrawny helped heighten the bird impression. We needed no introductions, of course. He had met us the night before. It was Mr. Simmons who had driven the hearse to pick up Joe's body.

We had so much to think about, Frank and I, and so many plans to make, and we were both still so stunned by Joe's sudden passing that we didn't have time to pamper ourselves with issues of social anxiety. Shyness was the last thing on our minds. So we simply did what we came to do, without the usual display of nail-chewing angst and histrionics.

Simmons eyed Frank up and down like he was measuring him for an eternity suit. "You don't remember me, but I remember you. I didn't want to mention it last night out at the farm, what with everything else going on, but I knew you when you were about knee-high to a woollyworm." Then he laughed. He seemed to laugh a lot, and when he did laugh, he sounded like he meant it. He was without a doubt the happiest undertaker I had ever met in my life.

"How's that?" Frank asked. "How did you know me?" He was busy casting nervous glances at the casket photos and other funerary paraphernalia scattered around, but he was still polite. Frank was always polite.

"Son, your pa and I go way back. I guess you don't know this, but we served in Vietnam together."

That caught Frank's attention. "You did?"

"Yes, sir, we did." And Simmons laughed again. A big old cackle. Just like a happy vulture. Or a jovial condor. One could almost imagine his feathers fluffing up in glee. "Your pa helped me through the loss of a loved one once." Simmons glanced at me, giving me a friendly nod in the process. "A loved one not unlike your friend Tom here, I reckon. He was a fine man, your daddy. And a good soldier too. Joe Wells had a good heart. And a fair heart. And a brave one. He surely did. I don't think he ever looked down on a soul in his life. Everybody was equal in his eyes, and that's a fact."

Frank glanced at me at the same moment I glanced at him. This was the guy Joe had told us about. The guy who lost his lover in the war. It had to be.

Simmons saw that we knew the story about the same time that we realized who he was. He could see it in our eyes, I guess. "I see he told you." Then Simon Simmons really let loose with a mountainous laugh that must have got the corpses chuckling in other parts of the building no matter what state of decomposition they were in. "He told me I put a curse on him, you know."

Frank was smiling wide, watching the little gay undertaker flap around like a bantam rooster. "A curse?"

"Yeah. A curse. A gay one, in fact. He said it was my fault his two boys ended up light on their feet. Said I must have done something to his chromosomes back there in the jungle somehow when we were fighting the Vietcong. Maybe when I drank from his thermos. Or when he drank from mine. I told your daddy he was nuts, but now seeing you boys, I'm not so sure. Lovers, are you?"

"Yes, sir," Frank and I said at the very same moment. It almost sounded rehearsed.

Simmons smiled. "It's nice to hear you say it like that, in unison and all, in the same voice with the same conviction. Maybe you'll beat the odds and actually make a go of it, like my buddy and I did until— well, until he died. I hope you do, anyway. There ain't nothing like living in the shadow of love, boys. Nothing. Remember that. Say, Frank, what was your brother's name? Stumpy?"

Frank laughed for the first time in two days. "Stanley. His name is Stanley."

Simmons knocked on his head with a knuckle like a maple farmer checking the sap on the inside of a tree. I could have sworn I heard a faint bonking sound when he did. "Oh yeah. Stanley. "

"A true putz," Frank said. And the three of us laughed. Simmons went so far as to turn beet-red and bend over and pound on his knees for about ten seconds. Lord, what a happy guy.

And in the space of a heartbeat, he turned solemn. Just like that. One second he was howling with mirth and the next second he looked like his favorite dog had just been run over by a dump truck. "I've got something for you, Frank. Your daddy left it with me to give to you when this day came. Either you or Stumpy. I mean Stanley. I guess Joe didn't put much faith in banks or lawyers."

"No, he didn't," Frank said, curious, watching Simmons go to a beat-up old filing cabinet in the corner of the room and fish around for a minute until he pulled out a business-sized manila envelope. This he handed to Frank. When Frank had his hands on it, Simmons took a step backward and clasped his hands behind his back, as if to say he now considered his obligation fulfilled to the letter.

"It's your daddy's will," Simmons explained. "He asked me a few months ago to put it away somewhere safe. It was right after he found out he was sick, I reckon. I've been holding onto it ever since."

Frank and I were speechless. We both stared at the envelope in Frank's hand. We didn't need to open it. We knew what it said. But if this was truly the will, then what the hell was Stanley's treasure map leading to? What was it Stanley was going to find when he finished looking for whatever it was Joe had sent him scampering off to look for?

Apparently the same questions were running through Frank's mind that were running through mine. It didn't take either one of us long to figure it out. At the very same moment, we turned to each other, and said, "The prank."

Frank looked back down at the envelope. "My God," he said. "Pop's going to lead Stanley on a wild goose chase for this will, and then we're gonna have to deal with him when he finds out it was all a joke. Shit, Pop. What were you thinking?"

Simmons cocked his head to the side and watched us for a minute, then said, "I don't pretend to know what you boys are talking about, but I can see you've got things to do. So let's finish up our business, and I'll let you be on your way. Now most of the business has already been taken care of. Your daddy was real insistent on how he wanted things done."

When Simmons was finished talking, twenty minutes later, we knew what had been done, what needed to be done, and how much money it would all cost, which in the grand scheme of things wasn't that much. Joe had been pretty thorough in his preparations.

Simmons gave us the name and number of a florist who wouldn't overcharge us for floral arrangements. He handed over a fistful of death certificates which he said we would need sooner or later for various things, and not to worry about the cost, that was his contribution to the enterprise. He gave us a phone number to the local newspaper for handling the obituary and made Frank promise to come right back with his father's suit as soon as we could go out to the farm to get it. We hadn't thought to bring it with us. We picked out the music for the service, a couple of hymns Frank remembered from Bible school when he was a kid, decided how many funeral cars we would need for the procession to the graveyard, and decided on a tent so everybody wouldn't have to stand in the hot sun during the graveside services.

And that was it.

Joseph Allen Wells would be on view at the Simmons Funeral Home by six o'clock that evening (if we got his suit to him on time) in the mid-range oak casket with the bronze handles and the silver damask lining which he had picked out and paid for a decade earlier. Two days later he would be interred at the Nine Mile Greene County Cemetery in plot #326, which he had also picked out a decade earlier when he buried his wife, Melissa Joanne Wells, in plot #325, right next door. The dual headstone was already in place. The stonecutter just had to carve a date on Frank's side of it to let posterity know when he died.

Simmons would send us a bill for that work when it was finished to our satisfaction.

Suddenly the business of Frank's father's funeral was completed and we found ourselves, Frank and I, a little breathless, back out on the street after Simon Simmons ushered us out the back door with armfuls of mortuary pamphlets, perpetual care brochures, a couple of ice-cold diet sodas from his vending machine since it was so goddamn hot, and a shoebox full of Amway samples.

In a state of shock, or close to it, we aimed ourselves toward the truck and home.

Now we had to go head-to-head with Stumpy, and neither one of us was looking forward to *that* confrontation, you can rest assured.

IT DIDN'T feel like going home, knowing Joe wasn't there. For either of us.

We parked between my Toyota and Stanley's rental car, heaved ourselves out of the truck cab like a couple of hundred-year-old men, that's how despondent and worn out we were, and headed for the house, still lugging all our booty from Simon Simmons. The Amway laundry detergent looked especially enticing. I wondered if it was formulated to work on ground-in cow shit.

When we opened the front door, it felt like we were stepping into an oven. A big, hot, silent oven.

Too silent.

"Pedro!" I called out.

Not a peep.

"Stanley!" Frank yelled.

Nothing.

"Well, this can't be good," Frank muttered.

We dumped all our crap on the kitchen table and went straight to Joe's room. Or what *used* to be Joe's room. Since he was no longer residing on the same mortal plane as the rest of us, we supposed it could be *anybody's* room now. Or nobody's.

Whoever it now belonged to, the place was a shambles. Stanley had done everything but bring in earthmoving equipment in his search for Joe's will. The dresser drawers were on the floor with all their belongings spilled out in every direction. The mattress was off the bed and leaning against the wall, and all the clothes in the closet had been flung, piece by piece, through the door and onto the bathroom floor. It looked like every pocket in every garment had been turned out.

Stanley had obviously been a man on a mission. The dick.

With a tsk, Frank bent and retrieved his dad's suit from the rubble. It had been removed from the garment bag it usually hung in, and it took Frank a while to locate the trousers that went with the jacket. When he had them both together, he arranged them neatly on a wooden hanger and carried them out into the living room. One of us would have to run it back to town.

I did my bit by finding a shirt and tie I thought would go nicely with the suit and carried them into the living room as well. I wasn't sure about shoes. Do dead men wear shoes to the grave? Just in case they did, I went back and found a pair of black dress shoes and a pair of black socks to go with them.

That was about all we could do as far as Joe's burial ensemble went. Now we still had the mystery of figuring out what had happened to Pedro and Stanley. Where the hell were they?

Frank and I spread out. He took the rest of the house, and I ran out the back door calling Pedro's name. Personally, I didn't give a rat's ass where Stanley was, but I was seriously worried about my dog.

I found all the other farm dogs lounging around the backyard, but Pedro wasn't humping any of them. I checked inside the washhouse on the off chance that Stanley was perhaps getting it on with a passing sheepherder since they are notorious for fucking assholes, and Stanley was certainly one of those, but that didn't pan out either. The washhouse was empty.

I was standing by the back gate, trying to decide where to search next, when Frank stuck his head through the kitchen window behind me.

"Did you hear that?" he asked in a hushed voice.

I hadn't heard anything. "No. What was it?"

"Sounded like Pedro." Frank pulled his head back through the kitchen window and two seconds later he was standing beside me by the gate. He cocked his head to the side. "Listen," he said.

I listened.

And off in the distance, somewhere out behind the barn I thought it was, I heard what sounded like a coloratura hitting a slightly off-kilter high C and sustaining it long enough to collapse a lung. The eerie note just went on and on and on. It was so creepy and so high-pitched that at first it didn't quite register on the human ear. Like a car alarm twenty blocks over.

But this was no car alarm. It was Pedro, all right. And he was in trouble.

Frank and I flung ourselves through the back gate and took off running. As we ran, Pedro's eerie cry grew louder and louder, until we burst around the east corner of the barn and plowed right into Samson's fence. We pulled up short in a cloud of dust, sweating like field hands. It was too damn hot to be running around like that.

At this range, Pedro's creepy cries made the hair on the back of my sweaty neck do a cakewalk. It was like the keening wail of a banshee swooping across the Scottish moors. Or fingernails on a blackboard. Take your pick.

But where was it coming from?

At first glance, Samson's pen seemed to be empty. There was nothing there but the hog trough, the half-carcass of the rusted out '52 Chevy pickup perched on its ass off in the distance, a couple of mudholes, and about two tons of pig poop scattered about. Samson's bowels seemed to be in fine fettle, even if he was crazy.

Then the wailing stopped, and a tiny trembling face peeked up through the busted-out side window of the derelict truck. It was Pedro.

His eyes were as big as golf balls in his little apple-shaped head. When he saw me, he let out a yip.

"Good Lord," I gasped. "What the hell is he doing in there?"

I started to climb over the fence to go fetch the little guy, but Frank pulled me back. "Are you crazy?" he hissed. "Where's Samson?"

And then we heard the other sound. It was sort of a wet, snuffling, guttural, chomping sound. The sound you might imagine a hippopotamus would make while it was eating a truckload of watermelons.

"What's that?" I whispered.

"I don't think I want to know," Frank whispered back.

While I watched, Pedro dropped down onto the truck seat and disappeared from the window. Then he popped up on the other side of the cab, and I saw the back of his head as he peered through that window in the opposite direction. A second later, he disappeared again.

The next thing I knew, Pedro was flying through the window on our side of that rusty old truck like he had been shot from a cannon. It was a pretty good drop, so he landed hard. He did a couple of somersaults when he hit the ground, but he didn't bother wasting his breath yipping or whining about it, he just took off running like Jesse Owens once he regained his footing. He headed straight for us, his tiny ears flapping in his jet stream, his tail tucked under his butt like it always did when he was having a bad day, and I figured this would certainly qualify as one of *those*.

Pedro was no more than twenty feet from the truck when Satan himself came tearing around the front fender and shot out after him like a freight train. It wasn't really Satan, of course. It was Samson. But I'd be hard-pressed to explain to you the actual difference.

Samson, for all his singleness of purpose, was no match for Pedro when it came to speed. Pedro was across that pen, sailing through the fence like a bolt of lightning, and leaping into my arms before Samson got all of his fourteen hundred pounds of lard moving in the same direction. But when he did, it was an awesome sight.

Samson hit the fence behind Pedro like a test car plowing into a brick wall. The impact of it knocked Frank and me on our asses, but it did even more than that to Samson. This time apparently, when he hit the fence, he hit it a smidgeon too hard. Even Samson's iron skull couldn't properly absorb the shock of the collision.

Samson's piggy eyes crossed, a slightly confused expression befuddled his ugly face, and he keeled over onto his side like Fatty Arbuckle doing a pratfall off the side of a building. *Whump!*

Frank and I pulled ourselves to our feet and warily approached the fence while Pedro growled and trembled and peed in my arms. I was so stunned, I didn't even mind.

It wasn't until we were really sure that Samson was out for the count that we leaned across the fence and looked down at him lying there.

Then we recoiled.

"Oh God," Frank said, looking over at me.

"Oh God," I echoed, looking back at him.

"Yip," Pedro commented, looking up at both of us as if he knew it all along.

Then the three of us looked back over the fence at Samson's gigantic head lying there in the dust.

His snout and jowls were smeared with blood, but we could tell it wasn't his.

In fact, the blood wasn't really what shocked us at all.

What shocked us from the tops of our heads all the way down to the soles of our feet was that pathetic orange shoe string dangling from Samson's tusk.

FOR the second time in two days, the Cadillac hearse from Simmons Funeral Home was parked outside the house. This time there was a squad car parked next to it that belonged to the County Sheriff.

"A waste of gas," Simmons was saying to whoever felt like listening. "I could have pedaled out here on my bicycle with a bucket on my arm to carry away the remains. That hog pretty much ate most of it. Biggest damn pig I ever saw in my life. Mean fucker too. Oughtta be shot."

Simmons had the good sense to look embarrassed when he realized Frank was listening. He mumbled an apology and shuffled off shaking his head. I wasn't sure if he was apologizing for saying Samson should be shot or for commenting on the fact that there wasn't enough left of Stanley to fill more than two or three burritos.

The County Sheriff wasn't so easy to get rid of. He was talking to Frank and me with a slightly bemused expression on his face and not even bothering to take any notes. I had an unsettling hunch that he wasn't believing everything we said, and frankly, I couldn't say I blamed him.

"*Why* did you say you think your brother was dumb enough to climb into that pen with that monster?" The sheriff had his hand up under his baseball cap scratching his scalp. He seemed to do that a lot when he was trying to think.

Frank scooted a couple of mud clods across the ground with the toe of his shoe. I could tell he wasn't comfortable with this line of questioning. Who would be? "Well—my dad sort of played a prank on my brother, and well—it ate him."

"Singular prank," the sheriff said.

"You bet," I said, and the sheriff looked at me like now would be a pretty good time for me to shut the hell up. So I did.

"So you're saying what we have here is a homicide." The sheriff pondered what he had just said, and I could see he wasn't buying that either.

I couldn't resist. "A hogicide," I corrected him.

"More like a dickicide," Frank said, and the two of us started laughing. And in the middle of our laughter, while the sheriff was looking at us like we were crazy, Frank stopped laughing and started crying. Needless to say, emotions were running high, and a lot of those emotions were bumping heads with each other. Creep or not, Stanley *was* Frank's brother. But Lord, what a ridiculous way to go. It was a confusing situation all around.

Frank sucked in a deep breath and tried to pull himself together long enough to explain things once again to the sheriff in the best and simplest way he knew how. "Look, Sheriff. It's like this. Before Pop died, he drew up a map for Stanley because he knew Stanley was all fired up about the will and he wanted to know what he was getting when Dad passed away. The bogus map, which was really just a practical joke on my dad's part, said the will was stashed in the glove box of that old pickup truck over there, so my brother decided to go and get it."

"And you know this how?" the Sheriff asked, looking askance at Frank like he had never seen anything quite like Frank in his life.

"We found the map in Pop's bedroom while we were waiting for you to get here."

"I see," the Sheriff said. "And by the way, son. I'm sorry about your dad. He was a good man."

"Thank you," Frank said.

With that out of the way, the sheriff looked over at Pedro who was still hunkered down in the crook of my arm, shaking like a leaf. "And where does the Chihuahua come into all this?" he asked, reaching out to give Pedro a commiserating pat on the head. Pedro snapped and snarled and growled with such insane fury that the sheriff did a little yip of his own and yanked his hand back in the nick of time. Pedro was in no mood for commiserating. He'd had a rough day.

Frank was still laughing and crying at the same time. I reached out a hand to steady him, and the sheriff gave me a funny look, like maybe he was wondering if I was one of those queer boys he had read so much about. If he'd have asked me, I would have told him and broadened his horizons.

"Well," Frank said. "We think my brother used the Chihuahua as a diversion to keep Samson, that's the hog, occupied. He threw the dog out into the pen and Samson took off after it. While Samson was chasing Pedro, that's the Chihuahua, who escaped the hog by jumping through the broken window into the truck, Stanley, that's my brother, climbed over the fence and took off for the truck, that's the Chevy, so as to snatch the will while the hog was busy chasing the dog. Guess he didn't make it."

"Guess not," the sheriff agreed, looking a little dizzy after Frank's long-winded explanation. He gazed over at Pedro yet again, but this time he kept his hands to himself. Smart man. Two worry lines formed between his eyes. "That was a damn mean thing for your brother to do, throwing that little dog in there like that."

Frank's tears were finally drying up. He sucked a little snot back up his nose and said, "You'd have to know my brother, Sheriff. He wasn't—well, let's just say, he—"

I chimed in. "The man was a dick, Sheriff. There's no other way to say it."

And the sheriff looked at Pedro one last time. "Lord, son, you might be right."

Frank gave his head a sad little shake. "Plus Stanley had been drinking all night. I'm sure Pop didn't mean for things to turn out the way they did. How was he to know that Stanley would be dumb enough and drunk enough and greedy enough to actually follow that silly map?"

"I guess greed does funny things to people," the sheriff said.

"Exactly," Frank agreed.

"And Samson was just doing what Samson does," I tossed into the pile. "No sense shooting the messenger. Or the pig."

The three of us looked over at Samson, and Samson gave us a grunt when he saw us all staring at him. He had woken up about fifteen minutes earlier. It might have been my imagination, but I thought Samson looked like he had a bellyache. I couldn't imagine why.

"That sure is one hell of a hog," the sheriff said, scratching his scalp.

And with that astute observation, the questioning by law enforcement pretty much petered out.

Chapter Seventeen

WELL, it was one hell of a double funeral. Everyone said so. Most of the county turned out, of course. Double funerals don't come along every day of the week, and in Indiana you take what entertainment you can get. It was a bit sad to see Stanley's tiny pewter urn parked next to his father's monstrous oak-and-bronze coffin in the Slumber Room of Simmons Funeral Home, but there wasn't much of Stanley left to put on display. A coffin for him would have been a ridiculous extravagance. His little dollop of remains would have been rolling around inside it for all eternity like a dead mouse in a fifty-gallon drum.

As it was, Stanley was lucky to be able to tag along on the old man's dime, dangling from his father's funereal coattails, as it were. If it had been a solo affair, meaning Stanley's funeral alone, there wouldn't have been more than three mourners present, and two of those would probably have been there for the air conditioning. As it was, Stanley got a packed house, even if every single person who signed the guest log had come to pay their respects to Joe instead of him.

I considered inviting Jerry to Stanley's funeral, what with him being Stanley's ex and all, but I was afraid he might actually accept. So I didn't.

With Stanley gone to his maker, Frank not only inherited the farm in its entirety, he also got the twenty grand that their mother had put aside. But even that wasn't the big news. The big news, and the shocker to beat all shockers, was that, since Stanley had died intestate, and since Frank was his closest living relative, Frank also came into more than thirty thousand dollars that Stanley had socked away in a savings account out in California. If Stanley wasn't roasting in hell already, I'll bet that burned his ass plenty, knowing that Frank ended up with his thirty grand.

Frank, being the sweet guy that he is, used a big chunk of his inheritance to buy Stanley a burial plot and a nice tombstone, which to my way of thinking was pretty much a useless extravagance as well. There was so little of Stanley left after Samson got done with him that we could have buried his ass in a flower pot on the front porch and saved five or six thousand dollars, but no, Frank wouldn't hear of it. The gravedigger buried Stanley with a garden trowel like a tulip bulb, patted the hole down afterward with the heel of his boot, and that was the end of it. And the man still charged four hundred dollars to plant him. I saw the bill.

And speaking of Samson, you'll be pleased to learn that Samson survived the ordeal. We thought for a while that the bellyache he came down with after gobbling up Stanley might do him in, but in the end he prevailed. (Which is more than one can say for Stanley). Two weeks after Samson fully digested Frank's brother and eventually pooped him out into a mudhole, in increments, of course, not all at once, thank God, Frank sold Samson to a carnival impresario known in the carny business as the Midwest Barker Baron, his business being sideshows and carnival attractions. The Barker Baron put Samson on display at the Indiana State Fair and made a fortune. Labeled as the Yorkshire Maneater, Samson is still touring in county and state fairs up and down the Mississippi and as far north as Canada, eating like a king and being pampered like a queen. I mean a *real* queen. He must have turned into an insufferable ham, if you'll pardon the expression, because we never did get so much as a postcard from Samson telling us how much he enjoyed being in show business and how appreciative he was that we hadn't ground him up into three-quarters of a ton of pork sausage, which was my suggestion.

Some people never appreciate anything.

So with Joe dead and buried, but certainly not forgotten, and Stanley dead and buried and forgotten every chance we got, life on the farm went on.

Eventually, there came a day when decisions had to be made.

THE cows were milked, the eggs gathered, the chickens and pigs fed and watered, and the last ball of August sunshine was just about to slide down the sky into September. Frank and I lay back on the pond bank, with our pant legs rolled up and our naked feet sloshing around in the cool muddy water to relax after another long, exhausting day of tending the farm.

Pedro was on the other side of the pond chasing a frog. He probably wanted to hump it. Off to the east, nine hundred chickens were settling down for the night, and a little farther down the hillside, the cows were milling about, all facing west, plucking up wildflowers, mindlessly chewing their cuds, and pooping all over the place. The setting sun hung so low on the horizon behind us that the shadows of the trees we were lying under stretched out all the way across the pasture to the fence line.

I was squishing my toes through the mud and piddling around with Frank's belt buckle while Frank watched me with a dastardly smile on his face.

"So how many people are interested?" I asked, pushing his T-shirt up out of the way so I could pluck gently at the little trail of hair which led from his belly button down to my favorite spot in all the world. "What's the latest tally?"

"Two firm offers for the whole shebang, a couple of semi-interested parties who would prefer we chop it up into parcels, and about six or seven friends and neighbors who are just nosing around and wondering what we'd settle for."

"They think you're desperate to sell," I said.

Frank nodded. "That's exactly what they think. They're hoping to get a bargain price from the sole remaining son of a tragic Indiana family, who happens to be a fruitcup, and who undoubtedly wants to get back to California and reconnect to the fruitcup way of life he had been leading before he and his boyfriend, who they say has a really big pecker, were forced to return to the homestead to care for his dying father, which was just before his asshole brother got devoured by a pig."

"Nice sentence structure," I said.

"You stole that line from me."

"Yes, I did. Thanks for the pecker comment," I said.

"You're welcome. I'm getting excited, you know."

"Good," I said, pressing my lips to his fly. He was right. Unless that was a hammer in there, he *was* getting excited.

Silence reigned for a couple of minutes while I waggled my tongue around inside Frank's belly button and loosened his belt a little more. Reaching down to stroke my hair and watching me like a hawk, he said, "Do you think Pop knows what happened? Do you think he knows Stanley died because of that silly prank of his?"

I gazed up past the smooth expanse of Frank's chest into his incredibly green eyes. "Naw," I said. And I said it not because that was what Frank wanted to hear, but because that was what I truly believed. "In the first place, who would ever think that Stanley would be dumb enough to actually do what he did? And in the second place, your dad loved that damn hog so much that I don't think he could see the meanness in him. He would never have pulled that prank on Stanley if he thought any harm would come of it. Your dad was a funny guy. He was just trying to be funny."

Frank seemed satisfied with my answer. After a couple of ticks, he said, "That's what I think too."

I pulled my tongue out of his belly button and scooted up a little so I could lay my ear on his chest and listen to his heartbeat. I loved listening to Frank's heartbeat. Especially when he had a boner. It had a different rhythm to it then. Like Ricky Ricardo pounding on bongos. "The pigs are going to be ready to sell soon, Frank. If they get much bigger they'll be taking over the farm."

He nodded. "They'll bring a good price. The market is up right now."

"The chicken prices too," I said.

He nodded. "Yep. The chicken prices too. It's going to end up being a good year."

Frank made that comment more calmly than he would have made it before the deaths of his brother and dad. Frank had money now. Not a lot of money, but enough not to have to worry about every little bill that came along like he did before. He didn't have to worry if the hog prices or the grain prices or the egg prices were up or down or in-between. It gave Frank a sense of freedom he had never known before, having several thousand bucks in the bank, not to mention being the sole owner of a pretty fair chunk of real estate, and it was a joy to watch him savor that freedom.

I smiled at the look of contentment on his face, and then, out of the blue, Frank asked the question I had been dreading for weeks.

"When do you want to head back to San Diego?"

"I'm assuming when you say 'you' you actually mean 'us'."

"Yes. Us."

I thought about it. "When do *you* want to head back?"

Frank shrugged and looked up into the branches above our heads. They were gently shifting around in the evening breeze, dappling Frank's face with shifting splotches of shadow. "I suppose we could sell right now and be gone by October."

I thought about that. "Or we could wait until winter's over and sell in the spring."

Frank looked down at me. His belt was undone, and I was dragging his zipper slowly open with my teeth. "If we wait until spring" he said, "it'll be planting season and time to buy nine hundred new chicks."

I spread wide the flaps of his jeans and let his pubic hair tickle my nose. "Then we'll wait until they grow up and go to college. What the hell's the rush?"

He hooked a finger under my chin and dragged my face up to study it. "What are you saying, Tom? Are you saying you want to stay here?"

When he said it like that, I wasn't so sure. Being the kind of person who usually says what he's thinking, I said, "When you say it like that, I'm not so sure."

A smile played at the corners of Frank's luscious mouth. I caught a glimpse of snowy-white teeth and a scrumptious pink tongue. "You like the privacy," he said.

"Yes, I do."

"Neither one of us has had a bout of social anxiety freakiness for months."

"No, we haven't."

"I don't remember the last time you had to breathe into a paper bag."

"Me either."

"You're even starting to enjoy the company of chickens."

"I wouldn't go that far."

"Do you miss the city at all?" Frank finally asked.

And I didn't miss a beat. "No," I said, truthfully. "I have everything I want right here."

Frank smiled. Then he laughed. It was a beautiful carefree sound that made Pedro come running. He plopped himself down beside us, panting like a steam engine, tail thumping, tongue dangling. One happy dog. One happy *farm* dog.

"What about all your stuff?" Frank asked. He was looking pretty happy too. His tongue wasn't dangling yet, but it *would* be by the time I finished fiddling around with his crotch.

I shrugged. "We'll hire movers to empty out the apartment and drive the stuff here. No sweat."

"What about Jerry?"

"He'll have more room."

"No, I mean what about Jerry and you?"

"There is no Jerry and me. There's only Frank and me."

He stroked my cheek. "Good to know."

And since the fates never get tired of screwing with people's heads, that was the very moment my cell phone started chirping.

Disgusted, I spat out Frank's zipper tab and yanked the phone out of my back pocket. While I was checking the number on the readout, Frank began to shrug himself out of his clothes. I guess he couldn't wait any longer.

"It's Jerry," I said, reading the numbers.

"Well, whaddya know."

Naked as the day he was born, Frank wadded his clothes up into a ball and tucked them under his head for a pillow. He lay back down in the grass and watched me, idly stroking his rock-hard cock and grinning that dimpled grin that promised all sorts of wonderful things to come.

He nodded toward my phone. "Better tell him then."

I reached out to lend Frank a hand. His cock filled my fist perfectly.

"I'll write him a letter," I said, and flung the phone into the pond. It gave one tiny pathetic gurgle and sank like a rock.

I shrugged quickly out of my own clothes and when I was finished, Frank pulled me naked into his arms.

"I thought you were shy," he said.

I scooted south to warmer climes.

"That was the old me," I said. "The city me."

"So now I guess you're a farmer," Frank said, arching his back as I nibbled at his groin.

"Yep," I grinned. "That's me. Farmer Tom."

And oh so slowly I took him into my mouth, just to hear him moan.

JOHN INMAN has been writing fiction since he was old enough to hold a pencil. He and his partner live in beautiful San Diego, California. Together, they share a passion for theater, books, hiking and biking along the trails and canyons of San Diego, or if the mood strikes, simply kicking back with a beer and a movie. John's advice for anyone who wishes to be a writer? "Set time aside to write every day and do it. Don't be afraid to share what you've written. Feedback is important. When a rejection slip comes in, just tear it up and try again. Keep mailing stuff out. Keep writing and rewriting and then rewrite one more time. Every minute of the struggle is worth it in the end, so don't give up. Ever. Remember that publishers are a lot like lovers. Sometimes you have to look a long time to find the one that's right for you."

You can contact John at john492@att.net or on his website: http://www.johninmanauthor.com/.

Also from DREAMSPINNER PRESS

dress up

joel skelton

http://www.dreamspinnerpress.com

All
ALONE
in a Sea of
ROMANCE
B.G. Thomas

www.ingramcontent.com/pod-product-compliance
Lightning Source LLC
Chambersburg PA
CBHW051634260626
47170CB00004B/1173